WALKING BY FAITH

A. M. Leibowitz

Supposed Crimes LLC • Matthews, North Carolina

This book is a work of fiction. Names, characters, places, and incidents are products of the author's imagination or are used fictitiously. Any resemblance to actual events or locales or persons, living or dead, is entirely coincidental.

All Rights Reserved
Copyright © 2016 Author

Published in the United States.

ISBN: 978-1-944591-05-2

www.supposedcrimes.com

This book is typeset in Goudy Old Style.

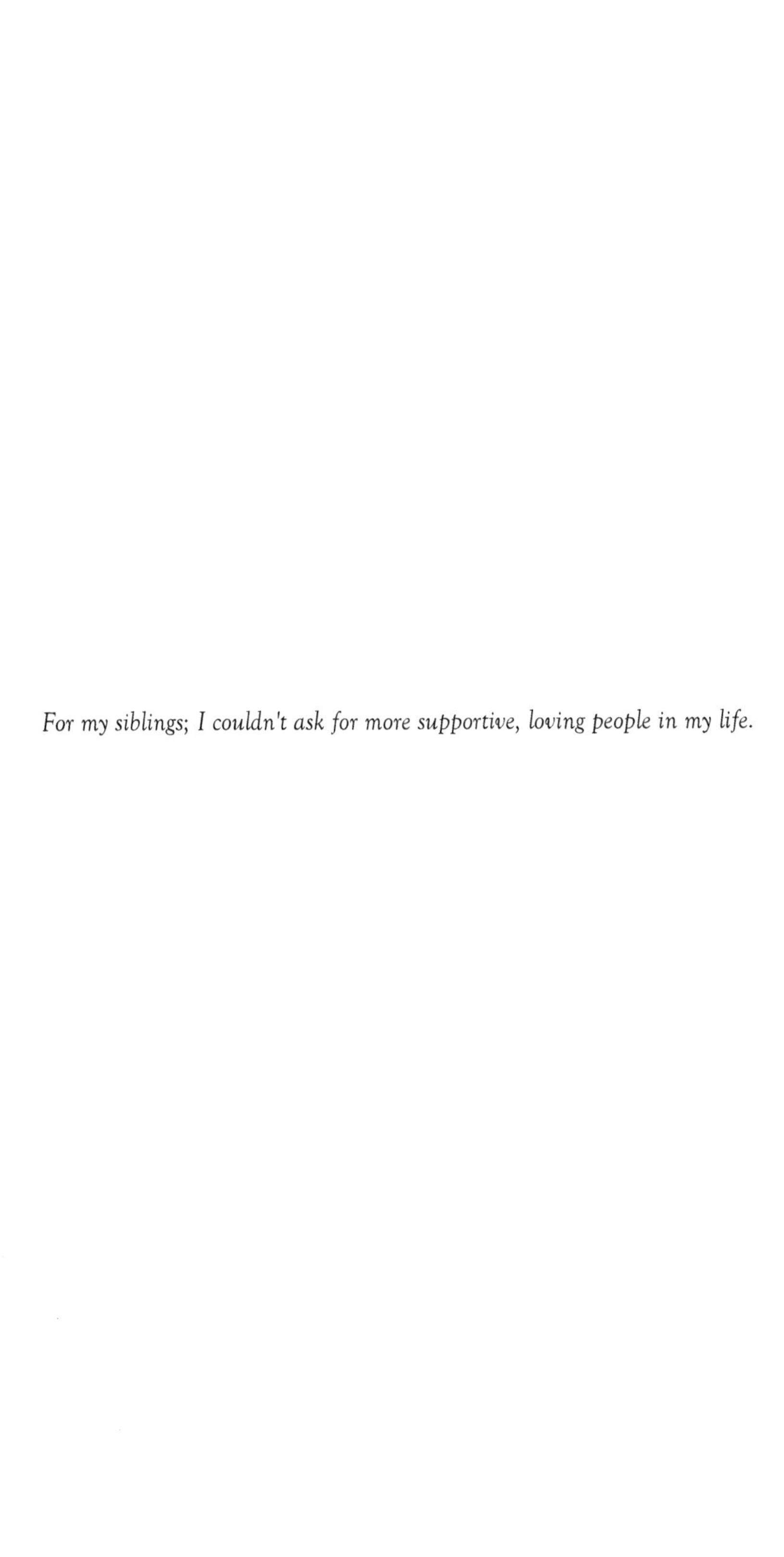

For my siblings; I couldn't ask for more supportive, loving people in my life.

Acknowledgements

I owe a special note of thanks to my beta readers, Bree West and Debbie McGowan, who saw me through all the trials of turning this novel from a mess into a viable story. Bree has been with me through a lot of novels at this point, and her careful attention to detail as well as her encouragement (and the occasional side-eye at my characters for their misbehavior) have kept me going through a lot of painful rewrites. Deb was new to me as a beta reader but not as an author. When one of your own favorite writers says she'd like to pre-read your story, you say yes, of course. Though you can imagine me sitting at my keyboard, trying not to fangirl scream as I typed my oh-so-casual, "Yes, that would be lovely, thanks." Both of these wonderful beta readers took my novel on a journey from disjointed scraps to completed work. Waiting for their emails kept me up at night, but receiving their feedback kept me going by day. I am in their debt.

CONTENT NOTE

This story contains mentions of sensitive topics such as physical assault and emotional recovery from trauma; religious content; HIV; and death of a partner.

PROLOGUE

IN THE NAME OF

AUGUST, 2013

CAT WASN'T running, exactly—more a fast lope. He was all the way to his own front door before he noticed his bare chest, having left his shirt next door. There was no chance he was going back for it, certainly not that night and probably not any other. It was fine; he had plenty of other shirts. A missing sunset orange V-neck was the least of his worries, even if it was one of his favorites and complemented his ginger-blond hair so well.

He hurried inside his house and shut the door, turning around to lean on it despite knowing his back would stick to it. His skin was damp, and his breathing was shallow. Every inhalation shuddered with longing and regret. He should have known better than to give in to his own wishful thinking. It was too much to ask that just once God might send him someone who could see past everything wrong with him to the real person he was.

No, that wasn't right. He didn't want someone to see past it—he wanted someone to embrace it. He'd done the whole "seeing past" thing once, and it had been all right in its way, but it wasn't what he needed. For all of a few minutes, he'd been sure this time he'd found the right person.

When Micah had turned up in their waterfront neighborhood at the beginning of the summer, he piqued Cat's interest for how similar he looked to someone from Cat's past. Cat had gone next door to have a better look. Naturally, he knew it couldn't be David; he'd been gone for years, and Cat had been with David's mother when she identified his body. Yet there were enough similarities to make Cat curious whether he might be a long-lost relation. As soon as Cat saw him closer, he knew there was no connection, but by then Micah had seen him.

Cat should have left Micah alone. He was a mess of his own problems, and he was only going to be around for the summer to fix up the house next door to Cat. Instead, Cat offered his help. As he got to know Micah, he began to long for more than friendship. The problem was, Cat's body wasn't fit for the kind of passionate summer fling which was the stuff of movies. His train-wreck of a body would always be in the way, the result of his severe hemophilia and the trauma it had endured years ago.

His usual trouble with the world of dating and mating was that many people saw him as a liability. Hooking up was largely out of the question, not that he was interested anyway. He never had been, no matter who believed he ought to be available. Being mistaken for passive was one lie of many which had followed him for eight long years. Cat hated how much people assumed about him because he was small and pretty and didn't hide his femininity. He refused to be reduced to a stereotype.

He also refused to make ill-advised, rash promises he couldn't keep, a lesson he'd learned when David was still alive. So what was his grand plan? Keep Micah at arm's length and give him a chance for summer love—or lust—with someone else. Which worked fine, until it didn't. Setting Micah up with his friend Reid had been a terrible idea for all of them. Not that the current state of affairs was any better; Cat never should have given in to temptation.

Cat sighed and shoved off the door, wincing as it tugged at his skin but appreciating the way the burn grounded him. He flopped onto the couch, tired and a little sore and a lot heartbroken. His mind wandered back to the previous five minutes, and he closed his eyes. Whether it was to block out the images or embrace them, he wasn't sure. It was his own fault—he'd made the first move. He'd kissed Micah.

Thoughts of soft lips on his own, of hands in his hair and on his skin and cupping him through his jeans sent a ripple down his spine, and heat rushed to his cheeks. It wasn't a matter of not wanting Micah; he wanted him more than he'd desired anyone in years. What worried him was how much more he needed when he wasn't convinced Micah felt the same way at all. It had been too long since he'd been with anyone, and he was sure it was his own foolish dreams interfering with reality. Micah couldn't possibly have meant he wanted more than taking momentary pleasure in each other's bodies. He hadn't been interested in Cat for who he was; he'd wanted anyone he could use to forget his own problems. Cat had to admit he found it a little strange how Micah thought making *him* feel good might do that, though, and it certainly wasn't going to happen by whatever mechanics Micah had been expecting. When he found out what Cat could and couldn't do and how much of a learning curve was required, it would lead to more pain and frustration for both of them. It was not a risk Cat wanted to take.

Anger displaced Cat's shame—some directed at Micah for kissing him back and for not being the person Cat thought he was. Some, if Cat were honest, was directed at God. They'd gotten along pretty well for the last several years, Cat and God, but Cat was more than a little annoyed by having his one long-standing request turned into something involving so much hurt. Most of Cat's anger was directed at himself, but he didn't like to examine that too closely. He certainly wasn't going to think about where the fire came from—not the years of relinquishing control to people who thought they knew what was best for him; not his regrets over which parts he still blamed himself for; and not the embarrassment over intentionally kissing a man who had admitted he used sex to avoid his problems. Certainly not anything at all to do with the resurfacing ache of loss and loneliness.

To guard himself from uncomfortable truths, he shucked his jeans, curled up on the couch, and buried his head in a pillow. It didn't help. All the reasons why he'd avoided situations like the one with Micah swarmed his brain, twisting in a familiar way to leave him feeling shame for his broken, sick body. He felt trapped by a disorder which left him looking whole on the outside while slowly destroying him from within.

Cat wasn't much of a crier. Sometimes he wished he could be, able to spill out his emotions as they struck. Micah was like that, openly pouring everything out—Cat had lost track of the number of times he'd found Micah sobbing that summer. Whatever else was wrong with him, at least he possessed the magical ability to release his pain; perhaps that was what drew Cat to him in the first place. Cat lay on the couch, wishing for tears that wouldn't flow. His eyes stung and his throat was tight, but everything remained trapped just below the surface. He closed his eyes and willed sleep to come.

It didn't. Instead, his mind supplied the details, the things he'd worked for years to shelve and forget. All the reasons Micah was a bad idea stemmed from one source, and in his loneliness and frustration, he finally allowed himself the luxury of reliving those moments. He rolled onto his back, staring up at the ceiling. More than eight years had passed—almost a third of his life. Yet here he was, still wondering if things might have been different if he'd chosen some other path. As he let his mind go there, he discovered what he'd been holding back even from himself. Now the thought had freed itself, he tried to suppress it, but the dam broke. At last the tears he'd prayed for began to fall, washing away the months and years of guilt and grief.

Oh, David, he thought. *I am so, so sorry.*

PART I

SPRING

CHAPTER ONE

AS IT WAS IN THE BEGINNING

APRIL, 2005

CAT ROWLAND chased after his best friend, Bryce Matthews, running from the community college's shuttle stop in town to Bryce's house. Bryce had said they were in a hurry because he had a surprise for Cat. Never mind that Cat could hardly keep up with him. Bryce flew down the sidewalk and reached his front door first. He stood there tapping his foot, arms crossed. Cat huffed and slowed to a walk. The last thing he needed was to twist something and end up with another injury.

He reached the end of the stone walkway and scowled at Bryce. "You could've waited."

"That would've made it easy. You need to work for your birthday present."

Cat shoved him. "Whatever. Let's go."

When Cat stepped onto the porch, Bryce tangled his fingers with Cat's. He dragged Cat into his personal space, giving him a light kiss on the mouth. Sure, they'd kissed before, but never anything out where someone walking by could see. It was always just messing around in their rooms—nothing serious. Cat jerked back, startled.

"You okay?" Bryce asked.

"Yeah, I just wasn't expecting that. I mean, not right here."

Bryce grinned. "I felt like kissing you. Is that so bad?"

"No." Cat leaned forward and kissed Bryce this time, his heart thumping madly, his head buzzing with the thought that Bryce might want them to be more than friends who sometimes kissed or explored.

"Come on," Bryce said. "My parents won't be home for a couple of hours." It didn't matter that Bryce was nearly nineteen and in college; his parents still kept tight watch on everything he did.

Cat hung back. "Your house? I thought we were going to Zee's to hang out tonight. I told my parents I was staying there overnight."

"Yeah, and we will. Later. I have so many surprises for you it's not even funny." When Bryce smiled, a dimple appeared in one cheek. Cat thought it was cute.

"It doesn't involve putting holes in my body again, does it?" Cat asked warily. The previous year, his surprise gift had been the guys taking him to Regal Ink, the tattoo place in town, to get his ear pierced. It had hurt like hell, bled all over the place, and gotten infected so bad he'd needed antibiotics.

"God, no," Bryce assured him. "I wouldn't put you through that again. It was a shitty idea."

"Okay. But don't feel bad. I like my earring." He bumped Bryce with his shoulder.

Bryce flicked the stud gently with his finger. "It's hot," he said. "I'm just sorry we couldn't have done both ears."

Cat let Bryce lead him into the house, a large, rambling old place with three floors. Inside, they dumped their backpacks and shoes by the door. Cat carefully lined his pink Converse up on the shoe mat, and Bryce rolled his eyes.

"Neat freak," he said, but his tone was more affectionate than scolding.

They sat on the couch, and Bryce flipped on the television. He handed Cat a game controller. For the first few minutes, they were quiet, but things quickly escalated as they tried to outrace one another. Bryce was good, but Cat was better, and they both knew it. Before long, they were both up on their knees, shouting at each other and jostling playfully. When Cat won, he let out a loud whoop and dropped his controller. Bryce tossed his aside as well and grabbed Cat around the middle. They tussled for a bit until Cat shoved Bryce a little.

"Be careful," he said.

"Yeah, yeah. Fragile and all. You weren't so fragile when you were beating my ass at that game." Bryce didn't let go; instead, he drew Cat closer.

Cat's heart sped up. He was sure Bryce didn't have more wrestling in mind at that point. One look at his face and Cat knew Bryce was going to kiss him again. He wanted it too, so he leaned forward at the same time Bryce did. Their mouths met with a little more force than either of them had intended, and Bryce laughed against Cat's lips.

They kissed for a few minutes, something they'd done plenty of times before. They'd been each other's experiment of sorts. Bryce had confessed his crush on their friend Zee—who was straight—back in high school, over a year ago. Bryce's family, like Cat's, was Catholic, but the difference was it actually mattered to them. Bryce had sworn Cat to secrecy, explaining that his parents would be really upset. Cat had agreed, naturally. He understood some things were best not shared with certain people, including parents. After suffering through his own overprotective family's hovering, he knew why Bryce wasn't ready.

Cat had been out himself since he was eleven, and his gender had been a source of confusion for most other people by the time he was thirteen. Still, he'd been behind the curve when it came to anything more than a few mild crushes and a bit of secret hand-holding. When Cat finally hit puberty, it was like an explosion. There was absolutely no question about his feelings, only a question of finding the right guy to mess around with. Too bad it had taken so long to find Bryce, but at least Cat had discovered any number of ways to feel good by himself. Only perk he could find for his health issues—he was amazingly responsive to touch pretty much everywhere.

Ezra, the anchor to their relay team of friends, and Zee had both left town for college. Cat and Bryce were enrolled in the community college where Cat got a free ride because his father was a professor. Just before Christmas break, Bryce had come to Cat with a proposal. Having abandoned his ill-fated crush on Zee, or maybe to act out the feelings he couldn't otherwise express, Bryce had suggested he and Cat try things out with each other. Not boyfriends, really, more like science lab partners. When they'd kissed sitting on Cat's bed, Bryce had slipped his hand up Cat's shirt and Cat had slid his hand over Bryce's ass.

Like an ignition spark, that had led to searching for excuses to feel each other every chance they got. Cat's house was often safer, if only for the proximity to his meds and the fact that it would be embarrassing rather than dangerous to have someone walk in on them. So far, the most that had happened was the one time Cat's sister, LR, had complained about hearing them making out while she was trying to study. They'd been quieter after that.

It was different this time. They could be as noisy as they wanted—no one was around to hear. Even their kisses were more intense; Bryce was licking into Cat's mouth like he wanted to devour him. Cat's stomach tightened with a combination of nerves and excitement. When Bryce began to feel him up beneath his pink, glitter-sprayed t-shirt, Cat gasped. His skin was so sensitive, and the way Bryce was fingering his nipples felt very, very good. He was afraid he'd shoot before they even had their clothes off.

"Aw, shit," Bryce groaned. "Come on, let's go upstairs."

He withdrew and held out his hand. For a moment, Cat looked up at him, not moving. His pulse bounded. He knew what Bryce wanted, but they'd never gone that far with each other. He swallowed and stood up.

"Um," he said, still rooted to the spot.

Bryce dropped his hand. "Don't you want to?" he asked. "I want to give you your first birthday present." He made a half smile. "It's not every day a guy turns nineteen."

"I want to," Cat said quietly. Now he understood why Bryce had said on Cat's real birthday he had to wait until the weekend to unwrap his gift.

"Then let's," Bryce said.

Cat followed him upstairs to his bedroom. Bryce shut the door and immediately yanked off his t-shirt, followed by his jeans. He lay down on the bed, watching Cat. Hands shaking, Cat stripped down to his underwear as well. He curled up next to Bryce, quivering a little.

"We don't have to," Bryce said. He reached over and put his hand on Cat's chest.

"I know." Cat flinched.

He wasn't sure how this was supposed to work. What if he got hurt? He'd already had one unfortunate incident, and that had only been jerking off in his own bed. The thought made anger bubble up inside him. He was so tired of being weak, tired of having to be so careful with everything he did. No contact sports. No climbing. No doing anything that might result in bumps or bruises. He assumed sex was probably on the no-no list as well, given his doctors' reluctance to bring it up.

Cat clenched his jaw. *Fuck everything*, he thought. He was going to do whatever he wanted. If that included getting naked and screwing his best friend, so be it. His parents could go to hell for making his life miserable and instilling in him such a deep fear and loathing for his own body. He reached out for Bryce and pulled him closer.

"I know we don't have to, but I want to," Cat said. He turned over and rolled on top of Bryce, rocking down against him.

Bryce relaxed and grinned, revealing the dimple. They kissed a bit more, and Bryce reached down to slip his fingers inside Cat's underwear. The touch was light, but it felt so good Cat was sure he wouldn't be able to take much of it. He grasped Bryce's wrist to stop him then dragged off the rest of his clothes, waiting for Bryce to do the same.

They lost themselves in a tangle of limbs and bodies, first rutting against each other until they were dizzy then moving further. Cat was glad Bryce had planned ahead—he had plenty of condoms and some lube. He was understanding, too, despite his teasing about Cat being fragile. He opened himself to Cat, saying he thought it was best for their first time so Cat wouldn't get hurt from their inexperience.

Even with all Bryce's preparation, it was still awkward and a little too tight. It took ages for Cat to figure out what the hell he was supposed to be doing exactly, and Bryce didn't look like he was enjoying it. Cat held still, hovering over Bryce.

"Should I stop?" Cat asked.

"N-no." Bryce tipped his head back. "Holy shit, they make it look so easy."

Cat laughed, ducking his head and resting it on Bryce's breastbone for a moment. "No kidding. Are you okay?"

"Mostly. It feels...weird." Bryce shifted, and his face relaxed. "That's a little better."

They slowed down, kissing a bit more and working back toward their earlier excitement. Cat wasn't quite flexible enough to put his mouth on Bryce's dick in that position, so he used his hand instead. When Bryce started moving underneath him, Cat put both hands on the bed and braced himself, letting Bryce take control from below. The feeling of being inside another person was so overwhelming Cat almost thought he was going to die. It took hardly anything before he was shaking with the most intense orgasm he'd ever experienced. Through the haze, he felt Bryce jerking himself until he cried out and splattered them both.

Cat withdrew, causing Bryce to wince and grunt, and they lay next to each other, panting. After a couple of minutes, Bryce peeked over at Cat. A look of alarm crossed his face, and he sat up.

"What's wrong?" Cat asked, thinking maybe Bryce had heard his parents' cars.

"Cat..." Bryce's eyes crinkled with worry. "You're all red."

Cat laughed. "Yeah, of course I am. We just fucked. That's supposed to happen. Even I know that."

Bryce shook his head. "No. Look at yourself." His voice trembled.

When he looked down, Cat gasped. His pale brown freckles were mingled in with pinprick red spots, all over his chest and down his belly. "Shit."

Having sex must have caused a few surface blood vessels to burst. It wouldn't send him to the hospital, but he needed to get home for his meds as soon as possible. Whether it was from the heat or the strain of sex, he didn't know, and it didn't matter anyway. He got up and began dragging his clothes back on.

"I gotta get home," he said. "I need my meds." He stumbled as he yanked up his jeans.

Bryce slid to the edge of the bed and swung his feet over. "Didn't you bring them?"

"No," Cat said quietly before pulling his shirt over his head. "We were at school. Dad has shit for me in his office."

"But you brought your stuff to go to Zee's." Bryce's expression reflected his bewilderment.

Cat turned around and stood by the door. He couldn't explain to Bryce that it was just one night at Zee's, and he'd wanted to pretend for a few hours he could leave the house and be *normal* for a change. It didn't matter that his parents were a phone call away if anything happened or that he wasn't likely to sustain life-threatening injuries from take-out Chinese food, birthday cake, and a few games of stripes and solids in Zee's basement.

"I forgot," he lied. "I have to go. My parents—"

"Are they home?" Bryce began putting himself back together.

"No, but they will be soon, and I don't want them asking me why I need an infusion. Shit!"

"Okay, okay. I'll get you there. Maybe Zee can pick us up early. He was supposed to come by so we could go get your second present." Bryce fumbled in his pants pocket for his phone.

"Fine. Hurry!" Cat urged.

Less than twenty minutes later, Zee showed up in his parents' car, and Cat and Bryce piled in. Their friend Ezra was already in the front seat. Once they got to Cat's house, he tore inside and stopped short. LR was sitting on the couch, doing her homework. Two of her friends were sprawled on the floor, engaged in the same activity. She looked up when he came in.

"What are you doing here?" she demanded. "Mom said you were going to be at Zee's house with the guys tonight."

"So that's why you have them here." He pointed to the other girls.

"Well, yeah. We're finishing up some stuff and then we were supposed to have the whole house to ourselves." She glared at him.

He rolled his eyes. "Only you would do homework on a Friday, *Libertee*." He emphasized her real name to annoy her, and he was rewarded with her scowl. "I came to get some stuff I forgot." He stomped up the stairs to his room.

Now what was he supposed to do? If he stayed long enough to take his meds, LR would know and tell their parents, or she would ask him why. Maybe he could do it back at Zee's house. He snarled, thinking what a pain sex was and how maybe he wouldn't ever do it again if it was going to be this much trouble.

That stopped him in his tracks. No, it had felt incredibly good, and if he had the chance, he would do it over and over. He had never felt so hot and excited as when he was pushing in and out of Bryce's tight ass. His own hand couldn't compare, though he still thought masturbation was pretty amazing. *Fuck fucking hemophilia*, he thought. If he had to, he would carry his medical supplies everywhere with him just in case, but nothing was going to prevent him from making his body feel that good ever again.

He grabbed the pills he took to boost the effect of his infusions and swallowed them hastily with a bit of water from the bottle he kept on his night stand. He shoved everything else into his bag and ran down the stairs. Calling a goodbye to his sister and her friends, he blew through the door and slammed it on his way out, barely registering the girls' protests behind him. He leaped into Zee's car.

"Drive," he said.

"Did you infuse?" Bryce asked, confused.

"No. Had to dodge The Sister and her minions. I'll do it at Zee's house."

"But we're not going there!" Bryce protested. "We were going to take you somewhere special."

"Where?" Cat asked. He wasn't panicking, but he needed to get where he could take his meds.

"Um." Bryce shuffled his feet.

"Tell me, asshole," Cat said.

"Fine. We were going to take you to dinner and then a club. We've been planning this forever."

Cat groaned. "All right. *After* my meds." He growled. "Please get me somewhere I can infuse. Then you can drag me to wherever you want."

Bryce relaxed. "You got it. Zee's house first."

"Good." His parents would be pissed if they knew, though he suspected not nearly as pissed as they would be if they found out he was having sex with Bryce without talking to his doctor first.

Once. They'd done it once. He reminded himself it didn't mean anything, really. Friends with benefits and all that. Bryce probably didn't want more. Cat's chest constricted at the realization he did want more. He wanted to be like all the happy couples he saw at school, holding hands and acting all goofy. That wasn't going to happen, though. It wasn't because Concordia was such a backwards town. In fact, they weren't—there was a huge LGBTQ population, and half the businesses in town had rainbow stickers, meaning they were explicitly friendly. The community college wasn't an issue either—there were lots of different kinds of couples there, too. It was more Bryce's family who were the problem. Maybe Cat's, too—at least about the sex. His mother in particular worried constantly, and sex was one thing neither he nor they had ever brought up.

Ezra broke him out of his musing. "This is gonna be one fabulous night, my boy," he said.

He opened a small bag and produced several small cards. Cat's eyes widened when he realized what they were. He glanced at Bryce, who grinned, and then he tapped Zee's shoulder.

"Where are we going?"

"New place north of town, just for you," Zee said. "Supposed to be hot, and Ezra happens to know a couple of people who work there and can sneak us in."

A gay club, then. Cat knew vaguely the one Zee meant. He let the idea settle in his brain. A slow grin spread across his face, despite the lingering worry over getting his meds in time. This was going to be one hell of a birthday.

Chapter Two

Lead Us Not into Temptation

There was a line outside the club. Cat balanced on the balls of his feet to peer over Zee's shoulder. There was no way they would get in; they were by far the youngest people in line, at least from what Cat could see. He knew he didn't even look like he was out of high school himself. They did have the fake IDs courtesy of Ezra's cousin, but that didn't mean much. Cat bounced a little with nerves.

"Will you cut it out?" Zee hissed, turning around. "You're making us look like we don't belong here."

"Well, we kind of don't," Cat said. "These guys are a lot older than we are."

Ezra elbowed him in the back. "Keith's got us covered. His boyfriend Preston is at the door, and he said he and their friend Landon will meet us inside."

Cat nodded, too full of nerves and excitement to say anything in response. When they reached the front of the line, he held his breath through the guys handing over their cards. He fumbled his way through passing his to the man Ezra had referred to as Preston. The man barely looked at it then gave Ezra a wink and sent them inside. Cat let the air out of his lungs and followed the others.

It was dim inside and more crowded than Cat had been expecting. He looked around, trying to figure out what the decor meant. There were neon palm trees and other tropical decorations, but there were also what looked like miles and miles of fishing net strung with rainbow lights. Were they going for a pirate theme? The idea made him giggle-snort, and he covered his mouth before the others heard. Bryce was always on him about that kind of thing anyway, being too girly. Cat composed himself and lowered his hand, still puzzling over the bar's theme.

The first floor had the bar and plenty of floor space with a ring of high tables and stools. The upper level—more of a balcony—had all the booths. It took Cat a moment to realize his friends were pushing him toward one of the tables, where they staked their claim. Cat breathed a sigh of relief to be out of the way of so many bodies so close together. He could easily see himself getting crushed in between people.

Ezra had disappeared, and Cat looked around for him. After a short while, he popped back up with two others in tow and multiple drinks between them which he set on the table. He pushed a glass toward Cat.

"Happy birthday!" he yelled in Cat's ear.

Cat flinched then looked down at his drink. It didn't look like a soda. He sniffed. Definitely alcoholic. He turned to Ezra and glared at him. "I can't have this."

"Sure you can! It's your day, and you're covered for it."

"No," Cat said, trying to hold back his annoyance at both Ezra and himself. "I can't have any alcohol. It fucks with my body."

Bryce rolled his eyes. "Just for once, play along. You don't have to get drunk."

Cat didn't want to explain all his stomach problems or his need to be clear-headed at all times. He knew the beer in and of itself wasn't a big deal. Unlike sex, his doctor had been very clear on a number of other things, and Cat hadn't been too embarrassed to ask about the ones he wasn't. His refusal to drink had more to do with some of his other chronic problems than his hemophilia, and he had no interest in reminding them he'd be spending the rest of his night in the bathroom.

"I said no," Cat told Bryce firmly. "But you guys go ahead and enjoy."

Bryce and Ezra both shrugged and turned away, but Zee pressed a palm on Cat's shoulder. Cat relaxed and let the sights and sounds wash over him. He was as overwhelmed here as he had been in Bryce's bedroom but in a completely different way. Knowing places like this existed was not the same as being in the midst of everything, watching a full range of men—and, surprisingly, a few women—enjoying their night out in a place they could be themselves.

He looked to see if there were any others like himself. There were definitely some who were overtly femme, maybe even more than Cat. He watched a group for a while, wondering if it was simply how they dressed for a night out or if they really were like him, always questioning his gender, trying to sort it out. He'd stopped calling himself gay when he found the word *queer*. It worked so well, and he didn't have to try so hard to guess his feelings day to day. It bothered Bryce when Cat used it, and Zee and Ezra always looked uncomfortable, but it fit like latex. Cat liked it.

Having gotten distracted enjoying the pretty men dancing together, Cat missed when a good-looking guy pulled up a stool next to him. He only registered it when the man said in his ear so he could be heard, "Hey, there."

Cat nearly jumped a mile. He put a hand on his stomach—conscious of doing anything someone might comment on later—and waited until his heart rate slowed before he said, "Um, hey."

"I'm Landon." The guy stuck out his hand.

Taking it, Cat suppressed a giggle at the oddly formal gesture. It was nice, though. He'd seen how a few of the men were getting handsy even when asked to stop.

"I'm Cat."

"Cat?" Landon laughed. "Interesting. So, you came with Preston's...cousin, was it?"

"No, his boyfriend's cousin. Oh!" Understanding dawned. "You're Keith's friend."

"Yeah." The man grinned. "Having fun?"

Cat shrugged. "I guess. I'm a little—"

"Overwhelmed?" Landon guessed. He nodded, not waiting for a response. "You'll get used to it. You should go dance."

"Um." Cat's face fell. "I probably shouldn't, really."

"No?"

"Not a good idea for me." He hadn't been going to tell a total stranger about his health, but he figured what the hell. Landon wasn't exactly a stranger if he knew Ezra. "I have a medical...thing. Like, I could get hurt."

"Not if someone's protecting you, right?" Landon asked.

"I'm not sure," Cat admitted. "Maybe—"

He was cut off by Ezra appearing at his elbow. "Hey, Landon."

Landon backed off from Cat. "Keith's cousin, is it?"

"Yeah." Ezra turned his attention to Cat. "Want to go upstairs, have a look from there?"

He didn't wait for Cat's reply, tugging him from his seat and leading him up the stairs. Cat followed, his brief conversation with Landon left behind him until they reached the top of the stairs. It was quieter up there, fewer people. Cat almost felt like he could breathe again.

"Thanks," he said to Ezra, not having realized he needed to be away.

"Sure," Ezra said. He fidgeted a little. "Listen, I'm sorry I butted in there, but Keith told me I should."

"Why?" Cat furrowed his brow.

"He said to me, 'Maybe you shouldn't let your friend talk to Landon.' I have no idea why not, but I get the feeling Landon's kind of a player, you know?"

No, Cat didn't know. He hadn't had a lot of opportunity to find out, either. It wasn't as though great-looking men were knocking down his door. Even being in college had taught him to tone down his clothing choices. Not to avoid being harassed but because it made people uncomfortable, especially some of the guys he liked. He'd figured it didn't matter once he was mostly with Bryce, but even Bryce reminded him not to act too much like a girl sometimes.

Cat didn't tell Ezra any of that. Maybe he could have told Zee, who was surprisingly cool for a straight guy. Ezra was good too, though Cat sometimes wondered if Ezra was bi even though he'd never said so. He was more of a guys' guy than the others, which made Cat hesitate to talk about it with him in case it made him uncomfortable. Bryce sometimes left Cat with the impression he thought Ezra was who they should all aspire to be more like. It might have been due to his ongoing fear of discovery by his super-conservative parents.

"Okay. I'll be more careful," Cat said. "I wasn't into him anyway. I thought he was being nice because he knows you."

"No," Ezra replied. "I've only seen him a couple times because of Keith and Preston. I don't know him too well."

They made their way farther along the balcony until they found Bryce and Zee. The two of them were in a booth, hanging back and sipping another couple of drinks. Bryce's cheeks were flushed, which Cat noticed even in the dim light. He sighed, hoping Bryce was only a little buzzed. Having his best friend-boyfriend-whatever puking all night wasn't the birthday fun he'd been looking forward to.

Fortunately, Bryce didn't seem drunk, only a little loopy and relaxed. He beckoned Cat over, and once Cat was on the seat next to him, he put an arm around him. It forced Cat closer, and he curled happily into Bryce's side. It felt good, particularly the way Bryce rested his other hand on Cat's thigh under the table where the others couldn't see. He traced patterns, inching higher, but he stopped short of doing anything which might give them away. As far as Zee and Ezra were concerned, there wasn't anything going on between them.

A song Bryce liked began playing, and he pushed at Cat a little. "Come on, I wanna dance."

Cat raised an eyebrow, but he let Bryce pull him to his feet. They made their way back downstairs, and Bryce eyed the crowd. He took Cat's hand, and they escaped to the fringe of the throng. Bryce wrapped his arms around Cat from behind and swayed in rhythm with the music. Cat leaned his head back on Bryce's shoulder, warm from the beat and the people and the press of Bryce against him. He closed his eyes and let himself simply feel Bryce's presence all around him.

Bryce ground against him, his breath stuttering in Cat's ear. His hand drifted down to the top of Cat's jeans, toying with his belt but not doing anything else. The feel of Bryce hardening against his ass made Cat shiver, and he inhaled sharply. Upstairs, sitting with the other guys in the booth, the idea of Bryce messing with him had felt weird, and he'd been grateful Bryce didn't go there. Now, on the edge of the dance floor, it felt sexy and a little filthy and plain wonderful when Bryce stretched his fingers a little to brush his zipper.

He turned in Bryce's arms, and they were pressed so close. The song they'd come down for ended and another started, but Cat ignored the change in favor of concentrating only on Bryce. He was here, celebrating his birthday, in the arms of...was Bryce his boyfriend? They hadn't determined it for sure, but he thought it's what they should be, after everything. He rested his head on Bryce's chest then tilted back until he had a good angle to kiss Bryce's neck.

Bryce twitched at the contact then settled back in. To Cat, it all felt like too much. Too warm, too sensual, too intense. He pulled away and took a few breaths. "I need a minute," he said.

"You okay?"

"Yeah. Just...bathroom."

It was the only thing Cat could think of to escape the sensory overload. They were already on the side where the bathrooms were, so he ducked around a few people and went inside, hoping to clear his head. He was out of luck. Despite the signs posted all over the bar reading "No sexual activity of any kind," that's more or less what several people were doing. Most appeared to be using the bathroom for its actual purpose, but Cat heard distinctly non-toileting noises in one of the stalls. There were a pair of guys at one of the urinals, one of them jerking the other from behind. A third kept reaching over and adding his own hand to the situation. Cat looked away, knowing his face had to be fire engine red.

He slipped into a stall and shut the door, leaning on it. A moment later, he heard Bryce's voice. "Cat?"

"In here."

Bryce knocked, and Cat let him in, not really caring if the other men made assumptions. "I'm sorry," Cat said.

"Hey, it's fine." Bryce rested their heads together. "Bit much?"

"A little. I don't know." He bit his lower lip. "I wanted you to keep touching me, but it felt weird, you know?"

"Oh." Bryce moved closer. "Because we were right out there, in front of everyone?"

"No," Cat said. "That was...I liked it. And that's what felt weird."

"Oh," Bryce repeated. His whole body was flush against Cat's. "What about now?"

Cat wasn't sure if it was better or worse, but in an instant, he stopped caring. He'd already done more in one day that he probably wasn't supposed to than in most of the rest of his life combined. It didn't make a difference now if he wanted to join the fun the others seemed to be having. He looked up at Bryce with determination and then pushed, shoving Bryce up against the opposite wall of the cubicle and crashing their mouths together.

Bryce made an mmph noise, but a few seconds later, his hands were all over Cat as though he wasn't sure which part he wanted to touch. Cat needed to feel it all, the rush of the blood in his veins and the throb of Bryce's cock against his and the adrenaline of mild exhibitionism with possible discovery. He didn't let up kissing Bryce, not even when they were both shoving at their jeans to get them the hell out of the way.

"I'm still—I can't—" Bryce panted, and Cat understood.

"Hands," he said, demonstrating by wedging his between them.

Bryce caught on. It took hardly any time before they were both spiraling into release, panting into each other's open mouths, eyes squeezed shut and bodies pressed together. They both shuddered and gasped, and Cat continued to shake for a long time afterward. He was overcome with a new feeling, one which left him on the edge—not crying, but covered in a deep sense of shame that maybe they shouldn't have been in there at that particular time doing what they'd been doing.

He took a long while to calm down, hoping Bryce would think it was nothing more than the after-effects of coming so hard. He straightened up, shifting his weight from Bryce. They didn't say anything to each other, avoiding eye contact until they'd managed to mostly clean themselves up.

"I need to piss," Cat said.

"I'll wait for you." Bryce buckled his belt and stepped out of the stall.

There didn't seem to be any further need to analyze their situation. Cat relieved his bladder, zipped up, and stepped out around a guy who looked like he might pee himself if he didn't get in there soon. As he washed his hands, Cat looked over his shoulder at Bryce, leaned up against the wall by the door with his eyes closed. Cat almost missed it, but when Bryce ran his wrist under his nose, the light caught the single tear sliding down his cheek.

Cat dried his hands on his jeans and stepped up close to Bryce. He reached up with his thumb and ran it down the side of Bryce's face, temple to chin, until Bryce looked down at him.

"Okay?" Cat asked, low.

Bryce nodded and pulled Cat into a tight hug, resting his chin on Cat's head. They separated after a minute, and they both pretended nothing had changed when they stepped out of the bathroom together.

PART II

CONTRITION

AUGUST, 2013

CAT WOKE with a jolt, heart hammering. He gasped and wiped his sweating brow with the back of his hand then sat up. Curling his knees in toward his chest, he rested his forehead on them until he'd calmed down. He stood up and glanced down at his nearly naked body. All he had on was one of his favorite pairs of underwear: a pink string bikini with a tiny bow in front. He shrugged; the advantage of living alone was not having to care about walking around his living room in nothing but his bare essentials.

Except for no good reason, he felt embarrassed and exposed. He wrapped his arms around his torso and closed his eyes. No one but his doctor had seen him like this in years, and now he remembered why. Scars of various lengths cut paths through his freckles, and his joints were all slightly misshaped. There were lumps where, beneath his skin, thicker scar tissue had formed. He eyed his jeans and decided against putting them back on, clinging to the rare feeling of shame as though it made better clothes.

A twinge in his shoulder pulled him into the present, and he rubbed at it gently. It wasn't bad enough to do anything about it, so he dropped his hand and headed for the kitchen. Once he'd fetched a glass of water, he returned to the couch and lay back down. He wouldn't be able to sleep again yet.

Cat tried to remember what he'd been dreaming about—it was hazy, but in the dream, David had been there. Or maybe it was Micah. Their similarities ended with their appearance. Cat ignored the pang of guilt over why he'd talked to Micah in the first place—

he'd looked so much like David it had piqued his curiosity. He closed his eyes and concentrated, but all he had of the dream were random images and the feeling of being pulled in two like a wishbone. Which of them would get the bigger piece?

Wait...no. He frowned. He hadn't been dreaming about either of them, it had been about Bryce. His first boyfriend, if that's what they were to each other. He hadn't seen Bryce or his other friends from those days in years. Cat thought he remembered hearing Zee got married recently, but he hadn't gone or even been invited. There was a good reason he hadn't spoken to Ezra or Bryce in almost eight years. He wondered what had become of them and whether Bryce had ever been honest with himself. Whether he'd ever forgiven himself.

Now wide awake, Cat slid his hand down to play with the bow on his panties. He entertained the idea of taking it further, but he didn't bother; he wasn't even a little bit aroused. On any other night when he couldn't sleep, he might indulge, maybe even break into his ample supply of toys, all of which were upstairs in his room. Not tonight. He was pretty sure he wouldn't be able to get it up or keep it there. It happened on rare occasions as a leftover from his injuries, but that wasn't the current problem.

Enough moonlight streamed in the window that there was a bright patch illuminated on the floor a few feet in front of the fireplace. Cat pulled himself partially upright and stared at it for a long time. Eventually, he rose from the couch again and stepped over to the hearth. He fumbled for the matches on the mantel and lit a pillar candle and then a stick of incense. For a few minutes, he stood in front of the fireplace, watching the flickering flame and the curl of smoke. Hooking his fingers into the sides of his underwear, he stripped them off and kicked them aside. With his eyes closed, he stood bare, breathing in the scent of burning honeysuckle.

Cat picked up a long box and the matches and knelt in front of the fireplace. He opened the box and drew out his rosary, running his fingers along the smooth glass beads. Until this summer, he had prayed nearly every evening, drawing strength and comfort from the familiar act. He'd been distracted lately, drawn into a tug-of-war between what he wanted and what he knew was right. Prayers were forgotten, lost to the consuming pursuit of coping.

"In the name of the Father, Son, and Holy Ghost." His voice sounded strange after hours of silence.

He kissed the Crucifix, and he couldn't help the shiver

running through him at the memory of the last thing his lips had touched. What should have been as holy a moment as his prayers was stained with the sin of his mistake. Repentance tonight, then. He lit four votive candles in the fireplace: one for himself, one for Micah, one for Bryce, and one for David. Two men he had once loved and one he would never have the chance to. Sitting back, he began his prayers, working his way around the chain until he had completed three full chaplets.

When he was through, Cat stood, his knees stiff from bracing on them for so long. He extinguished the candles but left the incense to burn itself out. With a slight flush at the realization he was still naked, he pulled his underwear back on. The night had turned cooler, and his sensitive skin erupted in goosebumps. A wave of sleepiness surprised him, and he yawned. Maybe he could rest a little after all. Shivering, he ascended the stairs, climbed into bed, and pulled the covers over his head. He fell asleep within minutes.

SUMMER

CHAPTER THREE

DELIVER US FROM EVIL

AUGUST, 2005

CAT FELT like he'd overdone it a bit. He'd made the mistake of telling LR he was going to a party. She'd asked, and he couldn't tell her the truth, which was that he and the guys were going back to the club one last time before Zee and Ezra left again for school. So he'd said it would be a "gay party," and she was back to being a generally fabulous sister instead of an irritable overachiever. She'd been all right most of the summer, but now that her senior year was a month away, she was stressed again. In Cat's opinion, LR was far too driven for a seventeen-year-old, but sometimes her intensity paid off. For example, when she was throwing her whole self into helping her big brother pick out something to wear and do his makeup.

Which was why he stood in the line wearing denim capris, a glittery silver tank top, and a blood-red stud in his ear. He'd painted his nails to match. When LR had done his makeup, she'd tried to get him to use eyeliner, but the most he would let her apply was mascara because the other stuff itched too much, and he'd messed it up with squinting anyway. She'd convinced him to let her put something slightly shimmery on his eyelids, though. He had the lip gloss she'd given him in his pocket in case he needed it. Watermelon flavored, with a juicy reddish tint to it. The idea of having someone lick it off his lips made his dick perk up a little.

That someone wouldn't be Bryce, apparently. They'd spent the afternoon sucking each other off before Cat went home to change, and somehow blowjobs had turned into a raging argument about why they couldn't have out with it and at least tell the guys they were official. Cat was sick of Bryce's hedging, but Bryce had numerous complaints against Cat, too, the number one being why Cat had to be *so gay*. When Cat corrected him and said queer, Bryce snapped at him that wasn't his point, he'd meant Cat should tone down the glitter and why the hell did he have to wear those damn lacy underpants and lip gloss and swish his hips like that?

So here they stood, waiting to be let in, and Cat was busy ignoring Bryce and talking to Ezra about his future plans. Zee had taken a summer class at the community college, but Cat had spent his summer working in his mom's cafe, Ezra had a job at Wegmans, and Bryce was doing construction with his older brothers. His job was a source of great entertainment for the others. It turned out Bryce wasn't the only one with secrets. His middle brother had made him swear not to breathe a word of it, but Cat and the others all knew he was having a fling with the boss's daughter. Bryce's boss was one of those extreme evangelical ex-Catholics, and while he was all right hiring Bryce and his brothers, he'd made it clear his daughter was to stay away from "their type." Cat, despite not having been to Mass in years himself, didn't follow what Bryce's boss thought was so awful; his crowd didn't seem a whole lot better.

"So, Cat, did you figure out what you're going to do after this year?"

"Nope. Looking at schools, though. I'm going to have to transfer if I want to do something besides work in the cafe when I'm done."

Zee, who hadn't been paying attention until then, turned around. "Yeah? Where are you going?"

"Probably one of the SUNYs. Cortland or maybe Brockport. I checked out a couple others, too, but I don't know." He shrugged. "Ithaca or maybe even Eastman."

"Up in Rochester?" Ezra asked. "I was thinking about transferring to the U of R."

"Yeah. It doesn't matter anyway. I'm going to study conducting eventually, but I'll probably end up giving private cello lessons in some tiny little town in the middle of nowhere." Cat laughed. "Kind of like here."

Zee and Ezra laughed too, but Bryce scowled at him. "Not dressed like that, you won't," he muttered.

"What's that supposed to mean?" Cat asked at the same time Zee smacked the back of Bryce's head and muttered, "Asshole."

"Nothing," Bryce said, but he made a show of looking Cat up and down.

Cat wanted to slap him, but instead he turned his back to Bryce and twitched his ass, just to annoy him. "Anyway, my alternatives are pretty limited, so I'll have to figure it out soon."

What he hadn't told the others was how even though he'd followed his father's footsteps—albeit with cello and not voice—he had other things he was interested in, too. He was torn between finishing his BA in music and changing to something else, starting over once he was away from his family. He'd taken two electric circuit analysis classes and two math classes at the community college, but he'd never gone anywhere with them. His coursework was otherwise all music, all the time. He'd have to be sure to choose a college with an orchestra, though, as he would miss playing too much if he decided on another course of study.

The line moved, and in a short time, they were inside the familiar club, music and people and lights all around them. As soon as they were past the entrance, Cat's future plans and past arguments were drowned out by their surroundings. He relaxed, glad for a few hours away from his family and relieved they were finally letting him have his own life for a change. They might not have been pleased to know where he had really gone, but for once they hadn't objected when he'd said he was going to a party. Time to let go and enjoy one of the last fun nights before classes started again.

By this time, they had a routine. Cat mostly avoided dancing—too many people, and he wasn't interested in being squished—but he liked sitting on the upper floor and watching everything unfold below. A small part of him wanted to be more adventuresome, throw out his habit of carefully monitoring every facet of his life. He was in charge of it now, and he could, in theory, do as he pleased. If only he could turn off the nagging voice reminding him his parents and his doctors were right, for the most part.

Bryce wandered downstairs, and Cat watched with a bit of sadness. They were already growing apart, and it had only been since April they'd been having sex regularly. He couldn't understand it; they'd both been so eager to take the next steps, but it was all coming apart instead of bringing them closer together. Now Bryce was being rude to him and disappearing to find someone or something else. Cat looked down at himself. Bryce didn't want someone like Cat after all. Too bad he hadn't mentioned it before Cat spent the summer in his bed.

While he mulled things over, someone sat down at his elbow. He glanced over at Landon, who offered a wide smile. Cat mustered the manners to smile back instead of rolling his eyes. He was sick of Landon hitting on him every time they were there, but he was too frustrated with Bryce at the moment to flip Landon off like usual.

"Hello there," Landon said, bumping Cat with his shoulder. "All by yourself?"

"One of my friends is down there." Cat pointed to the dance floor. "The others are...somewhere. I lost track." He wrinkled his nose. More like they got bored and wandered off to find Ezra's cousin. Come to think of it, Cat wasn't sure why Landon wasn't with them.

"You don't ever dance," Landon commented.

"Not in the middle of the crowd, no." Cat didn't feel like explaining again.

"Ah, okay." Landon leaned in. "We could find something else to do."

"Such as?" Not that Cat didn't have at least some idea where Landon was headed.

"Go somewhere quieter." His smile was charming in a way which reminded Cat of a salesman.

Cat looked over at him and gave him a *yeah, right* look. "You skipped a few steps, I think."

"Did I?" The way Landon was looking at him made Cat wish he could move several feet away without being rude.

"I don't really know you."

"Oh, are we playing that game, then?" Landon laughed; it wasn't mocking, but there was an edge to it Cat didn't like.

"What game? I'm sitting here people-watching." The night was not turning out how Cat had hoped, and Landon wasn't helping. Cat wished he would get the hint and go away.

"I like people-watching. Especially you." Landon lowered his voice. "You're very pretty, you know. And I like pretty men." He reached out and touched Cat's chin with his thumb.

Now Cat really did shift away. He stood up and faced Landon. "I'm going to go find my friends."

He started to turn away, but Landon put a hand on his wrist. His grip was firm without squeezing, but he could easily have tightened it. Cat stayed put, waiting for Landon to say his piece.

"You should know something about me," Landon said, his voice low and smooth but with a hint of bite.

"What's that?" Cat's heart thumped, and he tried to withdraw his hand, but Landon held fast.

"I always get what I want eventually." He smiled again, accompanied with a wink.

"Not from me," Cat told him, trying to sound firm despite the quiver in his voice. "Not like this."

Landon's expression changed, fading quickly from predatory to contrite, though he still didn't look sincere. He loosened his grip on Cat's wrist. "Look, I'm sorry if I was too forward, but I couldn't resist when I saw you sitting here alone." He brushed his thumb over Cat's skin, making a slow, sensual circle which didn't diminish Cat's feeling of unease in the least. "If you change your mind, you know where to find me, yes?"

"Sure," Cat replied. He took his arm back and left Landon alone.

Still feeling annoyed and wary, Cat descended the stairs. He didn't know where any of his friends had gone, so he walked the perimeter, keeping a lookout. Eventually, he saw Zee leaning against one wall, texting someone—probably his girlfriend—and Ezra was next to him with some guy's tongue down his throat. Cat was torn between exasperation and amusement; there went his suspicions confirmed. He wouldn't needle Ezra about it, though. Coming out was a process, and Ezra would talk in his own time. Later, Cat would work out some supportive but vague thing to say to Ezra.

At last Cat spotted Bryce. He was alone in the alcove by the bathrooms, and he didn't look happy. Confused and worried, Cat threaded his way over to him. He settled in next to Bryce and put out one pinkie to twist it around Bryce's.

"Hey," he said.

Bryce looked down at him. "Hi, Cat."

"Is everything okay?" Cat would have liked to add, *because you've been a real dick all day and now you're alone in a corner*, but he wasn't feeling quite snotty enough to start another fight.

"No," Bryce said.

Startled at his admission, Cat slid his hand so their palms pressed together. "Tell me."

Bryce closed his eyes and swallowed visibly. "I'm sorry I was an asshole to you earlier."

"Okay," Cat said. "You're forgiven. What's going on?"

"I can't do this with you anymore," he said.

Cat had known. He was surprised to find it didn't make him angry, only sad. "I thought maybe." He would never be who Bryce wanted or needed.

Bryce must have picked up on his thoughts because he said, "It's not you, Cat!" His sigh was full of anguish. "I want to be with you."

"Then why—"

"My parents suspect. It's why I kept telling you we couldn't be there when they were home. They said you're not welcome there because you're a bad influence on me, and they won't pay for college if I don't do what they say. I can't get stuck in this shitty little town doing construction with my brothers. I can't!" He was breathing hard, his chest heaving with the force.

"Hey." Cat pushed off the wall and stood facing Bryce. "It's okay. Maybe...maybe we can wait, right? It's only another year, and then we'll figure it out. We'll go somewhere else."

Bryce shook his head. "I don't know."

"That's all right." Cat reached up and touched his cheek. "I'll have faith enough for both of us." It was a hard thing to say, but after a long friendship and Bryce's admission of his feelings, the least Cat could do was give him something in return. The rest would surely work itself out. "I want to be with you too," he said.

Bryce gazed down at him and then let out his breath in a rush as his shoulders slumped. He put his hand on the back of Cat's neck and drew him in, kissing him long and deep. Cat melted into it, wanting to show Bryce how much he cared about him in the only way he knew how. They lost track of their position in time and space, kissing until both of them had raw lips and aching jaws, and yet they didn't stop. Every part of Cat's body was hot and alive, and he wanted Bryce—wanted to prove he would still be there when Bryce was ready.

He pulled back a couple of inches, and it seemed Bryce had the same idea. They pushed their way into the bathroom to the same stall where they'd gone the first time they'd been at the club. Cat wondered if Bryce had what they needed in his pocket but then giggled against Bryce's mouth as someone in the next stall flicked a condom over the wall, hitting Bryce in the back of the head. Bryce rubbed the spot and grinned, kissing Cat quickly before bending down to retrieve the offending–though welcome–item.

Their coupling was near-frantic, as it had been all summer. The first time they'd gone so fast was when Bryce had been afraid his parents would find them. After that, he'd often seemed like he needed to go quick and hard. It had become another of their experiments, Cat playing with the thrill of danger to his body and Bryce excited by the threat of discovery. Now, in the bathroom, it was simply because they were both too eager to go slow, especially knowing it was the last time for who knew how long.

Bryce propped himself against the wall behind the toilet, and Cat slammed into him until Bryce let go with a cry. Cat was so close himself, and he kept going, needing to come. Suddenly, he felt the pull and knew he'd done it again–torn the deep muscle in his abdomen. By then he was already at the point of no return. He didn't have an orgasm, but he ejaculated, and it hurt like the devil. The pain was so intense his agonized yelp echoed off the walls, earning a wolf whistle, a smattering of applause, and several calls of "Yeah, baby!" from the few other people in the bathroom. Cat added humiliation to the host of other things he was feeling at that moment. He and Bryce were usually quiet enough that people might have suspected what they were doing but would have ignored them.

Cat pulled out by way of collapsing onto the floor. "Bryce–" He grunted in pain.

Bryce looked down at him as he zipped his fly. "Cat?" he asked, his eyes going wide with fear. He crouched down and helped Cat shed the condom and clean up while assessing him.

"Please," Cat whispered. "It hurts."

Bryce was already on his phone, his fingers frenzied as he typed. He shook his head, hit a couple of buttons, and put the phone to his ear. A moment later, he shoved the phone back in his pocket.

"The guys aren't answering. I'm going to get help," he said.

He slammed his way out of the bathroom, leaving Cat writhing on the floor. Cat gasped and hauled himself up to sitting. It was bad, he knew. He had to call someone while Bryce looked for their friends. Fumbling for his phone, he thought of his parents. They'd be pissed off, but they would come get him. His hand shook, and he couldn't think clearly.

"Hey," a voice by his elbow said. "Here, let me help you up."

Cat looked up to see Landon, and he shook his head. He knew

he couldn't stand, or shouldn't anyway. "My boyfriend...going to get help..."

"Come on. We'll go find someone." Landon bent down to help lift Cat.

He didn't want to stay in the bathroom, so he let Landon haul him to his feet then leaned heavily on him while he struggled to fasten his jeans. "Thanks."

"Your friend do something to you?"

"No. I need...I need to get out of here." The pain had lessened a little, down to more of a cramping than burning, and Cat sighed with relief.

"Sure." Landon wrapped an arm around Cat's waist and led him out of the bathroom.

By the time they reached the bar, Cat was more numb than in pain, but he still couldn't fully straighten his left leg. Landon asked for water, and he handed it to Cat. Gratefully, Cat sipped at it until he felt a little better. He made to grab his phone again, but Landon stopped him.

"You need to get somewhere?"

"Home," Cat said. He needed medical attention, but it would be better to have his parents with him. "I need to find my friends first. They don't know I left the bathroom." His mouth felt like it wasn't moving right either. He worked his jaw, trying to loosen whatever it was.

"I'll drive you, and you can call them on the way."

Cat's head swam; he frowned, confused. He must have done more damage than he'd realized; the bleeding seemed to be affecting his brain, too. When he tried to stand again, he was lightheaded. Landon reached out to catch him, and Cat slumped against him. Shaking his head, Cat attempted to clear the weird sensation, but the motion only made it worse. He tried to think; had Landon offered to get him somewhere? He couldn't remember the question or whether he'd answered it. The bartender interrupted his almost-thoughts, but his voice sounded far away.

"Your friend looks like he's had a bit too much. Better get him out of here."

"Right, on my way."

Landon half-lifted him and sort of carried him to the door, where they slipped out around a few people coming in. It was warmer outside than inside, but the air was fresh, and Cat took a deep breath in a renewed effort to stay coherent. He let Landon guide him out to the parking lot, hardly registering where they were going until they were leaned up against a car. Landon didn't make a move to unlock it or help Cat inside. Instead, he leaned Cat against the door and pressed up to him. Cat grunted in pain at the contact, but at least Landon was holding him up, and he was a little more clear than he'd been at the bar.

Cat took the opportunity to reach for his phone again, and he hit Zee's number. While it was still ringing, Landon grasped it and tossed it aside into the dirt, and the sound stopped. He put his face right up against Cat's.

"Glad I finally got you alone," Landon murmured in his ear. "Didn't think you really meant what you said earlier, not after I heard you in the bathroom. So hot. Should have been for me."

"What?" Cat heard the slur in his own voice.

"I told you, I always get what I want." He bit Cat's earlobe, hard.

Cat's head buzzed, and he pushed at Landon. "Stop...I can't—"

His protest was muffled by the first blow, which caught him off-guard and knocked him to the ground. His phone lay next to his head, and he turned toward it when he heard Zee's voice. "Zee?" he said. "Please! I need—"

This time, what cut him off was a foot landing a solid blow on his side. Landon was saying things to him, but none of them made sense—something about it being his fault. Cat gasped, trying to piece together how he'd gotten where he was and what the hell was happening. He never arrived there; something hit his head, and everything went black.

Chapter Four

Begotten, Not Made

Cat opened his eyes and squinted at the sun coming in through a small crack in the heavy curtains. He tried to move, but everything ached, and a thick fog of confusion covered his thoughts. Where was he? The last thing he remembered was being back in the club with the guys. They'd been standing in line. Had they gotten inside? He couldn't recall. They must have, though, and gone to Zee's afterward. He had yet to test his joints, but judging by the way his body felt, he must have been doing something physical to precipitate the soreness.

Blurry around the edges, a memory surfaced of being in the bathroom with Bryce, and his face heated. It had been a weird night, but he couldn't remember all the details other than a vague recollection of making out with Bryce and stumbling into the bathroom. Had he been drunk? That didn't sound right, but he'd been so out of it. He wracked his brain, reaching for something to make sense of. He and Bryce...kissing...the toilet stall...He'd been hurt, and Bryce had left. That much he knew. Then someone...no. Not just anyone, Landon. He'd found Cat alone on the bathroom floor. Everything after that tumbled into his mind in fuzzy pieces, and Cat tried to curl in on himself as it reached the surface. The pain when he moved was so severe he cried out, and two women in scrubs descended on him.

"He's awake," the first one said.

"Only just."

One of the nurses put a hand on him, and pain seared through his shoulder. He wanted to tell her to stop, but the only voice he found was to yell again and continue until she let up. The nurse backed off and murmured, "shush, shush" over and over. Cat shook, whimpering. He was vaguely aware through the haze of agony that someone was administering meds, but he didn't care. Nothing made any sense, and the pain wasn't just physical. Even though the fire under his skin receded, the memories remained intact, more clear than they had been before.

Whatever the nurse had given him made him sleepy after a while, and the sharp edges of his mind blurred and softened. He settled down, drifting off again into the holy abyss of dreamless slumber.

When he next woke, the pain was much less severe, and he wasn't alone. His parents were there, along with a police officer. Cat struggled to sit up, but he felt weighted down. Giving up, he looked around the room. He was in the hospital, which he'd more or less gathered from the last time he was semi-awake. He wasn't in as much pain, but he was stiff. His side hurt as though something were pulling on it.

He tested a few motions and discovered his arms worked all right, aside from the ache in his shoulder. His legs, too. He could wiggle his toes and flex his ankles, but bending his hips or knees sent a flare of pain radiating out. All sorts of tubes and wires snaked their way inside his hospital gown, so many he couldn't follow which ones went where at first. As he shifted, he became more aware of the sounds around him—swishing and beeping at low volume. There was a surgical drain with a tube inserted somewhere in his abdomen. His face was sore, too, and a little stiff when he scrunched his nose. He reached up to feel it and discovered there were bandages there.

Panic crept slowly up his spine. He had next to no idea what had happened, only vague shapes and shadows after exiting the club into the parking lot. Something floated to the foreground of Cat's memory. The last thing he remembered doing was pleading with Zee for help because someone was—*Oh, God.* Landon. What had he done after finding Cat in the bathroom? If he was in this bad condition, he couldn't imagine how he'd managed to survive whatever Landon had done next. He looked around for someone who might explain things and finally caught the eyes of three people by the doorway: his parents and a police officer. He forced a noise from his throat in hopes of attracting their attention.

"Honey?" Mom moved swiftly to the bed. She reached out for his hand, but he withdrew, remembering how bad the nurse's touch had hurt. She looked pained, but she didn't try again.

Dad stepped forward. "Cat?"

Cat shrank back against the pillows at his father's worried expression. Something had to be very, very wrong for him to have that look on his face. The trembling started in Cat's hands and spread outward as his agitation increased. All he wanted was for someone to speak, to tell him what had happened. He tried to ask, but the only sound he managed was a fearful whimper. His mother sat carefully next to him and slid her arms around him. He leaned his head on her, grateful it didn't make anything hurt worse.

"Shh," Mom murmured. "I've got you."

He clung to her, closing his eyes and waiting for the fear to pass as she stroked his hair like she'd done when he was small. Eventually, he was calmer. As soon as his mother registered the change, she let go and helped him sit up a little. He grimaced, but once the throbbing subsided, he felt better with the new position. Mom looked over her shoulder, and Cat followed her gaze to the other person still stationed by the door. He stepped forward.

"This is Officer Kerwin," Cat's father said. "He wants to ask you a few questions about what happened last week."

Last week? Cat's head buzzed with renewed confusion. He must have meant last night. They were at the club, and then—Cat had no memories of how he'd gotten to the hospital or what had happened since. The officer approached the bed.

"Son," he began, and Cat winced. He hated being called that. The officer didn't notice, or perhaps pretended not to. "Can you tell me anything about the person who attacked you?"

Attacked. The only thing he recalled clearly was Landon hitting him so hard he collapsed. The memory of Landon's face next to his, hot breath on his ear, a hand groping him...and then being hit so hard he saw stars. Cat didn't understand why Landon had done it, why he'd gone from threatening rape to apparently beating him to a pulp. Maybe he'd done both—Cat simply didn't remember enough to make sense of it.

"Cat? You need to answer the question," Dad urged. "Is there anything you can tell the police?"

Yes, Cat thought then, *No*. For a long time he sat there, staring into Officer Kerwin's face. He might have been mistaken, but he was sure he read judgment there: Cat shouldn't have been at that club; what did he expect would happen? He didn't want to tell anyone anything. In fact, he didn't ever want to talk to anyone again. He pressed back against the pillows and shook his head.

The officer's expression relaxed, and he lowered his voice. "It's all right, son. No one is going to hurt you here. I can't help find the person who did this to you unless you tell me anything you know."

Cat cringed again at "son." He'd never liked it anyway, but now it made him feel wrong and vulnerable. He looked to Dad, who nodded, and Mom, whose eyes were red-rimmed. He wasn't going to talk in front of them, that was for sure, but even without them he had no desire to tell anyone a single thing that would give them power over him. Slowly, he shook his head again and put a hand to his throat.

The officer sighed and turned to Cat's parents. "Does he even know what happened?"

"I'm not sure," Mom replied. "He's been in and out of consciousness the whole time. He might not remember how long he's been here or why. Um..." She paused, then continued with a quavering voice, "I don't even know if he can talk. He hasn't said a word to us or the hospital staff."

Officer Kerwin nodded. "There's not much I can do without his statement. It's still potentially a hate crime, and it's certainly battery, but it'll be hard to find the guy unless Becket cooperates. We'll look for him, but I sure would appreciate something more to go on than...well, nothing." He gave Cat a pitying look, which only served to make Cat more determined not to tell him anything.

They moved the discussion out of the room, Cat's parents holding hands as they exited. Cat breathed a sigh of relief. No one would ever get a word out of him for any of it. In fact, if he made it out of the hospital—which he suspected was still up in the air, given how he was feeling—he would make a promise. No, several promises. Nothing like that was ever going to happen to him again.

Lying there, listening to the steady beep and watching the IV fluid drip, he made his first vow: silence. *No more talking, ever.*

It was another week before the doctors let him go home. He now had a second surgery under his belt—the first had apparently been to remove his wrecked spleen and repair the muscle he'd torn. After listening to enough conversation about it, he gathered he was lucky he didn't lose his whole leg. He'd had to learn in bits and pieces what all had been done to him during his two-week stay.

Multiple blood transfusions, naturally, and carefully regulated infusions of factor; bandaging his broken nose; injections of anti-inflammatories; close monitoring of intracranial bleeding and pressure; bed rest; and now a shiny new mediport. On the one hand, that was good, since he could use it to take his meds. On the down side, until he and his family were adequately trained, he would have to have his infusions done by someone else to maintain functionality. His level of being pissed off at the loss of independence rose steadily.

Thus far, he'd managed to avoid talking to anyone, exactly as he promised himself. It made the nurses irritable because he wouldn't communicate with them properly. For most of the time, he'd had Mom to translate. He was sure his mother thought at first something had damaged his voice, but Cat knew that was one part of his body which still worked fine. His throat had been raw for a while, but he'd tested it out when no one was in the room, and he could speak without it hurting. He'd been croaky and his speech had been mildly slurred for the first few tries, but it all smoothed out. He let the others think he still couldn't talk; he had nothing to say to anyone.

LR was onto him, though. She'd hissed it at him once when she'd been in with Mom to visit. Mom had stepped out to make a few quick phone calls, and LR had leaned over the bed to look him in the eye. She'd called him a drama queen and told him to stop purposefully doing things to upset their parents. Cat had been tempted to spit on her or yank her hair like he might have done if they were ten years younger, but he restrained himself and simply gave her the finger. It was currently his go-to gesture, useful in almost every situation.

On top of everything else, Cat had the impression he wasn't likely ever going to completely recover. The attending physician had wanted to keep him for at least another week, but given his history of infections, Dad and Mom advocated on his behalf to take him home and do all his physio outpatient. They'd gone so far as to call his hematologist, who agreed and took charge of his care despite it being above and beyond his usual duty.

The doctor discharging him also made noises about future surgeries, including joint stripping, to relieve the worst of the pain. A nurse brought Cat and his parents reams and reams of papers to read over and another stack to sign. Not one of them, from the doctors and nurses to his parents, said what Cat was sure they were thinking, which was that he had been monumentally stupid. Well, LR said it, but only once, and it was under her breath. Cat wasn't sure if he'd been supposed to hear it. In any case, he chose not to respond, much like he'd been doing for the whole week he'd been coherent enough to interact.

When his parents came to pick him up, Mom handed him what had been his second favorite outfit. The first had been ruined, torn and bloodied and then cut the rest of the way from his body in the emergency department. It was one less set of clothes to give away or, preferably, burn. Mom passed him a pale blue v-neck shirt and a pair of soft black capris. He'd always loved those, mainly because he thought they made his ass look hot. Now he hurled the stack of clothes at his mother, watching them unfold mid-air and land at her feet with a soft *plumpf*. He stared in shock that she'd brought him his beloved cherry-red thong and a lacy white double-A-cup bra. She'd always loved and supported him, right down to his choice of underwear, and not once had she questioned why her teenage mostly-boy wanted to go bra shopping with her. The memory, and her excellent taste, made him feel sick.

Mom didn't yell or scold. She looked down at the pile then swept everything up in her arms. As though she'd anticipated it might be one of his more masc days, she produced a second bundle—a pair of ordinary khakis and a white t-shirt with a band logo on it. Folded neatly on top was a boring pair of tighty whities. Cat sighed with relief and accepted them. He couldn't tell her he would rather have worn the other clothes because there was his second vow: simplicity. *No more glitter. No more acting or dressing "like a girl."* The only thing his overt femininity had gotten him was being left in a bloody heap. Without a word, he yanked the curtain around his bed and struggled to dress, fighting the lingering exhaustion and pain and resting in between each item but refusing to let anyone else help.

By the time he was through, he wanted to cry with frustration. Not one part of his body was cooperating. The antibiotics—which he gathered were long-term this time, due to his lack of spleen—messed with his stomach and made him feel like crap, and he still couldn't stand up unsupported. Obviously that was what the physio was for, and everyone seemed to think he would at least be mobile again eventually, but it still made him want to throw things. He would have, too, if every movement didn't make him feel seasick and like he'd been running marathons. He didn't want to live every day like this. Being tied to his meds and forbidden from reasonable, everyday activities other people enjoyed without worry were bad enough. This was into unbearable territory.

At last he pushed the curtain aside again, but he wouldn't look at Mom when she came to sit beside him on the edge of the bed. He did let her draw him against her, though. She might have been more protective of him than he'd liked, but at the moment, Cat didn't care so much anymore. Mom was holding him without judgment or anger, a change from the heavy sadness and fear he'd felt rolling off her on previous visits. Cat needed several minutes to regroup so he wouldn't upset this new delicate balance.

When Cat felt stronger again, he sat up and examined her face, not sure whether he wanted to see reassurance or disappointment there. He found neither, simply the quiet sort of love only his mother could give. He knew he looked exactly like her, save that her eyes were true green—unlike his own gray-green ones—and her hair was a deep red rather than a strawberry blond. He was similar to her in other ways as well, but that day, he felt as though he no longer resembled her at all. The person he had been was gone.

She brushed his bangs off his forehead, and Cat pushed at her fingers before sitting all the way up and adjusting so he could stand. Mom took the hint and stood up as well, helping him into the wheelchair by the bed. She called for the nurse, and with little other fuss or discussion, he was on his way out of the hospital.

Chapter Five

Into Your Hands I Commend My Body

September, 2005

The weeks after Cat was released from the hospital were tense. Everyone watched him every minute. He couldn't tell whether they were expecting him to fall over and die or whether they were still waiting for him to speak. Neither of those was going to happen, and whenever he sensed someone's eyes on him, he ignored it or escaped to his room.

His parents had changed things around in order to accommodate his inability to navigate stairs. He was slowly regaining strength, which he took as a sign he might eventually reclaim his own space rather than the converted office, but he was stuck on the first floor for the moment. He refused to acknowledge or be grateful for the small space. It afforded him almost no privacy, including the lack of a real door. Mom had gone to the trouble to hang a curtain on a tension rod, but it wasn't the same, and it fueled Cat's rage over one more way in which he'd lost control over his own life.

The night before he began physio, Cat lay on his bed fighting the ongoing nausea from his meds. He'd already made two trips to the bathroom to empty his stomach, and now he was down to a dull ache. When he pulled himself up to sitting in bed, his eye caught his cello, stranded in the corner of the room. The "office" had once been the family's practice room as well as Dad's space for grading assignments. They'd moved the piano but not Cat's cello, so there it sat, mocking him. He moved the fingers of his left hand almost involuntarily, patterning them the way he would have placed them on the fingerboard. It was too soon to know whether there had been any lasting effect on his ability to play, and he was undecided whether he cared. Come to think of it, he didn't care for much of anything at all these days, and he wasn't sure whether that was a side effect of his meds or of his confinement.

There hadn't been a big discussion about his classes, at least not one he'd been allowed to participate in. He'd heard his parents arguing over how soon he'd be able to return and whether or not he might attend or be given coursework at home while he regained strength. Mom had won out, and the only thing Cat had been told was that he didn't need to worry about taking care of anything. Dad had withdrawn him from classes. It seemed the college thought nearly being beaten to death was a fairly reasonable excuse for dropping out. Cat didn't bother trying to find a way to communicate his lack of interest other than ignoring Mom when she told him; it wasn't as though it had cost them anything, since all his classes were free anyway.

Cat struggled to organize his thoughts. Not only was he missing out on his own classes, he'd been in the hospital when Zee and Ezra went back to school. He had a fuzzy memory of them visiting him once, but Cat had still been too out of it to process anything. He'd only been out of the ICU for a day or so. The one thing Cat recalled was Ezra saying over and over that he was sorry. Bryce hadn't come at all. Now the three of them were back in school, and Cat wondered who Bryce was sitting with on the shuttle and if he missed Cat's company.

While he was thinking about Bryce, LR stuck her head around the curtain. He looked up at the rustle, and she gave him a half-smile. "I brought you something," she said. She held out a glass. "Um...I heard you puking."

Cat nodded, and she stepped inside. She handed him the glass, to which she'd thoughtfully added a straw so she could hold it for him. This was an old comfort between them. In moments of sympathy, LR would bring him ginger ale when he didn't feel good. She would sit with him, sometimes flipping through one of her magazines so they could admire the clothes together and pretend to dress each other. But that was before, back when things were some version of average. Back when the most LR ever had to worry about was if she would ace her chemistry final or whether Cat might steal her favorite lip gloss. Knowing he was the source of the unhappiness and fear he sensed from her made him that much more frustrated.

She rubbed his back and let him lean on her while he sipped. "Cat?" she said.

He pushed away and sat up, wishing he hadn't as his stomach cramped. He breathed slowly until the feeling subsided then looked at LR.

"I know you won't talk to the others, but at least talk to me." She sniffled, and when her eyes shimmered, Cat's stung too.

He shook his head and turned away from her, curling up on his side the best he could with his back to LR. She sighed.

"I wish..." She didn't finish telling Cat what she wished for. Instead, he felt the bed shift as she stood up. "Don't shut me out, please?"

Cat heard her footsteps and the swish as she pushed aside the curtain they'd hung in the office doorway to give the illusion of privacy. He waited until she was gone before carefully rolling onto his back and reaching for the bedside table. There was a small notebook next to the glass LR had left. In it, Cat had written down the first two vows he'd made. Now, lying on his bed in his wrecked state, a heaviness descended on him as he contemplated a third. If he hadn't been in the club...if he hadn't been with Bryce...Surely this was the natural consequence of his behavior. He'd pushed his limits, slamming into Bryce's body until his own couldn't take it anymore. Maybe Landon wouldn't have touched him if he hadn't been so foolish. The heat of his guilt burned in his gut, and he wondered if this was what people meant when they spoke of God's judgment.

He hadn't been to church in years, not since at age fourteen he'd figured out it meant committing to a lifetime of celibacy. Not for one minute had he believed God hated who he was. Cat's parents were agnostic, but they'd both been raised in the church and knew he believed. His father had taken care to tell him in no uncertain terms that if God's love was as wide as people said, then it was big enough to love queer people too. Cat did wonder what his grandmother would have thought; she had died when he was sixteen, and she had never made known her opinion about his being queer—only her opinion on his quitting church.

Maybe it wasn't too late to make it up to God now, though, to atone for everything he'd done all summer. He grabbed the notebook and pulled the pen out of the spiral binding. Slowly, he scrawled his third vow: Chastity. *No dating. No sex. No jerking off.* He snorted; dating wouldn't be an issue, not with his mess of problems. Where would he go, and who would want him anyway? The other two items on the list weren't problems either, given his lack of interest. He almost couldn't bear being touched in a non-sexual way by his own family, let alone anyone else. Sex involved the kind of physical contact he would gladly never experience again.

He read over what he'd written, and fury coursed through his veins over everything he'd lost. He winged the notebook across the room, hurtling it into the wall. It dug into the paint, leaving a small mark. Cat huffed, but a tiny part of him felt better.

The noise alerted the other three members of the household, and in under two minutes, they were all clustered in his doorway. Cat looked up at the sound of the curtain moving. He glared at the others with their worried expressions. Mom saw the notebook and bent down to pick it up, still open to the page where Cat had written his vows. Cat crossed his arms and waited while the others read over the list. Dad glanced up, and he looked mildly amused. LR rolled her eyes and gave an exasperated huff. Mom seemed defeated.

"You don't have to do this," she said.

Cat didn't answer.

Dad read the list out loud. Cat closed his eyes and listened to his father's voice.

1. Vow of Silence. No speaking whatsoever. Yes/no questions may be answered with nod or shake of the head. Everything else shall be answered with traditional prayers.

2. Vow of Simplicity. No clothes or jewelry other than jeans and t-shirts. Limit of one pair of ordinary sneakers. Absolutely no makeup of any kind.

3. Vow of Chastity. No dates. No boyfriends. No sex. No jerking off.

A muscle twitched in Dad's jaw, and Mom looked as though she had no idea how to respond. LR had no such hesitation. She snatched the notebook out of Dad's hand and waved it at Cat.

"You think this is funny?" she demanded. "Is this your way of telling us all to go to hell for trying to help you?"

"LR—" Dad began, but she turned her glare on him.

"No, Dad," she said. "I'm done pretending all we need is time, love, and tenderness or some shit."

"LR!" Mom snapped.

"Oh, shut up, Mom," LR retorted. "You heard what Dad read. Cat can talk. He's choosing not to. So we're all supposed to guess what he needs and when, while he figures out whatever is going on in his head. All the rest of this? It's such bull. You think I didn't hear what you guys said he was really doing that night? He lied to us! He lied to me." Her voice broke. "And I was the one who helped him—" she cut herself off with a near-scream.

"We can talk about this," Mom said. "Not now. We need to wait until Cat's ready. He'll tell us what he needs in his own time."

Which will be approximately never, Cat thought.

"He obviously needs something now!" LR yelled. "He's sick, Mom. They messed with his head, and now he thinks he has to do this. God knows neither of you seem like you want to do anything about it, though. I'm done."

She pitched the notebook onto the bed and stormed out. Cat shook all over, and he watched the doorway, wondering if she would come back. His stomach ached for a different reason. It was his fault LR was so upset, and he didn't know how to fix it. One more thing on his long list of sins to atone for. His parents turned toward him, but he refused to meet their gazes directly. He picked up the notebook and read over his vows again, ignoring Mom and Dad.

"Honey," Mom said, "is there something else you want to tell us?"

Cat finally looked up and shook his head. He held up the notebook and waved it.

Dad sighed and nodded. "I know you need some space right now. I hope when you're ready, you'll talk to us."

He put his arm around Mom's shoulders, and they stepped out of the room. Cat blew out his breath and looked down at his hand, realizing he still had hold of the pen. He scribbled a single sentence underneath the vows.

Lord Jesus Christ, have mercy on me, a sinner.

On the morning of his first physio appointment, Cat woke early. He was often out of bed before everyone else anyway, but for several weeks, he'd been sleeping later. To test his muscles, he flexed several before attempting to sit up. He only groaned a little at the shift in position. Even Cat had to admit he was better than he had been. While he still had healing wounds everywhere and a few places where the bruising had left swollen spots, he'd mended reasonably well after the surgery. He was weak, but at least he could move short distances without help. Ahead of him lay a long stretch of both recovery and boredom.

Cat tried to shower on his own, which resulted in throwing a bottle of shampoo weakly against the tiles. He had a shower chair, and that alone made him irritable, but he couldn't even lift his arms long enough to clean his hair. Alerted by the noise, Dad poked his head into the bathroom.

"Cat?"

With a growl, Cat shoved the shower curtain aside just enough to turn his frustration on his father. Dad stepped into the bathroom and opened the curtain farther. He adjusted the shower spray so he wouldn't get soaked.

"Let me?" he asked, picking up the shampoo bottle from where it lay in the tub.

The question startled Cat. So far, no one had asked him much of anything, simply doing or assuming things. Cat nodded, and Dad scrubbed his scalp.

"Can you soap up, or do you want help?" Dad's hands were gentle as he rinsed the bubbles from Cat's hair.

Cat flicked his wet bangs from his face and handed Dad the soap. Without another word or a complaint, Dad took over, washing Cat's body with firm confidence. Cat hated to admit it, but it felt good. Dad's touch was different from the hesitant, too-careful way Mom cleaned him or the complaining LR did on the rare occasion no one else was available. Cat relaxed into it, and when Dad was through and handed over the washcloth, Cat turned his face to his father again and offered a small smile in thanks.

"You're welcome," Dad said. He bent down and did something he hadn't done since Cat was small—he pressed a light kiss to the top of Cat's wet head. It hurt, but not in any physical way.

As soon as Cat was dry, dressed, and ready to go, Dad drove him to the outpatient building. Cat was grateful to have his father at his side rather than his mother. Mom was a worrier, and it wouldn't have helped Cat's already tense state.

They sat side by side in the waiting room until a woman with a long braid came out and called, "Becket?" He waved to her, and she crossed the room to him. "Hey, there. I'm Shannon Li, and I'm going to work with you. Ready?"

He flipped her the bird, and Dad glared at him, but Shannon only arched an eyebrow as the corner of her mouth lifted slightly. Cat was impressed, but he refused to let her know by way of crossing his arms and giving her a dark look, which only made her grin.

She wheeled him back along a corridor lined with physio rooms. Beyond them, he saw where the space opened into something like a haphazard gym, with equipment and wide benches everywhere and people in various states using them. He had no idea what it was all for. Shannon didn't wheel him that far, though. She entered one of the smaller rooms and closed the door. There was a mat on the floor, a sink, a shelf full of smaller equipment, and three chairs.

"All right, so the first thing we need to do is go through some testing to see what you're able to do so far. Are you ready?"

Cat huffed and angled away from her. He was tempted to flip her off again—if he were honest, he would have to admit it was fun to see people's reactions. Instead, he simply didn't answer. Shannon came around the wheelchair and put her hands on the armrests.

"Look," she said. "I've seen it all before. I know you're pissed as hell about things right now. But I promise, if you put all that anger to work with me, I will help you get your ass independent again." She straightened up. "And by the way, don't bother trying to make me lose my shit with your antics. I know that game, and you'll lose."

Open-mouthed, Cat turned his head to stare at her. She gave him a wicked smile before her expression turned professional again, and she grabbed a clipboard from the shelf.

"Now," Shannon said, "how about we get started?"

PART III

Self-Denial

August, 2013

THE SOUND of someone knocking on the front door woke Cat from his slumber. He rubbed his eyes and stretched, a couple of his joints creaking. When he licked his dry lips, he grimaced at how pasty his mouth was. Before he could contemplate brushing his teeth on his way to answer the door, he heard footsteps on the stairs.

"Cat!" a voice called. LR—of course.

He cringed. Because he hadn't returned any of her last three phone calls, she was checking up on him. Even if he'd wanted to, he couldn't have kept her out—he rented the house from her, and she had a key. He wasn't allowed the luxury of a chain on his door, and she knew it. She'd been respectful enough to knock first, but she'd obviously decided he wasn't going to answer. He growled under his breath; he had no desire to see or talk to anyone after what had happened with Micah. LR was intruding on his private moment of wallowing in misery. Maybe if he was quiet enough she would leave him alone.

No such luck. She walked right into his bedroom, which he hadn't bothered to pick up. There was a dirty cup on his bedside table and a pair of jeans on the floor where he'd dropped them. That was two things too many to be sitting out, and LR was going to notice. He suspected she'd already seen the downstairs, though, and he knew it wasn't tidy by his usual standards. He rolled onto his back and sat up, keeping the blanket tucked up under his chin. LR marched over to the bed and stood by it. Cat didn't look her in the eye, instead concentrating on the tattoo of a carbon chain on her left forearm.

"Why the hell are you still in bed?" She made an exasperated noise at his continued lack of response. "And why haven't you been answering my calls? What did that asshole do to you?"

Cat shook his head. It wasn't anyone's fault but his own for hoping he could move on. He shrank back against the pillows and drew his knees up.

She yanked the covers off him and rolled her eyes. "And you're in your underwear. Why are you in your underwear? I do not have time for this. I have work at the lab and classes."

Tugging the blanket back, Cat tucked it around himself again. He didn't bother telling LR she was lucky he'd had anything on at all. He was used to wearing boxers or pajamas around the house, but he slept bare most nights in the summer. Not that she cared; she'd been helping take care of him for years, and she was no longer fazed by his body. Any person who could tolerate being around him when he was at his sickest was all right in his book, but LR had done it more than anyone, at this point including their parents. She was better at it, too, even if he wouldn't tell her so. He frowned at her, hoping she would get the hint and go away.

"I'm here because Mom wanted to be sure you're all right," she snapped. "No one has heard from you in three days. Three fucking days, Cat!"

Cat blinked. That long? He sort of recalled doing things, more or less. He'd prayed in the middle of the night once, and he was sure he'd gotten out of bed for important needs like to get a drink or to piss. He might have eaten, and he supposed he probably remembered to take most of his meds. Now that he thought of it, maybe he hadn't. A hot flush bloomed in his cheeks because he *did* remember what he'd been doing the night before, when he'd finally been at ease enough to touch himself. If LR was paying attention, she might have been able to work that part out by a few items he'd left on the floor partway under the bed. He drew his brows together, trying to picture what else he'd done in the last few days.

LR's posture relaxed. "You didn't realize?" she asked. "Oh, honey. He really did a number on you, huh? Want me to go beat him up?" She sat down on the bed and tried to put her arms around Cat.

He pulled away and shook his head. It wasn't Micah's fault; it was Cat's. Why couldn't LR figure it out for herself? He shoved her, and she almost toppled off the bed before catching herself. She stood up and put her hands on her hips.

LR trained her glare on him. "Not gonna talk to me? Fine. Call your fucking therapist, Cat. I'm not dealing with your bullshit a second time. You know how much the last time almost destroyed you. You're a responsible adult. Call her." She growled. "On second thought, I know you won't, so I'm going to do it for you."

He didn't move, and she looked him up and down before pulling out her phone. Apparently, she still had his therapist on speed dial, even all these years later. She stalked out to the hallway, and he only caught snatches of her conversation. Five minutes later, she returned to the living room and eyed him before snatching the covers away again.

"Why the hell aren't you up? Go get dressed. Your appointment is in half an hour."

With a sigh, he rolled out of bed. Even if he decided to talk to his sister, he wasn't going to give her the details about what had happened with Micah. She would have too many questions about why he'd gotten involved in the first place. At least he would be fully clothed in the therapist's office and wouldn't need to justify himself there. He glared at LR when she suggested she drive him, and she backed off, telling him to get it together or she was calling their parents. He kept his back to her while he pulled on his jeans, and eventually, she gave him a dramatic huff and turned to walk away.

"I'm trusting you'll get yourself to the appointment," she said over her shoulder. "Otherwise, I'm coming back here."

He gave her the finger even though she was already out the door.

AUTUMN

CHAPTER SIX

LORD HAVE MERCY

NOVEMBER, 2005

SOMEHOW, THROUGH weeks of both physical and occupational therapy, Cat managed to keep all three of his vows. He'd taken to wearing t-shirts with slogans ranging from mildly rude to fairly offensive, but other than that, he'd found numerous creative ways to express himself. He tallied the score in his favor, since the other three members of his family had more or less resigned themselves to asking him yes or no questions. It had only taken a week of responding to *peanut butter or egg salad* with a Hail Mary and *what time is your appointment* with the Our Father before they all mostly stopped.

He'd ripped the page with his vows out of his notebook and tacked it to the wall in his temporary room. Dad shook his head in resignation every time he caught sight of it. Mom often pushed him to give her a real answer and had developed a perpetual frown in his presence because the most she ever coaxed out was a recitation of the Act of Contrition. LR had stopped speaking to him entirely after the day he responded to her a dozen times with the entire Nicene Creed. When she'd stormed off and slammed her door, it was the first time he'd smiled since That Night.

That Night was how he'd come to think of it. It gave him the freedom to refuse access to it even in his own head. He could lump his entire life into broad categories of "before" and "after" without having to entertain the tangled memories he still couldn't quite make sense of. He'd promised himself nothing like That Night would ever occur again, and he meant to give no room for it.

Once, Mom had asked him how long he planned to keep it up. It was the only question he hadn't tried to answer by reciting a prayer; he'd said nothing at all. The truth was, he didn't know. He was tempted to answer, to find a way to tell Mom it was forever. Except he held to the belief God would give him a sign when he had done enough penance, as soon as he was absolved of the guilt for his part in That Night. In response to Mom's question, Cat only shrugged.

In the meantime, Shannon had been right, and with hard work on both their parts, Cat had regained enough strength he didn't need so much assistance. Grudging respect for her had turned into trust as she worked his body until he was capable of nearly all his own care again. Pain was still a constant companion, but at least he was mobile. He'd even gone back to swimming once a week at the college pool with Dad. Those moments in the water were good; Dad was lower pressure than Mom and LR, and gliding along next to his father, hearing quiet words of encouragement, took Cat back to his years perfecting his technique for a race. He would never be so agile again, but at least it eased the aches and stiffness.

Fortunately, he was also well enough now he could pick up a few hours of work at his mother's cafe. She wouldn't put him on register, and his lack of communication made it hard to fill orders, too. He was reduced to sweeping floors, clearing tables, and restocking the bathrooms. He didn't care; at least it was work, even if he still tired easily and had to limit his shifts to half an hour here and there.

It wasn't until this had been going on for almost two months that Cat's parents finally did what he'd been expecting all along—they got fed up. He was well enough now they'd all anticipated he would go back to whatever they thought "normal" was, only he didn't comply with their plan. He could tell they were on the verge of making some Really Important Decision because LR crept around him and sneaked peeks at him when their parents' backs were turned.

Once, she waited for everyone else to go to bed and slipped into his room the way she'd done when they were much younger and she hadn't had to worry so much about things like college applications and why her older sibling wouldn't ever be himself again. They'd been close until his senior year. It wasn't as though they'd had some huge falling out; it was more a gradual slide while she became more studious and he rebelled against the entire previous eighteen years of his life. Somehow, they hadn't regained their footing.

She didn't speak a word at first, only laid her head on the pillow next to his and carded her hand through his shoulder-length hair. He could tell something was on her mind, and he waited for her to say it. She bit her lip and looked for all the world like she had no idea how to talk to him. He sat up a bit and motioned to her, hoping she understood the meaning in his gesture. She sighed and sat up too, curling her knees to her chest.

"I wish you would talk to us, Cat," she said.

He flopped back onto the bed next to her and stared up at the ceiling. Her words didn't justify an answer, not even in the form of a prayer. Everyone had been saying the same thing in a hundred different ways over the weeks, and he was out of patience for it. He'd made himself clear, and they all needed to back off.

"It's just...well, we don't know how to help you."

Cat huffed. He didn't need help. Couldn't they see that? He was perfectly fine. He was going to spend the rest of his life doing penance for getting into so much trouble, and that was as it should be. If nothing else, he would stay healthy. He could keep his vows indefinitely, just like being in a religious order but without the actual monastery. Much simpler this way, and he could still help out in his mother's cafe.

LR let out a tiny breath. She lay back too, and her fingers found Cat's. Out of the corner of his eye, he saw her turn her face toward him. "I love you, big brother. I miss shopping with you and painting our nails and picking out just the right lip gloss." She leaned in and kissed his cheek. "Speaking of which, if you change your mind, they're having a sale at Linder's Drugs this week on flavored gloss. I'll bet you'd like the pineapple one."

Without another word, she rose form the bed and slipped out of his room. For a long time, Cat stayed in the same position, wishing he could tell her he missed all those things too, but they were gone from his life forever.

Everything came to a head the next day. Mom shouted at him in the kitchen when he started the Our Father after she asked what he needed from the grocery store. She stopped mid-sentence, turned to the sink, and stood there with her shoulders shaking. Cat knew her well enough to know she was raging inside while simultaneously feeling guilty for yelling at him.

When she turned around, she said, "That's it. You will—no, I guess I will, since you're still not speaking—make an appointment with a therapist. I know you're hurting, baby, and we've all tried our best, but there's only so much we can do. You won't even find some other way to let us in, not even writing it down. This has got to fucking stop."

Cat knew it was serious if his mother resorted to swearing. She'd grown up having her mouth washed out more than once, and she'd always said she hated dirty language but would never punish her kids for it. This was the first time in Cat's memory he'd ever heard her utter the f-word. It made him step back a pace and stand still, waiting to see if she had anything else to say.

She sighed. "Understand?"

He nodded. His mother would call, and he would endure hour-long sessions of sitting in silence while the therapist threw questions at him he wouldn't answer. Or maybe he would, and the therapist wouldn't mind if he said the Gloria Patri every week. It was anyone's guess.

Cat curled his legs under himself then sat still as stone on the standard-issue doctor's office couch. It was his third try with a therapist; the first two had made it clear it wouldn't work out. She had a name, he knew she did, but he didn't care what it was. In his head, he referred to her as "the therapist" or "Dr. Something-or-Other." He'd been there less than five minutes and he hated her already, despite the fact that she hadn't yet spoken to him. She was sitting there, right in front of him, and her presence was all he required to develop deep loathing. Did she think she could make him talk? That was never going to happen. Cat possessed endless determination, capable of outlasting anyone. He was the one who had poured hours and hours into learning a single difficult line of sheet music on his cello until he had it perfect. He waited for the therapist to say something—anything—but all she did was sit with her chair swiveled to face him, her legs crossed and notebook open on the table beside her. Cat watched as she uncapped a pen and poised it over the paper.

At last she spoke. "Why don't we start with why you're here," she suggested.

My parents think I'm broken. They think I'm a fragile little boy who needs them to guard me. He wasn't going to confirm for this therapist that he did, in fact, agree with them. He'd probably agreed with them for at least ten years, maybe longer, but he simply hadn't known the word. The summer after his eleventh birthday, he'd overheard his mother say it when talking to his father and realized it was the term he'd been looking for. That was the year he'd had a reaction to his meds which put him in the hospital.

Out loud, he said, "Lord Jesus Christ, have mercy on me, a sinner."

She pursed her lips and scrawled something. "Maybe you'd like to tell me something about yourself instead."

Hell, no. "Lord Jesus Christ, have mercy on me, a sinner."

There was nothing to tell anyway. Cat was certain his parents had given his entire medical history and probably his social history as well. He wondered if they knew what he'd been doing with Bryce, both at the club and elsewhere. Then he wondered if they'd told the therapist. If so, they probably wouldn't have used the words he might choose. He pictured his mother's pinched expression as she sought a polite way to explain the fine art of bathroom fucking.

"All right," the therapist said. "Help me understand a little better. Your mother says you've taken some vows. Would you like to explain them to me?"

He paused. Maybe if he was rude enough, that would get her to stop. He barked at her, "Lord Jesus Christ, have mercy on me, a sinner," and he flipped her the bird.

She didn't even flinch. Cat couldn't decide if that made him proud of her or disappointed. He'd been able to upset the first therapist with his attitude, and the second one declared she couldn't help him even though he'd said absolutely nothing to her. This one clearly wasn't going for his usual methods; she would take some work.

"At least help me understand the vows so I'm not in the dark. Your parents gave me a list, but I want to have a clearer picture of where you're at."

It wasn't a question, so Cat felt no need to answer her. Instead, he gave her both fingers this time. Increasing his rudeness might make her impatient. If he couldn't shock her, maybe he could annoy her.

No such luck. She remained calm when she replied, "It

sounded as though you had a complicated system going." She scribbled something else on her notepad.

Of course it wasn't complicated. It was three simple vows, easy to maintain. Cat scoffed and slouched down in his seat. He had every right to decide how his own life was going to go. Whatever Landon thought he was stealing That Night, Cat was taking it back. The woman across from him wasn't entitled to part of him any more than Landon had been, and Cat wouldn't give her—or anyone else—a claim on him. He seethed, glowering at the therapist and trying to send waves of anger in her direction. All she did was sit quietly in front of him with her pad of paper, waiting for him to make a move. He wouldn't give her the satisfaction that day or any other. He gripped the armrests of his chair and leaned forward. The therapist didn't move, but she blinked and swallowed visibly.

When a lengthy period of time passed without Cat moving or making a sound, Dr. Something-or-Other changed tactics. "It might be best if we work through these one at a time. The big one, which I suspect is why your parents brought you to me, is your vow of silence." She glanced down at the folder on the table. "The other two are chastity and simplicity. Those sound like they might be rooted in a religious tradition. Is faith important to you?"

Technically, Cat should have answered her question, since it required a yes or no answer. However, he had no inclination to lead the therapist on, making her think he might eventually talk to her about anything. If her goal was to wear him down, he would prove impossible to crack, even if he had to show up every week, sit in her office, and refuse to talk to her. He curled his lip in a sneer and made no response.

The therapist made another note on her paper. "As much as I would like to start with helping you find your voice again, how about you let me know which of your other two vows you'd like to begin with."

Cat gritted his teeth and poured as much loathing into the words as he could. "Lord Jesus Christ, have mercy on me, a sinner."

The therapist sighed and backed off. At last she said, "It's going to take some time to unpack everything going on for you. We won't accomplish it in a single day. I'm willing to give you some time to process."

They spent the rest of the hour in silence; score round one for Cat.

CHAPTER SEVEN

PRAY FOR US, O HOLY MOTHER OF GOD

CAT SAT in his real bedroom, a pair of scissors in hand and a pile of clothes on the floor in front of him. It was a painful but necessary step, and he was finally well enough—more or less—to take it. He held up the first skirt he'd ever owned. LR had bought it for him for Christmas two years ago, right after he'd admired the one she'd just gotten for herself. It was calf-length and deep maroon in color; LR's was blue. The bottom layer was soft cotton overlaid with black lace. It hugged Cat's barely-existent hips and swished against his legs when he moved.

He sat there holding it for a long time, his hand with the scissors shaking. Eventually, he set it aside; he couldn't destroy it. Instead, he picked up the next item, which he mercifully had less emotional attachment to, and proceeded to shred it, taking out his frustration on the unsuspecting fabric. An hour later, fifty percent of the pile was in long strips which he could repurpose as cleaning rags or give to LR for one of her creative projects. The other half he folded and placed in plastic bins, too weary to continue cutting. He set them on the floor in his closet, thinking he might donate them when he was feeling up to it.

It wouldn't be right away, that was for sure. The headache he'd had when he started had radiated out to include his neck and shoulders. The left one in particular was sore—not just aching but a deep, throbbing pain. He grimaced and hauled himself to his feet, intending to take something for it. The moment he stood up, a hot flush rushed down his body, and he swayed. The pain in his shoulder increased, and a prickling sensation rose on his skin.

He knew what it was, and he had to get help or he would end up sicker. Stumbling into the hallway, he braced himself on the wall and crept toward the stairs. He should call out, get someone to come, but he wouldn't break his silence even for that. Unable to walk further on his shaking legs, Cat sat down on the top step and put his head in his hands. What else could he do? Drawing on all his strength, he spoke softly into the dim light of the stairwell.

"Pray for us, O holy Mother of God, that we may be made worthy of the promises of Christ."

His voice was barely above a whisper, so he repeated it a little louder. Rocking slightly where he sat, his head gripped in his hands, he raised his voice, repeating the prayer over and over, each time a little louder until he was calling out.

"Pray for us, O holy Mother of God, that we may be made worthy of the promises of Christ!"

LR's door opened, and she emerged. "Cat? What the hell?"

She stepped over to him, and he felt her irritation when she bent over him, but it quickly drained away and her brow creased with worry. Her hand went to his head then slid down his cheek. He closed his eyes, her cool fingers soothing against his heated skin.

"Holy crap. You're burning up. I'm getting Mom."

She thundered down the stairs, hollering for their mother. Relieved, Cat slumped against the wall under the railing to wait.

"Hey there. I'm David, and I'll be your nurse today."

The voice at his elbow caused Cat to stir, floating into awareness from a dream-free stage of sleep. He flung one arm over his eyes to block the light which had just turned on over his hospital bed. He extended his other hand and gave the intruder his middle finger.

A deep chuckle. "Good morning to you too, sunshine. I need to give you your meds."

Cat groaned and struggled to sit up. The minute he did, his abdomen cramped, and he gasped as the urgent need to empty his bowels hit. He flung off the sheet. To his credit, the nurse—David, apparently—understood. He helped Cat up and to the bathroom, depositing him on the toilet and stepping back to wait. Cat gagged, and David reached for a basin just in time for everything to explode from both ends.

"Okay?" David asked.

Cat grunted as a second round of cramps rolled through him and he expelled more bodily fluids. He panted, regaining the wind that had been knocked out of him. He waved his hand at the basin, knowing at least that part was over, and waited for the diarrhea to stop.

David took care of the basin while Cat finished clearing out his intestines. His eyes stung, but he refused to show anything in front of the person he'd decided to blame. It didn't really matter that David had done nothing more than wake him up for the day; it was still all his fault.

"Let me know when you want some help," David said.

Out of his peripheral vision, Cat saw that David kept his side toward Cat and his head facing the sink where he was washing up, but their eyes met. David donned a fresh pair of gloves. Cat sneered at him in reply and shook his head.

"You're going to change your mind. I'll be right here." David leaned against the wall, arms folded and legs crossed at the ankles.

Cat's stomach cramped, but nothing else came out. He sighed in relief. Shaking, he tried to shift so he could clean himself, but the stiffness in his joints made it difficult. He put his head in his hands.

"It's okay," David said, his voice softening. "That's why I'm here. Please, let me help you."

Cat's shoulders slumped and he nodded. While he cleaned Cat up, David made a few comments about unrelated topics to which Cat paid little attention. His touch was surprisingly gentle. When he was through, he applied a thin layer of something cool and soothing before shedding his gloves to clean his hands. He then helped Cat stand at the sink to wash up and led him back to bed. Cat slipped gratefully between the fresh sheets someone had installed while he was in the bathroom. He inhaled deeply as the nausea and cramping finally faded to a low level.

"No doubt that felt awful," David remarked. "Probably from the antibiotics. I'll see if you're okay to have something for the nausea, and I'll be sure to have the doctor take the stool softener off the scripts." His lips twitched.

Cat finally cracked a smile, though he remained silent. He was feeling slightly more amiable than he had when David first arrived.

David grinned. "Looks like you have a sense of humor after all. They come in to check your vitals yet?"

Cat shook his head.

"All right. Should be here in the next ten minutes. Think you can eat something? It'll probably help your stomach. Maybe I can sneak you some crackers from the kitchen."

Cat's eyebrows went up. He doubted David was supposed to offer such a thing. He shook his head again and leaned away.

Laughing, David said, "I was kidding about sneaking it. You're allowed to have whatever you can tolerate." He glanced at the clock on the wall. "It's at least an hour till they bring you breakfast. I was serious about the crackers."

Another shake of his head. Cat shifted a little and groaned. He didn't feel as sick, but a dull ache radiated out from his chest, his head throbbed, and despite whatever David had used on him, his ass was sore from the diarrhea. It was clearly going to be one of those days.

"You don't say much, do you?" David remarked. He shrugged. "No worries. We'll figure out what you need."

That was a change. The other nurses were exasperated with Cat for his various forms of non-verbal communication. He never asked for a single thing, nor did he complain. Cat was impressed with David for picking up so fast on what he needed. The night nurse had let him throw up in bed because she couldn't grasp that he'd needed the basin, and it had been too far to reach for himself.

David broke into his thoughts. "So, you know why you're here, right?"

This time Cat nodded. He'd had septic arthritis before, but this was particularly bad. The previous doctors had warned that with the surgeries, his lack of a spleen, and all the weaknesses related to his assault, he was likely to have more problems for at least a while, if not permanently. Fortunately, he'd come in early enough this time that his stay would be comparatively brief. Even so, the heavy doses of antibiotics always left him feeling like garbage, aggravating his already sensitive digestive system.

"Well, looks like you'll only be with us a short time. I'm pretty new here, so I'm not familiar with all the procedures, but they might be transferring you to HemOnc."

Not pediatrics? Cat hauled himself up in the bed. That was where he usually stayed, much to his ongoing annoyance. Not that he minded children, but he was over eighteen and didn't want to have a six-year-old for a roommate anymore. Slowly, his mind registered what David had said. Hematology-oncology was blood cancers. He gasped, his heart speeding up and fear gripping him. He turned his panicked gaze on David, hoping to convey his confusion and worry.

David's eyes reflected his understanding, and he reached over for Cat's hand. "You're fine. Trust me, someone would have told you—and already moved you—if you had cancer. That's just where they're putting adults with complications from hemophilia and other blood disorders since they've expanded the unit. Technically, you qualify because you're over eighteen."

Cat closed his eyes, the fear draining away. He squeezed David's hand to let him know he understood.

David made a few notes on the clipboard by the door. "Well, anyway, I'm not sure. If you're doing well enough, they may send you home from here. All right, Becket, I'm going to finish visiting a few other people. Do you want me to help you get washed up in a bit?"

Cat shot David a glare for using his real name, not caring that the hospital records probably didn't have his nickname. He flopped back against the pillows and immediately wished he hadn't. His back hurt. He scowled at David, who he decided was annoying despite being nothing but helpful all morning.

"I'll take that as a no. Just ring for me if you need something, okay?" He retreated to the door, glancing over his shoulder. When Cat didn't reply, he exited the room, leaving the door ajar.

Cat made a face at the place where David had been standing. There was nothing about this that didn't suck. He huffed and closed his eyes, hoping to get a few minutes of peace before another overly cheerful hospital employee showed up to do something else to him.

The staff decided not to move Cat after all. By the end of the third day, he was feeling better and was bored. The unit was quiet, which surprised Cat, but flu season hadn't come into full swing yet, so there weren't many people hospitalized for illness. Outside of the few books his parents brought and his regular walks around the unit, there was nothing to do. He had a roommate, but the middle-aged man in the next bed wasn't a great conversationalist, and Cat wasn't exactly holding up his end either. Cat didn't even know what the man was there for, and he was moved elsewhere eventually anyway.

Most of the nurses didn't bother hiding their annoyance or amusement with Cat's unusual brand of communication and his irritability. He was well enough to manage most things without their help, for which he was grateful. He wasn't fond of having someone hover while he peed. The only tolerable nurse had been David. To his credit, David at least talked to Cat. It was slightly more fun when he switched shifts to evenings because everything slowed down around eight. After he finished his responsibilities, David came to sit with him. Listening to David share his opinions on various subjects was better than lying around moping.

One night, to Cat's surprise, David opened by saying, "I have something to show you. Want me to go get it?"

Cat shrugged, but he couldn't completely hide his curiosity. David grinned and ducked out of the room. A moment later, he wheeled a cart in with a television. He'd beaten the other nurses to the game system and signed it out to Cat, which was a welcome change. Cat hadn't even known the unit had one. The only option was an ancient racing game, but Cat hardly cared; at least it was different. David set it up for them and handed Cat a controller. For the next twenty minutes, they chased each other around the various worlds, and David eventually conceded to Cat—but it was a close game.

"I figure you'll be out of here soon," David remarked as he packed the system away.

Cat shrugged. He was still feeling good from beating David's ass as well as from having a worthy opponent.

David coiled the cords of the controllers and set them on the cart. "Good thing you're going home tomorrow—hopefully I'll stand a chance against whoever's in here next."

Cat laughed then covered his mouth. It was the first sound he'd made outside various indications of pain or frustration and his prayers. An odd sensation gripped his stomach at the thought of David playing video games with someone else, but he banished it as quickly as it had come. Annoyed with himself, he turned away from David.

"Listen," David said, and Cat rolled his eyes, preparing for a lecture. He knew how conversations went when he was expected to pay attention. "There's something you should know, and I want to tell you now since I won't see you tomorrow."

Cat looked back over his shoulder, and David shifted so he was turned toward Cat.

"You know it wasn't your fault, right?"

A frown crossed Cat's face. He had no idea what David was referring to. Cat had been hospitalized lots of times over the years, and no one had ever suggested it was his fault. Even he knew better, aside from That Night.

"Just..." David hesitated. "I read your chart, and even without the details, I do know your medical history."

Instead of answering, Cat turned over again so he wasn't looking at David. He wasn't going to dignify him with an answer. David shouldn't have pried, and he had no business talking about it now.

"Your illness doesn't define you, and neither does one night. It doesn't have to be that way." David pressed lightly on Cat's shoulder; his fingers were warm.

Cat shrugged him off and remained resolutely turned away.

"It's my job to listen, if you change your mind and decide to talk." David stood up and stretched. "Back to work. Unit's slow, but I need to start meds. I had fun hanging out with you."

Cat peeked over his shoulder and found David grinning down at him. A sudden flash of heat bloomed in Cat's chest that was nothing like the fever he'd come in with. He rolled back over and looked up at David—his warm smile, his curly brown hair, his summer-sky-blue eyes—and he began to sweat. He had to duck his head. How had he not noticed before how good-looking David was? He answered his own question with the realization that he had, but he'd been pretending not to. He indulged a little, given the fact that he was unlikely to ever see him again. All of those thoughts were enough to reawaken one thing that had been somewhat absent over the previous few months. The emerging feelings were pleasant but unwelcome, given his promise to avoid them at all cost. He shifted uncomfortably, his mood hovering between pleased and frustrated. He'd thought his personal commitment and months of recovery had created the lack of interest he wanted. The return of those feelings surprised and upset him, and he didn't know what to do with them.

"What is it?" David asked.

Cat shook his head, and David didn't press. There was no way to communicate his conflicted thoughts. Cat closed his eyes, hoping to indicate his need for rest and encourage David to leave. A moment later, the door clicked shut and Cat was alone once more. He turned back over, trying to block out a fresh sense of exactly how broken he felt.

Chapter Eight

That We May Be Made Worthy

Miraculously, Cat managed to stay out of the hospital after that, although not through any extra effort on his part. While he focused on avoiding people, LR was busy stressing over her schoolwork and all the classes she was taking. Unlike Cat, who had intentionally stopped taking anything he didn't need for graduation, LR had gone out of her way to add classes *for fun*. Cat didn't hide his exasperation with her. She was smart enough to do whatever she wanted with the rest of her life, a fact which their parents reminded her of repeatedly. They'd only ever considered him good at one thing, probably due to his lack of interest in schoolwork. Neither of them had asked if a career in music was something he wanted; it was the expected, safe path.

At least LR had stopped accusing him of creating drama. Possibly she—and their parents—had decided Dr. Something-or-Other would sort him out eventually. They'd all settled into a comfortable routine, and Cat had some peace for having agreed to sit with the therapist once a week and not talk to her, either.

During one session, she said, "Let me try something different today. I know you're not ready to talk about more recent history, and maybe not even think about it. I'm not going to ask you to say anything, just think. Okay?"

Surprised, Cat nodded, and he was rewarded with a small smile. It irritated him; she obviously thought she'd won some important victory. He wasn't going to give her the satisfaction of letting her know he was annoyed, though. He tamped down the urge to respond with a rude gesture. She'd probably have taken reacting to her as a sign of his giving in. For whatever reason, she was more amused by his flicking her off than she was upset by it, and feigning disinterest had a more profound effect.

"All right. When was the first time you were aware of how your hemophilia affected everyday things in your life?"

Cat snorted at her odd question. When had he *not* been aware? *Oh, you want to hear about the time when I was six and tried to climb the tree outside our house, and Mom came running. She yelled at me and startled me so bad I nearly fell out of the tree. When I climbed down, she lectured me for five minutes straight about how I'm not like other people and I have to be more careful.* He knew why. It wasn't only the injury which scared her; it was the treatment.

He kept his mouth shut, scowling at the memory. The therapist watched him, but she didn't say anything more. She made a few notes. Her eyes met his, and he flinched and turned away when all he saw was her openness.

"Good," she said, as though she'd been able to see into his mind and know he'd come up with something. "You'll have to trust me that this is relevant. Keep going with whatever you were processing just now." She had made a guess about his life prior to That Night, and she hadn't been far off. He was undecided whether he was impressed or furious.

No one had asked him—ever—how he was affected by his health and his limitations. They were always too busy calculating every risk and weighing those in balance with the benefits to make sure he wouldn't end up hospitalized or sick or dead. They whispered behind closed doors and cried on his behalf and fought with doctors and school employees, but not once did they talk to him directly about what he wanted or needed.

Once he started, he couldn't control the rush of memories. How had he not realized the effect of keeping it all in for so long? He stared at the therapist, trying to breathe steadily through the painful recollections. He shook with the effort of holding back years of rage. *How about never being allowed to sleep at friends' houses or go to birthday parties unless my parents knew the family or take school field trips unless one of my parents could chaperone? Maybe you want to hear about constantly missing school or daily nosebleeds or how I always changed in the bathroom for gym class so the other boys wouldn't see fresh needle tracks or how skinny I was or my swollen joints or any number of bruises. What about years of hospitalizations and antibiotics and so many times I couldn't keep food down? I could tell you about the time my new teacher saw marks on me and told the principal she thought my parents were beating me. Even though they both knew what was wrong with me, they still called a social worker. I spent an hour crying in the nurse's office trying to explain to the social worker that no one had hurt me. When the nurse—who was actually pretty cool—came back in, I was a fucking mess. She spent another hour trying to calm me down while we waited for my parents to show up. Afterward, I heard her telling off the teacher for not coming to her first.*

He didn't share any of it aloud. Instead, he curled his knees up and sat there clenching and releasing his fists until he could speak. After a round of reciting the Act of Contrition, the therapist requested Cat let his parents in for the last few minutes of their session. At first, Cat was irritated; she hadn't warned him, but she'd obviously told his parents—it explained why Mom had left her business partner in charge at the cafe in order to accompany Cat. The annoyance melted into curiosity and then resignation, and he assented by nodding his head. The therapist rose to let Dad and Mom into the room. They sat stiff-backed in the chairs on either side of Cat. The therapist returned to her seat and sighed, allowing a few moments of silence before speaking.

"I'm happy to continue having you pay me to sit here for an hour a week, listening to Becket recite prayers. However, I don't feel that I'm helping him in any significant way yet at this point." She pressed the tips of her fingers together and turned her gaze on Cat. There was no pity or pain in her hazel eyes, and the genuine concern Cat saw made him wince. He tried to look away, but it was impossible. She lowered her voice and spoke directly to him. "Maybe you think I don't notice much, but I do. I'm not making random doodles on my page while you keep your silence. You *are* making progress, and I'm still thinking about ways I might be able to help you. But on my own, it won't be enough." She turned her attention to his parents. "Becket has a lot—and I do mean *a lot*—of anger, and it would be ideal if we could sort out all the places it comes from and what it's really covering—preferably before it all comes out at once."

"I see," was all Dad said; he sounded disappointed.

Mom was more useful. "I suppose you have a suggestion? Because God knows, we've tried everything at this point."

The anger the therapist mentioned surged through Cat. There was nothing wrong with him for making a decision about his own life. They could like it or not, but they had no business telling him what he did or didn't need. It wasn't as though he sat in his room all the time, brooding and snarling at everyone who passed. He kept himself and his space clean, contributed to the household, and worked in the cafe when he felt well enough, which was most of the time now. So what if he wanted to stop talking? If the therapist didn't think she could do anything, he would be glad to stop going.

Dad reached across Cat to put his hand on Mom's and glanced at Cat. "I don't know that it's a problem so much as I worry about when the dam will break."

The therapist nodded. "Which is exactly why I think it would be a good idea for us to try two new things. First, I'm going to suggest meeting with the two of you." At Cat's enraged growl, she held up a hand. To Cat, she said, "Before you get too upset with me, I'm not asking them to come here and tell me how much your trauma has disrupted their lives. Nor am I going to share anything you say or do in here. That's not fair to you, and it won't help anyone. I'm asking them here for your benefit as much as theirs." She addressed all of them. "Second, I suggest Becket find a group. I can recommend several, and I've made a list. Some are therapy groups, which means if he wants to join, there's an additional process and a referral, and he may need to wait until there's an open session. Most are simply for support. They range from trauma survivors to living with chronic illness in general to specifically hemophilia groups."

She handed over a piece of paper, which Cat intercepted. His mother shot him a look, but she didn't grab for it. The message was clear—find a way to make his life work or get a different doctor. His parents were tired of dealing with him, and so was she. Cat didn't particularly care. He made a show of crumpling the paper and flipping off all three of the people sitting there.

"Just think about it," the therapist urged, ignoring his rudeness.

He didn't wait for his parents, storming out of the office without looking back.

Dad and Mom didn't bother keeping their thoughts to themselves on the way home. They expressed their opinions freely—to each other, ignoring Cat's array of angry sounds from the back seat. He wanted to tell them both to go to hell.

Hell, it turned out, was more or less where *he* ended up. Back at home, they called LR and then sat down in the living room, all facing Cat. It took a while, but eventually Dad cleared his throat.

"We were willing to be patient with you," he said. "We understood, and we weren't expecting anything overnight. But when anyone tries to help, you shut us out. We're not doing this to punish or fix you. You need more than we can give you right now."

There were more words, more things Cat didn't want to listen to because he knew there was some truth to it. If he could have, he would have told them he wasn't punishing them, either. When he was sure the family meeting was over, he climbed the stairs to his room and lay down, never having given them a proper answer on whether he would take the therapist's suggestion.

For the most part, every person in his immediate family moved around him as though he was part of the furniture. No one asked his opinion or offered him anything anymore. His mother had begun leaving notes regarding what she wanted done around the house and when she expected him to be ready for work. His father didn't so much as utter a "pass the peas" at dinner. He took Cat to the pool, but he'd stopped doing anything other than swimming. LR holed up in her room doing homework, and when she emerged, she didn't even look him in the eye. At least once a week, he heard LR crying or his parents murmuring about wishing there was more they could do, but they didn't dare express any of it to Cat himself. He supposed even if they had, the most response he'd have given would be spitting a Hail Mary or two at them or flipping them off, so they weren't entirely unjustified in avoiding a direct confrontation.

They'd turned the silence into an art form, and now they'd made their wishes clear. The only benefit Cat saw to joining some group would be to spend a portion of each week away from them. He decided an online search to look up the groups on the therapist's list wasn't breaking his rule about talking, since all he was doing was gathering information and not having a conversation online. He rose from the bed and pulled out the crumpled list. At his computer, he typed in each website, rolling his eyes as he read through, thinking they all looked either uninteresting or irrelevant. When he got to one about two thirds of the way down the paper, he paused. With shaking fingers, he entered the address.

Cat clicked the link for more information. He almost laughed—a group for queers with hemophilia sounded like a joke in such a small town; there couldn't possibly be that many people in both categories. Yet there it was, right in front of him. It was twenty-five minutes away, but they only met once per week. If he could convince his parents to let him borrow the car, they wouldn't even have to trouble themselves getting him there.

It was easy enough to provide information to his parents by printing only the location and time for the meetings. They questioned him on why he didn't find one closer to home, but he put them off with another Our Father. They didn't press after that; he suspected they were grateful he'd taken their threat seriously and didn't want to jeopardize their tenuous agreement.

Which was how he ended up in a different kind of hell.

On the night of his first meeting, Cat dressed carefully. If he was bound to attendance, that didn't mean he had to actually make friends. He thought it was unlikely people would dislike him merely because of his wardrobe—especially since these were other queer people—but he decided he might as well try. Since he no longer had anything pink or glittery in his closet, he pulled out every shirt he still had hanging before deciding on something baggy, black, and lettered with the proper grammatical conjugation of "fuck." A pair of black jeans and his favorite ancient black Converse completed the picture. He looked longingly at the box where he kept his small collection of earrings before deciding it wasn't worth breaking his vow to wear one.

Dad knocked on Cat's door and handed him the keys to his Nissan. Cat considered taking the car, driving to his destination, and simply waiting it out in a cafe. Unfortunately, his parents were smarter than he gave them credit for, and without him saying a single word, they told him he'd better return with some proof he'd been where he was supposed to be. He should have been old enough to make his own decisions about where he wanted to be and when, but his parents didn't see it the same way. Unless he was prepared to live on his own—and with his ongoing health problems that was still in question—he had to comply. He hoped the group had something there he could bring back.

He thundered down the stairs, waved over his shoulder in case anyone was looking, and jumped into the car before he could change his mind—both about the meeting and his clothes. Too bad he had the entire drive to second-guess both of those decisions.

The meeting was in a small complex of medical offices. Cat snickered when he saw that one of them was a veterinarian. So the tiny town of Raccoon wasn't all that different from Concordia, then—treating dogs and people in the same building. He parked and entered the door lettered with Delia Brenner, LCSW; she was the social worker who hosted the group. The outer office was eerily quiet, but he heard voices drifting from the back. He followed the sound, the door closing behind him with a thump. A sign on the inner door read: *Ring bell for assistance*, so Cat pressed the buzzer and waited.

"Be right there!" a voice called.

A moment later, a man with an open round face, bright blue eyes, and a head full of long, loose curls peered out. For a moment, he and Cat stood there, staring at each other. It was David, the cute nurse from the hospital. A bolt of nerves shot up Cat's spine, and he trembled as he unzipped his jacket. David was gay or bi or maybe, like Cat, identified as queer? Cat fiddled with the hem of his shirt, still frozen to the spot.

"Becket?" David's eyes lit up. "Oh, my god. How are you?"

At Cat's continued silent staring, David seemed uncertain, but he held out a hand and motioned to Cat. "Come on through. We were just getting started." He eyed Cat's shirt and a trace of a smile played on his lips, but he said nothing.

He led Cat through the maze of rooms at the back to a cozy area that looked like a family waiting room. There were soft chairs arranged in a circle and a table with water, coffee, tea, and cocoa. Next to all that was a stack of name tags and a black marker. Cat stood in front of the table, debating, his hand hovering over the name tags.

David must have misread his hesitation because he said, "You can get something to drink if you want. The meeting hasn't officially begun. Here, let me hang up your coat."

Cat nodded and handed over his jacket then grabbed a name tag, hoping the sticker on his chest would be enough proof for his nosy parents. He didn't relish being called by his given name all night, and he wasn't planning on talking to correct the group, so he used his nickname. He pasted the sticker on his shirt in such a way that it didn't cover up any of the words. When he was through, he helped himself to hot cocoa and followed David back to the circle. As they sat down, David eyed his tag.

"Cat?"

Cat shrugged.

"Oh, okay. So that's what you want to be called?" David asked, grinning at him.

Cat nodded, and that seemed to satisfy David. While David blew on his tea, Cat settled into his chair, cocoa in hand and knees drawn up to his chest. Delia introduced herself, then the other group members took their turns. Most of them also specified which type of hemophilia they had but not which kind of queer they were. David, it turned out, had the same type as Cat, hemophilia A, but his was moderate rather than severe. When it got to Cat, Delia prompted him, but he wouldn't answer, instead curling in on himself further. David put a hand on his arm.

"Do you want me to introduce you?" he asked. When Cat nodded, David turned to Delia. "Is that okay? I know how we usually do things, but Cat..." He glanced over, and Cat shrugged again, figuring David might as well explain. "He doesn't talk."

Throughout the meeting, Cat struggled to stay focused. That was a daily challenge anyway, but it was even more so at a meeting where the hot nurse he'd crushed on only a few weeks before was sitting next to him. He couldn't even look David in the eye. It was all he could do to listen to Delia's questions and the answers people gave. He was fairly sure he wouldn't remember anyone else's name. How would he get through the next session, let alone the next however long his parents and therapist made him do this?

When the meeting ended, he grabbed his jacket and nearly sprinted to the parking lot. While he was fumbling with the keys, a soft voice spoke behind him.

"Hey."

Cat whirled around, dropping his keys. Before he could get them, David bent down and retrieved them. He handed them over. Cat's face flamed.

"It's okay." David stood there for a moment, hands in his pockets. He cleared his throat. "Look, I can tell it makes you uncomfortable that I'm here. I know I'm not your nurse anymore, but it's definitely awkward to be around the person who's cleaned your puke and wiped your ass."

Cat wanted to explain that he had it wrong and it was a very different reason why he felt funny around David. Instead, he ducked his head and flattened himself against his father's car.

The corner of David's mouth lifted. "I can stop coming to this group. I've been here for a while, and I probably could move on. Sounds like it's more something you need."

Cat shook his head. He would find another group or he would somehow—wordlessly—convince everyone he was fine and didn't need any of this. David wouldn't have to worry that he was making anyone uncomfortable. Cat balled his hands into fists, digging his nails into his palms while he tried to work out how to make David understand.

David tilted his head. "You're thinking awfully hard over there. Let me guess. You're considering finding a different group yourself."

Nodding, Cat twisted the keys in his hands. He wasn't sure which was worse—the thought of seeing David every week or the thought of never seeing him again.

"You know, we could both stick it out and see if we can be friends," David offered. He smiled, and it brightened his eyes.

Cat's ears heated. Not seeing David was definitely the less appealing option at that point. Wanting to convey that it was all right, he was willing to try, Cat smiled back.

"Good." Two pink spots bloomed on David's cheeks, and Cat's mouth dropped open in surprise. David wasn't merely being polite; he wanted Cat to stay.

The rush the realization gave Cat hit him forcefully, and he had to breathe slowly through his nose. He jerked his thumb at the car. David gripped Cat's upper arm briefly, squeezing gently before dropping his hand and turning around. Shaking, Cat climbed into the car. It was several minutes before he was clear-headed enough to start the engine and drive home.

CHAPTER NINE

SAVE US FROM THE FIRES

DECEMBER, 2005

CAT WENT to the outpatient clinic for a check-up with Dr. Stern, his hematologist. Now that Cat was back to giving himself his own infusions, he was hoping for more good news. He was still using donated plasma, as he had been for over eight years since he'd reacted to the synthetic factor. Dr. Stern was confident they could switch to the synthetic now, but he would have to schedule Cat for an inpatient stay. They would bolus Cat—give him a large dose at once—a couple of times in hopes of reducing his immune response. Afterward, he could potentially self-infuse with somewhat higher doses of factor. That was a relatively new way to manage low-reactive inhibitors, and it had fairly good success in other people. Cat's age was a point in his favor, but his recent injuries were a strike against him. He couldn't try the treatment until he was medically cleared for takeoff.

Before heading in to see the tech for a blood draw, Cat waited for Dr. Stern, stripped to his underwear—a well-chosen pair of plain blue bikini briefs—and wrapped in a hospital gown several times too large for his slender frame. He swung his feet like a small child, banging his heels lightly against the exam table until Dr. Stern knocked and entered.

The doctor was a muscular man in his early fifties with thick gray hair and even thicker glasses. He greeted Cat cheerfully and washed his hands, whistling the whole time. He snapped on nonlatex gloves and began the exam, starting at Cat's head and working his way down.

He directed Cat to lie down on the table, gently probing around his navel and below. Cat swallowed heavily, aware that Dr. Stern knew he'd torn the muscle again. So far, Dr. Stern hadn't done any more at his check-ups than examine Cat; he was clear on the fact that he couldn't ask anything but yes or no questions. His exasperation with the whole thing was no secret, but Dr. Stern had been Cat's doctor for nearly his whole life. A few unspoken words weren't going to break the deep trust they'd built.

Dr. Stern completed his examination and told Cat to sit up. He sighed and leaned against the sink, legs crossed at the ankles. For a few minutes, he said nothing, just made notes in Cat's chart, which was thicker than a stack of Bibles. When he was through he closed it and set it aside, folding his arms and looking at Cat. There was something on his mind, and he was working up to whatever it was. Cat held his breath.

The doctor cleared his throat. "Are you, uh, sexually active, Cat?"

The question caught Cat by surprise, and he exhaled with force. Dr. Stern sounded uncomfortable, as though he didn't quite know whether he wanted the answer to be yes or no. Cat's heart thumped. He didn't know how to respond. On the one hand, he had been; on the other, he wasn't currently. He had no way to communicate his internal conflict over the way his heart raced and his stomach fluttered every time he saw David. But Dr. Stern knew about his semi-religious vows, so Cat opted for nodding, shrugging, and then shaking his head.

Dr. Stern startled him by saying, "You were but not anymore?" At Cat's affirmation, he continued, "Okay. So the abstinence commitment is more recent. Well...we should...talk about this anyway."

Cat clicked his tongue. It was like being in high school health class, where the teacher desperately wants to offer more than "wait until you're married" and a few words about how sex can make you pregnant or dead. Only they can't say more because it would enrage the parents. He gestured at Dr. Stern to go on, making a show of rolling his eyes. Dr. Stern chuckled then sobered.

Dr. Stern closed his eyes and pinched the bridge of his nose under his glasses. When he looked back at Cat, his eyes flashed. "Oh, to hell with this. You're an adult. I wanted to have this conversation with you years ago, but I've learned that it pisses parents off to no end when I try. They would rather their kids either not talk about it or talk to their primary care doctors. You didn't bring it up, other than that one time when you injured your psoas muscle and we discussed how you'd need to use caution in sexual situations."

Cat remembered that vividly. He'd been embarrassed beyond words. Outside of someone with a bleeding disorder, who the hell gets hurt from ordinary masturbation? Dr. Stern had been more than kind, right down to showing Cat a diagram of his abdominal anatomy. Cat shrank into himself, knowing half the reason he'd been in such bad shape after That Night had been his own damn fault. Thanks to Dr. Stern's explanation, Cat had discovered how to play roulette with his body—how close to rabbit-fucking Bryce he could go without getting hurt. He'd learned the hard way that his actions had consequences.

"I regret my decision to avoid it until you took the lead," Dr. Stern said. He held up a hand when Cat growled in protest. "Look, I'm not here to judge you. I already suspected you were having sex. There was definitely evidence you had the night you were attacked—"

Cat cut him off with his sharp inhalation. Having no memory beyond when Landon began kicking him, he didn't know if Landon had made good on his implied threat. Cat gripped the exam table and drew his brows together, hoping Dr. Stern would clear things up for him.

Dr. Stern's answering frown was concerned rather than angry, but he seemed to have misinterpreted Cat's anxiety. "I'm not going to tell anyone without your permission." When Cat shook his head, Dr. Stern studied him for a moment. The light bulb went on. "There was no indication you were penetrated. I only meant that you had the same type of injury as before, and there was some semen left on your genitals, which was determined to be yours. I'm hoping this was consensual?"

Letting the air out of his lungs slowly, Cat relaxed and nodded.

"Since you won't tell us what happened, I'm not even going to try to guess any further. I just hope you were using condoms." Dr. Stern looked relieved at Cat's nod. "Good. Now, you haven't had sex since?"

Cat shook his head.

"That's probably good too, given what I'm going to tell you."

He sighed. "You may have permanent nerve damage. You're lucky you didn't lose a leg—the injury to your deep abdominals was extensive, and I'm guessing that's not solely due to the attack. Have you had an erection since?"

A deep flush burned Cat's cheeks and extended down his neck. In the hospital, reacting to David, was the first time he'd been interested in anyone at all, and even that hadn't resulted in getting aroused. When he'd seen David at the meeting, he'd been too flustered to feel anything but crush-induced embarrassment. He raised his eyes to look at Dr. Stern, trying to convey his worry.

As though expecting Cat's answer, Dr. Stern nodded. "There could be a number of reasons you haven't. It might be psychological—you've been through a traumatic event. But I should tell you that it might be permanent. If nothing else, you are going to have to be very careful. Both being sexually aroused and having any kind of sex—and I mean any—could be painful. You'll need to avoid jarring your abdominal and pelvic muscles. At this point, you're best off choosing partners cautiously. You need people who are patient enough not to hurt you."

Shit, Cat thought. He nodded his understanding, but the words bit into him. He reminded himself he'd made a commitment to avoid dating, sex, and relationships, but now it felt as though the choice hadn't been his in the first place. He sighed; maybe it was for the best. He'd never intended to involve anyone else in his medical problems even before That Night. It was why he kept some information from Bryce—it wasn't part of their relationship.

Dr. Stern rested a hand on Cat's shoulder. "We can always talk about this more. You know nothing you say will bother me—I'm pretty open-minded. None of it will leave this room, either. If you decide to talk, I'm here." He picked up the folder. "Go on and get dressed, then go see the nurse. I think we can schedule you for that bolus and move on with getting your reactivity under control."

Once Dr. Stern was out of the office, Cat shrugged out of the gown and put his own clothes back on. He was held captive by his own body, no longer free to make his own choices—if he ever had been. He gritted his teeth and faced the exam room door. If his body wasn't his, at least his mind still was. He walked out, more determined than ever not to give anyone else access to either.

Later, Cat lay in bed, grateful it was warm enough in the house to strip down. He stretched out with the covers pulled up to his chin for the time being, one hand on the bed next to him and the other resting at the juncture of his hip and thigh. He massaged the spot with new understanding of why he still had some residual pain there and some difficulty flexing. He hadn't touched himself since That Night, not even after he'd recovered from his septic joint. Now he wanted to know if what the doctor said was true and he wouldn't be able to even if he wanted it. Briefly, he considered whether it was a violation of his vow but decided it was only an experiment to see if he *could*, nothing more.

Slowly, he inched his fingers inward. He toyed with his pubic hair, reluctant to do anything else yet. There was no sign of any response. His hand wandered until it met the soft skin of his penis. Nothing. Not a thing was stirring. Frustrated, he opened his eyes, peered under the covers, and glared down at his flaccid dick. He didn't even feel the slightest bit turned on. Of course, he was thinking about his doctor visit, which under the circumstances was the least sexy thing possible. Propping himself on his elbows, he considered that. Naturally he wasn't getting hard if he wasn't feeling horny. That was definitely more in his head than his body. Relieved, he flopped back onto the mattress.

The slight bounce he produced reminded him what he had stashed underneath. Cat's fascination with romance novels had started around eighth grade. He already knew both the basic health ed facts and some key things about himself, but reading trashy 1980s drugstore novels had given him a whole new set of things to explore. Over time, he'd discovered some delightfully naughty reads, his favorite of which featured a rather clinical description of the main characters having sex—complete with proper names for all their body parts. It was neither erotic nor romantic. Why that in particular got him hot was anyone's guess, but he had those pages dog-eared, and they'd fed his imagination for a long time despite his lack of interest in women.

Cat had gotten a new book months ago, but he'd never had a chance to read it before That Night. He'd given up on his guilty-pleasure reading as part of his vow of chastity. Now he reached out and flicked on the bedside lamp then fished under the corner of his mattress near the headboard. His fingers grasped the edge of the book, and he dragged it out. It had a shirtless pirate on the cover which made Cat snicker. The model's long, blond hair flowed out behind him, and he had a lot of gleaming teeth. He posed with his fist on his hip and one leg up on a crate, his other elbow on the ship's wheel. There was no woman in sight.

Cat began reading. By a third of the way through the book—whose back cover he hadn't bothered examining—he figured out why there wasn't a woman. By the halfway mark, Cat was absorbed in reading the *very* kinky adventures of the pirate captain and his not-at-all-female first mate. He immersed himself in a sensual, graphic scene of the first mate using his lipstick-painted mouth to lick and suck the rope-bound captain's hot, throbbing tool—in those words, to be precise. As the scene unfolded, Cat shoved the covers off and squirmed at the pleasant swirling in his belly. He was even more turned on than he had expected.

It surprised him when he felt the shift, just enough stirring that he recognized the sensation. Drawing in his breath, he looked down and grinned. It wasn't all the way, and he suspected there was still something not quite back to full health, but there it was—he was erect enough for the tip to peek out from the foreskin on its own. Cat couldn't hold back the relieved laughter.

He must have been noisier than he'd realized because next thing he knew, there was a knock on his door. He threw the covers over himself and rolled on his side just as LR stuck her head in the door.

"What in the world are you doing?" she demanded, but the look on her face was far from angry.

Cat held up the book he'd been reading, and LR put a hand over her mouth. A giggle sneaked its way out around her fingers.

"Oh, my god. Is it as cheesy as it looks?"

He grinned and nodded.

"Let me borrow it when you're done?" she begged.

Heat flooded Cat's cheeks. He wasn't sure whether LR would want to read about gay pirates, especially ones who had a fondness for being tied up. Then again, her reaction would amuse him. He shrugged and gave her a thumbs up.

"Good." LR smiled at him. "Night-night, Kitty Cat." She blew him a kiss, and he pretended to catch it just before she shut the door.

Nothing like a visit from his sister to kill his buzz. Cat looked at the book in his hand and decided to finish it another night. Turning back over, he nestled down in his blankets, feeling better than he had since before his doctor appointment. He sighed and closed his eyes, scenes from the pirate novel replaying in his mind. While he was enjoying the pleasant feeling of being aroused but not achingly so, his thoughts wandered, and David's face floated to the foreground. Cat inhaled sharply as the fluttering in his stomach mingled with the lingering fullness in his groin. An embarrassed prickle rose up his neck, and he quickly tamped down those feelings. Even if there was a remote chance David returned his interest, it wasn't right for so many reasons.

Caught between the tension of his crush and the relief over his body being perhaps a little less broken than he'd thought, Cat drifted into an uneasy slumber.

PART IV

HUMILITY

AUGUST, 2013

HALF AN hour later, in the therapist's office, Cat perched in a chair and ran his palms over the smooth wood of the armrests the same way he always did. He didn't look at Dr. Elyse. They sat there for about ten minutes in silence while Cat considered how much to tell her and how to say it.

"You decided to stop talking again?" she asked when the silence stretched on long enough to be uncomfortable. "Did you at least bring your rosary?" She reached into a drawer and pulled out hers, setting it on the desk in front of her.

He closed his eyes for a moment. As he opened them, he sighed. "No, I'll talk."

"All right, good. Can you tell me what happened?"

Cat swallowed several times, clenching and releasing his fists. He took a deep breath and let it out. "I met someone."

"Well, that sounds fine so far." She smiled.

"It's not." He scowled back.

"Ah, I see." Her smile faded.

"No, you don't."

He knew what she was thinking—that he was afraid it would be like the last two times he'd tried to get serious with someone. They'd bailed—the first time, the man was uncomfortable any time Cat needed his meds. He kept asking if Cat was all right, and he had next to no idea how to handle a relationship with someone who had a list of medical problems. The second time, the man had made assumptions about how sex would work between them, and none of them had been accurate. He'd actually used the line "It's not you, it's me" on Cat without irony.

Dr. Elyse tapped her lips with her pen. "I know we've talked before about starting a new relationship after you've lost someone. Does that have anything to do with it?"

So she thought he felt guilty about loving someone else. Maybe he did a little, but that wasn't the primary problem. David had been gone long enough that intellectually, Cat knew there was no shame in having other lovers. When nothing worked out long-term, he'd tried being casual, with mixed-to-disastrous results and lots of failed expectations. Even so, there wasn't anything in him that feared either David or God were looking down on him with disapproval. If he was worried about judgment, he might as well have stopped jerking off, too, and that wasn't going to happen anytime soon.

"It's not guilt. Not the way you're thinking," Cat said.

"Tell me what part I have wrong," Dr. Elyse encouraged.

Instead of answering, Cat said, "It hurt so much when he died."

"Of course." Her gaze stayed on him.

"I'm not in love yet. It's too new," Cat said. "But I want to be."

"Both of those are all right feelings to have."

"I know!" Cat snapped. His knee bounced, and he put his hand on top of it to stop the motion. "That's not the problem."

"All right." She leaned forward. "What would happen if you let yourself enjoy getting to know a new friend or lover or partner?"

"None of those are all right in this situation. I want to be more than friends, and I know he does too. But he's only here for the summer, and we can't be casual lovers because we're both going to end up angry when it's not—" His face was hot. "When it's not porn-quality fucking."

Dr. Elyse didn't flinch at his words. "Have you told him any of this?"

"No." Cat stalled by way of rubbing the side of his face. "I avoided it by setting him up with a friend. It...didn't work out."

"What would be wrong with letting him know how you feel about him?"

"Nothing, if it weren't me we were talking about," Cat answered. "You know what my life is like."

"Yes, I do. So this new man wouldn't be able to handle your disability?"

And there it was. Just like that, she found the weak spot. Cat knew this new man absolutely *would* be able to handle it—remarkably well, in fact. He'd already visited Cat in the hospital and held a bin for him to throw up in. He'd brought soup to his house and hadn't batted an eye at the long row of pill bottles or at watching Cat inject meds into his port. Handling Cat's illness wasn't a concern, except for one problem.

"He wouldn't have any trouble at all," Cat replied. "Do you know what he said to me?"

Her eyes crinkled at the corners. "I'm hoping you're about to tell me."

"He—we were—" Cat cleared his throat. "While we were half-naked and kissing in his living room, he told me he wanted to make me feel good."

"That's a first for you in a long time."

"Yeah." Cat sighed. "I want to believe him, but he says he's used sex to...I guess the right word is self-medicate, I think?" He furrowed his brow.

"That's a way some people describe it, yes," Dr. Elyse confirmed. "It might not be the phrasing I would choose, but it functions adequately. Sounds like he has his own troubles."

"He definitely does," Cat agreed. "I think maybe...that might be what I like, though. He's not hiding them, and I don't think he wants me to fix him, either. But my body isn't up for whatever he's sure will happen between us."

"Then maybe you're better for him than you believe."

"How so?"

Dr. Elyse gave him a gentle smile. "If he can't avoid his problems the way he's used to, he'll need to learn something better. You physically can't enable his coping patterns, which means his only option is to make it work a different way. If he meant what he said to you, then he'll be willing to listen to you and to try. If not, then he wasn't interested in you to begin with."

"He told me he would do anything for me." Cat put a hand over his mouth, the power of those words hitting him hard enough he wanted to hold in his reaction. *He likes me for me,* he thought. *I've known it all along, and I've been pushing him away.*

Dr. Elyse was bright enough to figure out what he wasn't ready to say. She sat back and tilted her head, her eyes narrowed as she considered his words. Cat saw the exact moment it clicked for her.

"It's not the sex, and it's not your limited time together. You're worried about him," she said. "You don't want him to get too attached, but you're afraid he already has."

"Yes." His voice was barely above a whisper. "When I get sick..." He sniffled. "I know how much it hurts."

She nodded. "But you also know how good it can be."

"I've been thinking about him."

"Your new friend?"

"No." Cat twisted the hem of his shirt. "About David and about the promise I made to him and couldn't keep."

"Ah," Dr. Elyse said. "I understand."

Did she? "I won't make the same mistake again," Cat replied.

Dr. Elyse nodded. "I can't tell you what to do—it has to be your decision. All I can say is that it's okay to let someone else in, and you don't have to make any promises."

"Until I do," he countered. "There are always promises."

She studied him for a moment. "No," she said. "I don't think there are. There is opening your heart, and there are commitments. But you do not ever again have to make a vow you cannot keep." He knew what she was referring to, and it was beyond what he'd once sworn to David he would do.

"Maybe..." Cat trailed off, turning the words over in his mind. He and David had never been good at communicating verbally, perhaps because for a long time they'd needed to find other ways. Cat had a feeling empty reassurances wouldn't do much for Micah; he needed something else, if Cat was willing to give it. "Maybe you're right," he finished.

"Are you ready to talk to your friend, then?" Dr. Elyse cocked her head, waiting.

Cat straightened up and met her gaze. "I think I am." He teared up again, hopeful for the first time all summer.

"Start with that." A smile spread slowly across her face. "I know how you are when you get talking, Cat. Not much stops you."

He wiped his eyes and gave a short, hiccupy laugh. "I told him about you. Sort of."

She chuckled. "I don't think I want to know what you said." Turning serious, she continued, "If it would help, you can bring him with you sometime."

"I might," he replied, startling himself. He'd made a decision, apparently even without his own knowledge.

"Did you want to finish out by praying?"

"Yes, please," he said. He pulled his rosary from his pocket while Dr. Elyse picked hers up off the desk.

When his time was up, Cat scheduled another appointment. He had a feeling he might need it, depending on how things went.

Winter

Chapter Ten

Where There Is Hatred, Love

January, 2006

Cat almost whistled while he wiped tables in the cafe. He caught himself and stopped, looking around to make sure no one had noticed. The cafe was almost empty at that hour, past lunch but not yet to the post-work rush. The only patrons had their eyes on their own tables and not on Cat. He breathed a sigh of relief and went back to work.

For the first time in forever, Cat felt reasonably good. He still ached when he moved, but it wasn't the exhausting, soul-crushing pain he'd had nor the constant, nagging soreness he'd felt in the first couple months of physio. He was down to bi-weekly appointments with Shannon because he was doing so well. Despite warnings from his doctors, he hadn't had any more rounds of arthritis. He still had some lingering stiffness from the surgeries, and he knew he had at least another one or two operations in store for the future, but for the moment, he was all right.

The holidays had been good too. The most excitement he'd had was the annual Christmas party at his grandparents' neighborhood by the lake. Every year, it was hosted by a different family. This time, Ms. Carter, who lived three houses down, had done it. She lived alone, but her daughters were there, and one of them was hugely pregnant. Meanwhile, Grandpa Rowland had spent the entire time complaining at top volume about the "religious weirdos" who only lived in the house next door during the summer. Cat remembered having met them once or twice, and they had indeed been a bit strange. Then again, he'd only been a kid, so most adults had seemed odd to him.

He still hadn't seen any of his friends. Zee had gone to Alaska—of all places—to visit his girlfriend's family. He'd sent Cat a couple of postcards. Ezra had taken a winter course and stayed at school. Bryce...well, radio silence from him, but Cat hadn't expected anything else. They weren't together anymore, and knowing what Bryce had said about his parents, it wasn't unexpected. It didn't hurt as much as Cat thought it should have, and some days he wondered if what they'd had was mostly infatuation and sex and fascination with forbidden fruit.

Cat had a few new friends. Besides David, the rest of the group had become accustomed to his non-verbal communication. They'd never known him any other way, so they had welcomed him in. One of the women seemed to pay particular attention when he showed up, looking to see what slogan might be on his shirt that week. Her reactions delighted him. Equally delightful was how entertaining David appeared to find it as well. Cat didn't see them during the holidays because there were no meetings, and he didn't know the others well enough to get together with them outside the group. Besides, what would they talk about with someone who didn't speak? He looked forward to connecting again now the break was over.

Once he finished the tables, Cat moved on to sweeping the floors, thoughts of David making him warm all over. He considered how he might be able to maintain his half of a friendship. David was the one person Cat wanted to spend time with beyond meetings. They couldn't call each other, of course. Cat couldn't, anyway. A smile slowly spread across his face. Even if he couldn't respond, maybe David would be willing to take his number and text him. Cat could communicate via emoticons, if nothing else. He finished sweeping in record time, still feeling happier than he had in ages.

He didn't have to wait until the meeting after all. As Cat picked up the bin of used cups and plates from beside the trash can, David came in. Cat almost dropped the bin, but he caught it in time. He stared at David, who finally looked his way, his eyes widening. David bypassed the counter to step over to Cat.

"You work here?" he asked.

Cat nodded.

"Well, I have the day off, and I was in town for some post-holiday shopping. I thought I'd come in because this place looked so warm and cozy. I had no idea I would see you! Let me go get coffee, and I'll be right back."

Cat tried to catch his attention again so he could explain that he was working and couldn't visit, but David had already turned away. A few minutes later, Mom was out from behind the counter, showing David to a cozy table in the far corner. To Cat's mortification, she came right over to him and took the bin out of his hands.

"This young man says he knows you. Yes?" she said.

Cat affirmed her words.

"Good. Take a break. You can finish this later." She patted Cat's arm, kissed his cheek, and returned to the counter.

David's eyes crinkled with humor. "That's your mom?" He laughed at Cat's flush. "She seems great." He took a sip of his coffee. "Mm. And she makes a good espresso."

Cat rolled his eyes, at which David laughed again. He put his hand on top of Cat's.

"This isn't any different from when we're at group. I'll talk, you listen. Fair?"

Cat ducked his head to show his approval, and David smiled.

"Good. Want to hear what happened yesterday? It was a zoo on the unit, and it all started when the patient in room eight threw a shoe at the guy from transport..."

For the next hour, Cat listened to David talk, laughing at the humor and trying to look appropriately scandalized at the more bizarre parts of his tales. At last he knew it was time to get back to work, so he stood up. David followed him to his feet.

"Now that I know you work here, I'll have to find you more often," David commented.

The thought warmed Cat from the top of his head down to his toes. He wanted to show David what it meant to him, so he reached out his hand. Hesitating for only a moment, he placed his fingertips right over David's heart and pressed gently. David caught Cat's hand and held it briefly before drawing him into a hug.

Everything in Cat came alive at the contact. He felt David's heart beating against his own, and his senses were filled with the scent of David's soap combined with his warm skin. For a few seconds, Cat almost gave up his control, like the exhilarating few seconds of free-fall on a roller coaster—letting go and trusting the ride to catch him. He drew on all his resolve and pulled out of David's embrace, stepping back before the risk of crashing became too great.

"Cat?" David asked. "Are you okay?"

Cat nodded and breathed slowly. He put up his hand to indicate David should wait, knowing it was futile but hoping anyway that David wouldn't catch on to the real reason Cat needed space. In the time they'd known each other, David had demonstrated a remarkable ability to understand, presumably because he'd worked with non-verbal patients on his unit before. Whether he'd interpreted Cat's behavior correctly or not, David gave no indication either way. He nodded and put his hands in his pockets, waiting for Cat to make the next move. Cat counted to ten in his head until the feeling of being overwhelmed passed.

Taking hold of David's arm, Cat pulled out his phone and motioned to David to do the same, which he did. Cat handed over his phone, hoping David would understand and enter his phone number. David returned the gesture, and Cat put himself in David's contact list. They traded back, and Cat slipped his phone back in his pocket. A moment later, it vibrated. Cat withdrew it, giving David a half-amused, half-annoyed smile.

Hi, was all it said.

Cat texted a smiley then made to turn around. David put a gentle hand on Cat's wrist, and Cat stopped. His heart rate sped up for a different reason this time. He stood frozen to the spot, unable to look at David or rid himself of the feeling his skin was crawling at being held. David must have registered the change because he let go. Cat breathed a sigh of relief, and David smiled.

"So I can't call you, obviously," David said. "I can text you, though, right?"

The last of Cat's near-panic drained away. When he nodded his consent, another grin flashed across David's face. Cat knew he must be blushing; he'd never been able to hide his reactions. When he was embarrassed, not only did his whole face turn red, it made his freckles stand out even more. He'd nearly let his panic show through, and what would David think of him then? David didn't seem to be concerned, though.

"Hey, will I see you at the meeting this week?" he asked. At

Cat's nod, he said, "Good. I'd better go and let you get back to work."

Picking up David's empty cup, Cat waved to him with his free hand. To avoid having to figure out how to manage everything he was experiencing at the surprise visit, he hurried into the supply closet without waiting for David to leave. Once inside, Cat leaned against the wall and wrapped his arms around himself, rocking a little. He'd almost lost control with David in too many ways. If he broke his vows now, it opened up the risk of repeating That Night. Yet the thought of not seeing David again was worse than the idea of sitting with him every week and never being able to show David how he felt. He would have to keep tighter rein on his emotions next time.

Taking a deep breath, Cat stumbled out of the supply closet, broom in hand, ready to return to work.

After meeting up with David at the cafe, Cat kept his phone on him at all times. He never knew when he would get a message. He could tell when David was on shift because the texts were fewer and farther between while he was working. Still, he sometimes managed one or two, often commentary on how the hospital was. A quick *Sorry, puke to clean*—which made Cat laugh—or another note about what he was doing kept Cat going through the day.

Cat liked best when David had the day shift. In the evenings, Cat lay in bed with his phone, and David sent him stories about his day or random pictures he'd taken with his phone of cats he said looked like Cat. Not being able to reply with anything other than various versions of smilies, Cat got creative and sent his reactions using different configurations of symbols. When David replied, Cat pictured his wide smile and sparkling eyes. Eventually, Cat would drift off to sleep, warm and content.

The night before Dad's spring semester of teaching began, Cat was on his way up to bed to wait for David's texts when he was halted by the big argument he should have seen coming. Mom called after him the minute his foot hit the first step.

"Do not move," she said.

LR peeked around the corner from the kitchen and looked between them. Her eyebrows shot up, and her gaze met Cat's. She drew her lower lip into her mouth, and Cat saw the question she wanted to ask—did he want her to stay and take his side? For a moment, he was angry because she'd known it was on the horizon and didn't warn him. His fury dissipated when he remembered he'd known too and hadn't wanted to acknowledge it.

He backed down and trotted obediently into the living room to perch on the couch. On his way past, he made a tiny motion to LR, indicating she should be on standby. It was an old habit of theirs, a way in which they'd protected each other over the years. Cat couldn't do much to defend her the way she could with him—she'd gotten in her fair share of trouble in middle school because she wasn't afraid to punch boys who threatened Cat. He could, however, make sure she was covered in other ways. For someone who spent the bulk of her time on her studies, she was surprisingly capable of finding all kinds of ways to rebel. Their parents still didn't know about her navel piercing or the tattoo of an atom she had on her hip. Leave it to LR to turn her teenage mischief into something appropriately geeky.

Mom and Dad sat across from Cat, and he felt like he was on trial with them. Dad cleared his throat. "You withdrew from all the classes I helped you register for."

Cat nodded. He was sure there would have been a way for him to remain enrolled despite his lack of verbal communication, but he wasn't interested. Withdrawing online had been easy. With a shrug, he tried to look bored and non-committal.

"I'm not so much angry that you did it," Dad said, and Mom shot him an irritated glance. He ignored her. "I'm upset you didn't even talk to me about it. Or, well, whatever it is you would have done to explain yourself. You can't drop everything without a word."

"You've been doing so much better," Mom added. "I can't understand why—"

Anger flared again, and Cat turned his frown toward Mom, causing her to leave her sentence unfinished. He knew what she'd been about to say: *why you can't go back to how you used to be.* He *was* doing better, and he didn't know why they didn't trust him to know what was best for himself. His whole life, someone else had made decisions for him, from his parents and doctors to Bryce and Landon. For once, he was making his own decisions, and quitting school was one of them. He didn't want to study more music theory and take more lessons. He didn't want to go back to the person he'd been before. And he definitely didn't want to see Bryce every day and be reminded of the long string of choices which were taken away That Night.

Furious, Cat shook his head. He stood up and made a firm *no* with his whole body. Mom and Dad began to protest. Fed up, Cat snapped at them, "Breathe in me, O Holy Spirit, that my thoughts may all be holy."

"Not this again," Mom muttered. Louder, she said, "Stop it. Just stop. We're trying to help you, and both of us feel—"

"Act in me, O Holy Spirit, that my work, too, may be holy," Cat shouted at her.

"You can't spend the rest of your life—" Dad tried.

"Draw my heart, O Holy Spirit, that I love but what is holy." By then, Cat was shaking all over.

"We only want to talk to you," Mom said. She looked like she might cry.

Unmoved, Cat replied, "Strengthen me, O Holy Spirit, to defend all that is holy." He would not let her get to him.

"Calm down," Dad said. "Please, both of you. Can we work this out?"

Cat turned his glare on Dad and answered, "Guard me, then, O Holy Spirit, that I always may be holy."

LR stepped into the room and slid an arm around his waist. "Hey," she said in his ear. "I'll talk to them, okay? Go upstairs."

He looked over at her and nodded. At least one person understood. With one last scowl, he pulled away from LR and retreated up the stairs. He heard LR start in on their parents, asking them if they were going to control her life the same way. Part of him was surprised. She'd been the one who was angriest at him over making what she considered ridiculous vows, but she'd also been the one to adapt most easily to the change. She'd always been able to read him better than either of their parents. Mom wanted to protect him from himself, and Dad wanted him to be "a normal kid." Neither of them had left him room to become who he wanted to be. It had never occurred to him they might have unreasonable expectations for LR, too.

Cat lay on his bed, his thoughts racing. He needed to calm down and take his mind off whatever was going on downstairs. No doubt LR was assuring them she wasn't abandoning her studies—as though that would ever happen. She would be miserable if she couldn't spend most of her time absorbed in scientific text books. He sat up again and reached for his pajamas, changing quickly and lying back down. Eyes closed, he tried to drown out the argument with his parents replaying in his mind. His father had said he wasn't angry, but then he was after all. Like always, Cat couldn't live up to whatever they wanted. Why couldn't they see he'd achieved his own kind of life?

Needing a distraction, Cat reached under his mattress for his latest book conquest, a novel he'd found at the indie bookstore in the village. LR had taken him as a Christmas gift, and he'd found their section of queer lit. It wasn't even small or buried in the back of the store like he'd expected; it was prominently displayed. He hadn't found any more pirate books—the look on LR's face when she skimmed through had been priceless—but he had found a number of other gay romance novels. They weren't all to his taste; he got a little tired of cowboys and firefighters and military men, none of whom were his type to begin with. Still, there were some decent finds.

The current novel featured a rock star and a violinist. Cat liked it because they were both a bit more like him, if still less feminine. He began to read, immersing himself in a hot shower scene which had his cock taking notice the minute the characters had their clothes off. Without thinking, he slid his hand down, massaging himself gently over the top of his pajamas as he read. He pushed his hand inside the waistband, his fingers brushing lightly against his erection and causing a ripple of pleasure. As soon as he touched himself, he realized what he was doing, and he froze. He wasn't supposed to, not according to the paper still sticky-tacked to his wall.

He looked up at the notebook page. What did it matter, anyway? He wasn't breaking his promise to stay away from men. It was an old comfort, stroking himself before sleep, a way to relax his body and ease the all-too-frequent pain. Bringing himself off didn't need to mean more than that. He pushed his hand all the way into his pajamas, using a slow motion while he continued reading.

The way the author described the violinist reminded Cat of David. As Cat lost himself in the story, he pictured David in place of the character. He groaned, unsure whether it felt wrong to think of David that way, especially if David didn't feel the same. Tension built, and Cat moved his hand a little faster. Anxiety and mild pain swelled along with pleasure, and Cat gasped, his mind and body each fighting for control.

As if on cue, the phone on his nightstand chimed and vibrated against the wood surface. Startled, Cat yanked his hand out of his pajamas and picked up the phone. His whole head, from his ears to his neck, went hot when he saw it was a message from David.

Hey. Still up?

Cat sent a Y.

Good. Whatcha doing?

Cat harrumphed, embarrassed and frustrated at having been interrupted. He took his time, crafting an elaborate text picture to send in reply. It served David right for having such terrible timing. It took so long David sent him two more texts to get his attention, but at last Cat hit send.

Oh. My. God. Did you really just send me a dick? Pause, then another text. *I'm laughing so damn hard.*

Relaxing at last, Cat sent a grin and a tongue-out face.

Sorry I interrupted you! Should I let you go?

Cat sent a wink.

Nothing like a random text to kill a mood, huh? I really am sorry.

Smile.

Did I ever tell you about the time I caught a couple of patients going at it...together?

Cat sent a series of question marks and exclamation points.

I know! Want to hear about it, or would you rather finish jerking off?

Even though David couldn't see him, Cat stuck out his tongue. He sent back an ellipsis, not sure how to tell David he should go ahead.

Looks like you want the story. Ok, well, this one time...

Cat read through David's series of texts on the subject, laughing and sending back what he hoped were appropriate replies in the right places. He was no longer disappointed at not finishing what he'd started, warmed all over by connecting with David over the messages. His attention was split between reading the texts and thinking about how much he wanted to see David again in person, but he didn't know how to convey that. He couldn't ask, and he didn't want to be a bother anyway. He knew David liked talking to him, but would he want to spend time with Cat face to face when he had to keep up the conversation by himself? Cat couldn't discern the answer. At last David finished the story, and Cat sent him a series of grins.

Well, I'd better go. Early day tomorrow. Good night, sweet dreams. There was a pause then David sent him a kiss-smiley.

Even though he knew it was only a silly emoticon, Cat's stomach did backflips anyway. He sent one back then laid his phone aside. He shoved the book back under his mattress. He wouldn't need it; thoughts of David were plenty to take his mind off any other worries. He curled up under the covers and closed his eyes, still smiling as he drifted off to sleep.

CHAPTER ELEVEN

WHERE THERE IS INJURY, PARDON

IT WAS BOUND to happen sooner or later, the first crack.

As usual, Cat sat in the group meeting, listening to others talk. This time, his still-too-thin body was covered up by a gray t-shirt with a suggestive picture of a hot dog and a ketchup drip that resembled a tongue. When David saw it, he smirked, and Cat had to stifle a laugh behind his hand. At that, David's eyes lit up, resulting in a funny tickle deep in the pit of Cat's stomach. Delia's brow creased, and several group members rolled their eyes, but no one commented.

Delia didn't push Cat to speak. Cat wondered if she, like the others, thought he couldn't or if she'd guessed the truth. She did occasionally direct questions to him. Sometimes, if they could be answered with a nod or a shake of his head, Cat voluntarily responded. Sometimes, he allowed David to speak for the few things he knew. Otherwise, Cat remained seated in his chair, legs drawn up with his arms around them and his chin resting on his knees. He hadn't felt comfortable reciting his prayers, sharing that part of his soul outside home or his therapist's office. He'd been embarrassed to speak them in front of the group.

Other group members were going over their weeks. Cassie, a graduate student, shared about returning to classes and having to face someone she'd had an enormous crush on years ago in high school. "He looked exactly how I remembered him. It took me forever to work up the nerve to talk to him after class."

"What happened?" someone else wanted to know.

"Well, I always thought he was a little weirded out by me because I'd dated a girl before him and because I had all these health issues." She giggled. "It turns out he's gay, and he's already in a relationship. Either way, nothing was gonna happen between us." She sighed dramatically, producing laughter. "But, damn, he's my type. He is so, so pretty."

Cat's reaction was immediate and unexpected. He inhaled at the word *pretty*. For a moment, he tried to control the kaleidoscope of emotions surrounding her words, but they hit too hard and fast. *You're very pretty, and I like pretty men.* It rattled around in his mind until he couldn't hear anything the others were saying. He had no idea how the rest of the group had responded to Cassie because the noise inside his head was too loud.

"Lord Jesus Christ, have mercy on me, a sinner," he mumbled. He gasped for air. "Lord—Jesus Christ—have mercy on me—a sinner." His ribs hurt as though he'd been punched, and his heart galloped. He covered his head with his shaking hands. "Lord Jesus Christ, have mercy on me, a sinner." The back of his neck prickled with sweat.

A hand on his arm shocked him, and he pushed at it. His face was wet; it didn't fully register why. Around him, he heard the voices of the other people in the room, but he couldn't follow what they were saying. In a moment, someone was in front of him.

"Cat? Cat, look at me." David's gentle voice. "You're safe. Stay with me. You can get through this."

"Lord Jesus Christ, have mercy on me, a sinner!"

Delia was there too. "Breathe with me," she said. "I'm going to count while you inhale and exhale. Whatever you're feeling is scary, but you are not in danger here."

Cat breathed in and out slowly on her count while keeping his eyes on David's. Around him, the room came back into focus and other voices became more clear. Someone asked what was wrong with him, and another person said they thought he couldn't talk. Delia shushed both of them by saying they would work it out when Cat was feeling calmer. He began to relax as his heart rate dropped again.

"Okay to touch you?" David asked. At Cat's nod, he put his hand on Cat's arm, and this time, Cat didn't flinch. David said, "Good. I'm going to get up again, but I'm right here still." He moved back to his own seat then reached over to take Cat's hand. Cat squeezed.

Delia returned to her chair. She looked at Cat for a moment. "Is there anything else we can do to support you right now?"

He shook his head. Everything hurt, and he was cold. He shivered, and David stood up.

"Want your coat?"

Cat wasn't sure. He wanted to warm up, but he didn't want David to move. He put a hand on David's sleeve, wishing he could make him understand. It took a moment, but eventually he did.

"Cassie, can you get Cat's jacket?" David asked. "It's the black one on the end."

Cassie was back in a moment, draping the coat around Cat's shoulders.

"Are you okay?" she asked. She looked upset, and Cat shrank back from her. He hated being the cause of the tension he felt rolling off her. She looked over her shoulder at Delia then back at Cat. "I know I said something wrong when I told that story, and I'm sorry."

So she wasn't angry or upset with Cat. He sighed, relieved then shook his head.

"Wait," one of the others said. "I thought you couldn't talk at all. But you were saying something...like, praying?"

"It's the Jesus prayer," a guy named Braden answered. "My mom's Lutheran."

Cassie said, "David, you hang out with him all the time. Did you know about this?"

David replied, "Sort of. Not the praying part, though. I didn't feel it was my story to tell." He looked at Cat. "Can I?" Cat nodded, so David continued. "He chooses not to talk for his own reasons."

"So, what, we have to listen to him spout religious crap all the time now?" one of the other guys demanded. "I got over that ages ago, and I don't need it here."

Delia kept her voice low and calm. "We're all in different places. You were sitting here while something put Cat in a panicked state. I don't think he was able to help it. I'm going to ask that we all be patient until we can work through this. Our group is for supporting each other because we've had similar experiences in one way or another. Tonight, we have the chance to do it beyond talking." She turned to Cat. "Do you need some space? Or are you ready to go on? Even if you don't want to talk, this might be a good opportunity for others to bring up things they'd like to be open about. I understand if you need to step away."

Cat shrugged. He was still cold, though the jacket helped, and he was sleepy. Without meaning to, he leaned against David and closed his eyes. David adjusted, making room so Cat could settle in. He put an arm around Cat, adding to the heat.

"I think it's all right to talk," David said. "I've got him."

Warmer now and comfortable, Cat let the conversation wash over him. He listened, surprised when several others shared their experiences with panic and anxiety. One of the women said she'd been diagnosed with a panic disorder, but she'd never felt comfortable talking about it. She said she was sorry about whatever had gotten to Cat, but she thanked him too. He wasn't sure what to do with her revelation, so he nodded at her.

At the end of the meeting, only a few people stayed to socialize, and the atmosphere remained subdued. David walked Cat to his car. Outside, the cold air revived Cat. When he turned to go, David said, "Wait." Cat faced him.

"Are you all right to drive?" David's face was lined with worry.

Cat nodded, and David reached for his hand, but Cat pulled away.

"I know you don't want to talk about it, but can you at least help me understand what happened?" David sounded like he was trying to control his voice, but Cat heard the anxious undertone.

He didn't want one more person to be concerned for him. He'd had enough of hearing the fear and pain in every exchange because no one trusted him enough to manage himself and not break at the slightest provocation. Cat backed up, shaking his head.

"Are you sure—"

Cat's patience snapped. He stepped closer to David, allowed anger to show on his face, and gave him a small shove before turning around. He ignored David's plea for him to wait, climbing into the Nissan and sitting with his hands on the steering wheel to control the shaking. He faced forward, not even looking in the rearview mirror to see when David walked away. Cat remained there for a long time before he started the engine and pulled out of the lot, headed for home. Whatever had happened at the meeting, he didn't want to repeat it. One more way in which Landon was still stealing from him—or maybe he was stealing from himself. It was anyone's guess.

Cat lay on his bed, hands behind his head, thinking about what had happened at the meeting. The word Cassie used haunted him. *Pretty*. He'd been pretty once, but not now. He didn't say the word aloud, but he mouthed it, testing the shape of his lips and tongue around the letters.

For as long as he could remember, he'd been somewhere in the uncharted middle between *boy* and *girl*—swirled like the colors in a child's paint box. Sometimes he expressed that in fluid ways, but more often, it felt like its own thing, both/and instead of either/or. He'd been all right with being perceived as a very pretty boy, though he'd never known what to call his gender. There were so many words, and new ones all the time. He'd never bothered using anything but *he* to identify himself. It worked all right, since *she* didn't quite fit either. Until That Night, it had always been fine— he'd had so many ways to show on the outside what he felt on the inside.

Sex, as much as the way he dressed or moved, had been an affirmation of his identity. That might have been why he'd enjoyed burying himself in Bryce until they both exploded—he felt as though he transcended gender then, so much so it was almost holy. He'd loved whispering naughty, sexy things in each other's ears or using their mouths on each other or being intimately joined and ejaculating together. It made the masculine and feminine parts of himself feel connected, whole. He occasionally wondered if that's how sex felt to other people too, but there wasn't anyone to ask, and anyway, that was a bit too personal even for anonymous Internet discussion boards.

What had always frustrated him hadn't been his sense of self; it had been the way others always seemed to want him to pick a side and stick with it. They wanted everything about him to reflect their perception. He'd never been able to make that choice. He sat up, realizing what struck him. *Boy. Girl. Man. Woman.* It wasn't that he felt the need to choose. It was the knowledge that whether he did or not, nothing he did would change his genetics. He would still have to face the long-term consequences of the disorder that ravaged his body, made him bleed into his joints and kept him from healing properly. Things that only happened because of his damaged chromosomes. People who said it didn't matter hadn't lived their whole lives knowing if they'd been born with a different set of genes, they'd have been healthy.

Now, lying on his bed, he wondered if any of his identity had been real or if it had been his own attempt to fix what was wrong with him. He'd tried being only a boy when he was younger, but maybe he hadn't tried hard enough. Maybe his parents had given in too easily when he'd said he wasn't. He squeezed his eyes shut, wishing he could block the intrusive thoughts and the doubt. In that moment, he didn't want to have to be any gender at all anymore. Relinquishing it just like he'd given up sex and speech and the prettiness which had gotten him nothing but pain.

He rested his cheek on his knees. An ache developed in his gut. He *missed* being pretty. There was a fine art to choosing his clothes every morning. Every day had been an adventure. He would stand in front of his dresser, stripped down to nothing, and close his eyes. How did he feel? What would be nice against his skin—soft cotton or lace or satin? Sometimes, this made him partially hard, especially if he chose something that felt sexy. More often, it only made him excited, the pleasure in choosing based only on the joy of expressing himself.

He'd loved knocking on LR's door once his outfit was complete, twirling for her and asking her opinion. Rarely, she'd tell him to change, but only if he'd chosen something she thought looked awful with his ginger-blond hair or his numerous freckles. She was more casual with her wardrobe, earthy and flowing, but she—and some of her friends—loved to turn him into their life-size doll. Most of his collection of tinted lip gloss was thanks to LR's friends, and LR had picked out his favorite clothes.

Everything he hadn't shredded was in boxes in his closet. It would be so easy to take them down, open them up, and try it all on. He raised his head to look at the closed door. *No,* he thought with conviction. He would never wear any of it again, not ever. Shifting, he swung his legs over the edge of the bed. He rose slowly and made his way to the bathroom, where he shut the door and then stood in front of the full-length mirror.

He pulled off his shirt and then his pajama pants and underwear, studying his naked body with its pale peach skin and scads of light brown freckles. A long, pink scar trailed diagonally across his stomach from his breastbone to his side under his ribs where he'd been cut open to remove his spleen. Cat touched it gingerly, but it no longer hurt. He lowered his hand to rake through his sparse orange pubic hair then skimmed his thumb over his flaccid penis. He'd never wished it gone, not even on his most feminine days. He liked the soft skin and the way it firmed when he stroked it. He loved the tight ache in his balls and the slippery, messy feel of semen when he came.

Sliding his hands upward, he pinched his nipples. He never really thought of his pecs as breasts, exactly, but if he could change one thing, that might be it. Sometimes—not always—he wanted real ones. Small and firm, enough to cup them. He wanted to feel their weight against his palms and see how they might fill out his shirts, making them taut across his chest. He squeezed a larger area, slight pain mixing with pleasure. He'd always wanted to ask Bryce to fondle him differently *there*, but he'd been afraid Bryce wouldn't like it. Cat wanted to call them *tits*, enjoying the sound of the word for how taboo it was. He knew lots of girls hated that word; LR said it sounded, and made her feel, dirty. He also knew lots of girls felt as though boys in general made them feel filthy, the way they talked about and looked at and grabbed their bodies. He understood.

Bryce had made him feel dirty.

Why do you have to be so gay?

Landon had made him feel dirty.

You're very pretty.

Cat stifled a tiny, wounded noise, letting go of his nipples and raising his eyes to look at his face. His hair had grown so it brushed his shoulders. He'd always liked it longer, though not enough to tie it back. When he was with Bryce, he'd had it chin-length. A memory surfaced of being in Bryce's bed, thrusting into him while Bryce reached back and tugged at his hair, his grip tightening when he came. Bryce had loved Cat's hair, at least until he started pulling away and claiming Cat was too girlie.

With a snarl, Cat pushed the memory aside. It was his fault for always wanting what he shouldn't, and now he was going to make it right. He turned to the sink and grabbed a pair of scissors LR kept in the vanity drawer for trimming her bangs. Standing in front of the mirror again, he lifted handfuls of hair and cut them off, not caring how jagged he made the locks. He cut and cut, clumps of red-gold landing on the tiles at his feet.

Not pretty. Not pretty. Not pretty.

Dry, angry heat burned behind his eyes in his cheeks as he shredded his hair, and a sob caught in his throat. When he couldn't cut any more, he let the scissors clatter to the floor. He dropped down too, leaning against the vanity with his knees drawn up. He felt so lost, no longer sure who he was.

He almost missed the knock on the door. "Kitty Cat? You okay in there?"

Cat wrapped his arms around his knees when LR opened the

door a crack and peeked in. She looked from Cat to the piles of hair on the floor, and her face turned from worry to shock back to worry.

"Oh, Kitty," she said. "Oh."

LR stepped in and closed the door again. She sat down with him, not even complaining that he was stark naked when she folded him into her arms. She rocked him, stroking what was left of his hair and waiting for him to stop shaking. When he was calmer, he sat up and rubbed his eyes.

"Let's get you fixed up, okay?" LR said. Cat nodded, and LR picked up the scissors. She began to trim, neatening up the places where he'd done the most damage. "You could have come to me, Kitty Cat. I'd have done this for you any time. I love playing with hair, and yours is so—"

He cut her off with a smack to her arm then shoved at her. He didn't want her to say he was pretty. She sat back, a frown crossing her face.

"I was only going to say yours is so soft. It's easy for me because it's not too thick, either. Here, let me finish, then I'll show you."

Relaxing, he moved closer and let her resume her work. She took her time, making sure it was even. It seemed like an eternity before she set aside the scissors with a satisfied expression. She stood up and offered Cat a hand. He looked up at her, his cheeks burning. LR glanced down at his clothes on the floor.

"I've seen you naked way more in the last five months than probably the entire rest of my life, not counting when we were really little. I think I can handle it."

Cat nodded and stood up. He faced the mirror, and LR grinned when his mouth dropped open. His hair was mostly short all over, but she'd left his bangs longer so they fell over one side of his face in layers. The blond highlights stood out more, stylish and—dare he say it—sexy. He wondered why he hadn't asked LR to do this for him long before That Night. Turning to her, he flung his arms around her, almost knocking her down. When she laughed, he did too. He planted an extra sloppy, wet kiss on her cheek.

"Ew, Cat!" She giggled and wiped it off. "Guess you like it, then?"

He backed up and nodded then looked down ruefully at the mess on the floor.

"Don't worry about it," LR said. "I'll sweep up. You shower so you don't get hairs all over your sheets."

While he washed up, he listened to LR moving around on the other side of the shower curtain. She called goodnight and shut the door with a click, leaving him alone to rinse and step out of the tub.

When at last Cat sank beneath his covers, still a little damp from his shower and utterly exhausted, he reached up to touch his new haircut and run his fingers through the fine strands. The texture was fuzzier because of the way LR had sheared the ends, but he liked it. Soft, but in a different way than before. He lowered his hand and nestled down with a yawn.

He didn't need to be pretty. Not at all.

CHAPTER TWELVE

WHERE THERE IS DOUBT, FAITH

DARKNESS, PRESSING IN. Something heavy weighing on Cat's chest, smothering him. He gasped for air and clawed frantically, wanting to call for help but unable. A voice, inches from his ear.

"You're mine."

Cat opened his mouth to scream, but no sound came out. Then pain, sharp and twisting, and he was falling...

Cat's eyes flew open, and he sucked air into his lungs. He was drenched in sweat, and his heart thundered. It took a moment before he registered what had woken him. The buzz of a text message broke through Cat's sleep-fog. He picked up his phone and saw it was David, but he ignored it, not sure he wanted to face David after the previous night. He lay on his back, eyes closed and fingers curled around his phone, trying to calm down. Just as he was beginning to doze off, the vibrations startled him and he sat up. His phone buzzed again, and he looked down at it.

Please talk to me. Or whatever it is you do. Are you okay?

Cat winced. David needed to leave him alone. He was embarrassed enough already, and now he was on edge from his dream. To put David off, he sent a smiley, wishing there was a way to convey both sarcasm and "fuck off" in a wordless text. He might be able to figure it out, given enough time.

David's reply was fast. *I can hear the sarcasm in that smiley. Come on, how are you really?*

Cat returned the volley with a frowning face.

I figured, David answered. *You took off so fast last night.*

Cat sighed and closed his eyes. David had treated him like a child, and Cat had behaved like one in response. He thought for a moment before playing around to create what he thought might resemble a "sorry" face.

No, don't apologize! My fault, not yours. I'm sorry.

Puzzled, Cat sent a question mark.

I should have trusted you. I didn't mean to hurt you, but I think I freaked you out.

Cat replied with a Y.

It took a few minutes before David answered. *Will you forgive me?*

Of course Cat would forgive him, but they hadn't exactly talked about what happened. Cat sent him a smiley.

It's okay, you know. Do you need anything?

Cat sent him an N.

Want to hang out later? I can stop by the cafe. Today's my day off this week.

Without his permission, Cat's stomach did enthusiastic flip-flops. He tried not to feel too excited, but it was impossible. As humiliating as it had been, David wasn't put off by anything Cat had done the previous night. Unbelievably, even Cat's skittishness hadn't made David want to avoid him for the rest of forever. Mirroring his facial expression, Cat sent a grin.

Cool. Wanna hear what happened to me the other day? You won't believe the weird shit I put up with from work, even when I'm not supposed to be there.

For the next hour, they messaged, same as before as though nothing had changed. When David said goodbye, Cat kept his phone in his hand, re-reading the last message until he realized it was long past time to get up.

I'm here for you. Tell me if you need me.

After a shower, Cat passed the time until his therapy appointment by reading another new book, less sensual and more intellectual than the others. The knock on his bedroom door startled Cat out of his concentration. He shoved the book under his mattress before rising to answer the door.

Mom stood there, hands on hips. "There's someone here to see you," she said, her voice somewhere between too excited and too mysterious for Cat's liking. He glared at her, and she relented. "Bryce is here."

Shit. Shit, shit, shit. Cat didn't want to see him, not after months of Bryce avoiding him even when Zee and Ezra had finally made a couple attempts. For a moment, Cat stood in his doorway, undecided. He must have hesitated too long because Mom sighed.

"You can't avoid your friends forever," she said. "No one said you have to talk to him—just see him and hear what he has to say."

Resigned, Cat nodded and followed her down the stairs. He did a double take when he saw Bryce. He looked like his older brothers now—less polished and trendy, more filled out and muscular. He'd stopped spiking his hair. How could he have changed so much in six months?

Bryce cleared his throat. "Hey, Cat."

He reached out and gave Cat a one-armed hug. Cat wrinkled his nose when he inhaled. Bryce used to smell good, like a cross between his cologne and the thick gel he put in his hair. Now, he only smelled like soap and skin and some kind of ordinary deodorant. Cat pulled away and gestured at him to come farther in. They sat on the couch side by side, not touching. Bryce's fingers twitched like he wanted to reach over and take Cat's hand, but he didn't. He kept his hands on his knees, bouncing a little.

"Um...how—how are you doing?"

With a huff, Cat curled his lip in disgust and crossed his arms. How, exactly, did Bryce think he would be doing? Cat silently cursed his mother for making him endure this awkward non-conversation. He deflated a little when he remembered she didn't have any idea he and Bryce had been more than friends.

"You look different." Bryce moved his hand this time, putting it close to Cat's bangs but not touching. "You cut your hair."

Cat would have liked to snap back at him that Bryce was different too, as though he was trying too hard to be whatever his parents wanted. Instead, he withdrew and folded his arms around himself. Bryce backed off, and there were pain lines on his face. Cat softened, curling further in on himself. One more person he'd disappointed in the last several months.

Bryce surprised Cat when he angled himself toward Cat and said, "The guys said you stopped talking. Is it true?"

Cat nodded.

"Why?"

Cat made a sound in his throat, low and angry. He stood up, wanting Bryce to see for himself what had changed. For a few seconds, Cat's hands hovered over the hem of his t-shirt before he dragged it off and turned to show Bryce the long scar on his stomach. He pointed to it, watching Bryce's face fall apart.

"Everything is so messed up," Bryce said. "God. This is so bad. I don't even know what to say to you anymore."

Of course not. He hadn't been to see Cat since That Night, not even in the hospital. He hadn't called. No word, just disappeared from Cat's life. With a snarl, Cat said, "Glory be to the Father—"

Bryce said. "Your mom said you were doing this weird religious shit, but I didn't believe her. You know what it's like for me. Please don't."

Don't what? Cat wanted to demand. *Don't show you the truth?* Out loud, he continued, "—and to the Son—"

"Shut up!" Bryce said. He rose to his feet and stood facing Cat. "You're not the only one who suffered here. Stop!"

"—and to the Holy Ghost. As it was in the beginning—"

"Do you know what it's been like?" Bryce demanded. "We saw you, Cat. We saw you lying there covered in blood and nearly dead. Zee blames himself. He's stopped hanging out with anyone but his girlfriend, and now that she's pregnant, he's all wrapped up in buying diapers and baby clothes and telling the rest of us to fuck off if we say anything at all to him. Ezra spends his nights shredding the insides of his arms then getting wasted, or sometimes the other way around. I can't watch them like this anymore."

Cat paused his recitation. They'd been back long enough for Bryce to see all this? What happened to college? All this was because of him, because of what he'd done—messing around with Bryce and then letting Landon lead him away from safety. He was the cause of all their distress. Cat stared at Bryce, his mouth open but no sound coming out.

He'd been quiet long enough Bryce lowered his voice. "Look at you," he said. "You're different too. What happened to you?" He reached for Cat, but Cat shrank away from his touch. "Everything that made you special—"

In the same way Cassie's use of *pretty* hit Cat at the meeting, Bryce's words sliced him open. A chill raced up his spine, and he shook head to toe. *Everything that made you special.* All the things Bryce had complained about when they were together. His femininity, his glitter, the very core of his being was what had painted a target on his back for men like Landon. *You're very pretty.* Cat had hurt everyone, himself included, by being *special*.

"Lord Jesus Christ, have mercy on me, a sinner," he said as the world around him narrowed and faded into his spotty memories of That Night.

"Please listen," Bryce begged. "I'm sorry! I'm sorry for it all. But you left! You weren't there when I went back. I searched and searched for you. A couple of people told us you'd gone with some guy. And that call—fuck, we *heard* him beating the shit out of you. Why? Why would you go with someone else? Did you think he would give you something I couldn't? That he would care about you more than I—"

So that was it, the reason Bryce had never visited or called or texted. "Lord Jesus Christ, have mercy on me, a sinner." Cat sat back down on the couch and curled into himself, his arms around his knees, rocking. He tried to block out Bryce's voice and the jagged edges of his pain. "Lord Jesus Christ, have mercy on me, a sinner."

Bryce stopped shouting. "Cat? What's wrong?" His voice sounded far away.

Over and over, Cat repeated his prayer. He was distantly aware of Bryce calling for his mother, but he didn't look up even when he felt the couch dip next to him and Mom's arm was around him.

"Come on. Talk to me."

It was the same damn thing that had happened at the meeting. Somewhere in the panic and confusion, Cat recognized it. He fumbled in his pocket for his phone. David's last text to him was still on the screen. Not knowing what else to do, he gave Mom his phone. She took it, and in the background, Cat heard Bryce ask what was wrong again followed by Mom's voice on the phone.

"Is this David?" she said then paused. "This is Audrey Rowland, Cat's mother. For whatever reason, he meant for me to call you. He's having some kind of panic attack, I think." She listened for a moment then lowered the phone. "Cat," she said. "You're safe. David says I should help you breathe. Do you want me to put you on the phone with him?"

Cat held out his hand. While Mom counted, Cat breathed with her, and David's soft voice spoke into his ear through the phone. "You're not in danger. Focus on us, okay?"

Slowly, so slowly, Cat's heart rate returned to normal and the sick feeling ebbed. He took long, shuddering breaths until the terror receded and was replaced by the now-familiar fever-like ache. He kept his eyes closed, concentrating on Mom's and David's words, calm and soothing. After several tense moments, he relaxed enough to sit back against the couch cushions.

"I'm going to go now," David said. "I'll text you later, and I'll see you this afternoon."

Mom took the phone. "Thank you," she said before ending the call.

"Who's David?"

Cat had almost forgotten Bryce was still there. He looked up and shook his head when he saw Bryce's slight frown.

"He's a friend of Cat's. I'm sorry about this," Mom said. "Obviously this isn't a good time to visit right now."

"Obviously," Bryce said. "Must be a really good *friend*." There was such deep hurt in his eyes it made Cat need to turn away.

He shifted so he could lean against Mom, his face hidden in her shoulder. For a long time, they stayed that way, her fingers smoothing his hair. Eventually, he heard footsteps and the sound of the door opening and closing. When the exhaustion lifted, Cat sat up, and Mom took his face in her hands.

"Okay?" she asked. He nodded. "I'm sorry. I thought it would be good for you to see your friends again, but it was a poor choice today." Her sigh was heavy with anguish. "Go on up and lie down for a while. I'll make you some tea."

With Mom's help, Cat rose from the couch, and she handed him his shirt. He watched her turn toward the kitchen before ascending the stairs, still wobbly. Somehow, he didn't think tea and a nap were going to solve anything, but at least they might take his mind off the visit with Bryce for a while.

Cat flopped into the chair in the therapist's office. He reached into his pocket and pulled out his old rosary, depositing it on the table next to her. Before his appointment, he'd heard Mom's hushed voice on the phone with her, telling her what had happened. When she hung up, Mom had told him the therapist had asked if he had a rosary. Surprised, he'd nodded, and Mom had told him to bring it to his appointment. He'd contemplated ignoring her, but since he saw neither harm nor benefit to the therapist's strange request, he complied.

Attempting to appear annoyed and sarcastic, he gestured at his rosary, hoping to conceal his curiosity. The therapist, whom he'd grudgingly begun referring to by her actual name—Dr. Saliers—saw right through him and smiled in a way which both irritated and amused Cat. She had balls, he'd give her that much.

Dr. Saliers picked up the rosary, and Cat twitched. It was old; his grandmother had given it to him for his fifth birthday. At the time, he'd been fascinated by watching her say her prayers, her voice soft and gentle and the beads sliding through her fingers. Her rosary had been beautiful, made of hand-painted wood. The one she'd bought for Cat was a child's rosary, smooth blue faux glass beads with a simple Crucifix and a medallion of Philomena, Patron Saint of blood disorders. Nana had meant well.

"Do you know how to use it?" Dr. Saliers asked.

Cat nodded. No point in denying it. Nana had taught him patiently, explaining the meanings of each part and going over the prayers until he'd memorized them. She'd taught him dozens of other prayers as well, something for every situation. He'd forgotten some of them, but he'd spent so long committing them to memory that many remained. For years, Nana took pride in his ability to recite the prayers and the central tenets of the faith; at one point, she'd proclaimed he might someday be a priest. If only she'd known.

"Good," Dr. Saliers was saying, bringing Cat back to the present. She stood up and walked around to the other side of her desk, pulling out a string of prayer beads from one of the drawers. She returned to her seat.

Raising his eyebrows, Cat pointed to the beads. Now that he had a closer look, he could tell they weren't identical to his. There were fewer, for one thing—only seven small beads between the larger ones, where his had ten. He tilted his head. Despite his intent to feign disinterest, he was too curious to be successful.

Dr. Saliers smiled. "I grew up in the Episcopal church. Did you know many traditions—most of which aren't Christian—use beads? I learned how many years ago. I don't attend church often these days, but if I went back, I know my denomination would welcome me."

Cat wondered what she meant, but he wasn't going to break his silence to ask. He reached out, and Dr. Saliers dropped her beads into his hand. The rosary was heavier than he'd expected. Marbled gray beads were interspersed with larger black ones, and the Crucifix was a slim, silver cross. She didn't have a medallion on hers. Cat ran his fingers along the rosary, rolling the beads. He handed it back to Dr. Saliers in exchange for his own.

She changed the subject. "Your mom mentioned on the phone today that you had something resembling a panic attack. Without your description or witnessing it myself, I'm hesitant to say that's what it was, but it wouldn't surprise me."

Sinking low in his seat, Cat frowned at her. He didn't like how his parents had been seeing Dr. Saliers themselves. He was sure it was because they had to *figure out what to do with him*. As though they hadn't been doing the very same for his entire life. They'd learned new ways to handle situations like the one with Bryce, including keeping communication open on their end with Dr. Saliers. It wasn't her fault his parents were so invasive, but he wasn't pleased Mom had told her. A small part of him knew his mother was concerned, and he had to acknowledge after seeing Dr. Saliers for a month his parents had been significantly more relaxed around him in general. But if it was going to lead to even more awkward questions and silence in Dr. Saliers' office every time he did something *new* and *unexpected*, he wanted no part of it.

"Because you're always reciting prayers, I thought I might teach you a way you can center and calm yourself if something like that happens and you're not with anyone who can help you right away." Dr. Saliers held up her beads. "I'll show you what I learned with mine, and you can show me how to do it your way. Then we'll work on how to use it to help you. Fair?"

Cat hadn't been expecting that. He debated with himself whether or not to hear her out. In the end, it didn't sound like too bad a deal after all, so Cat nodded. He allowed his mental tally to score a mark in Dr. Saliers' column on this one for giving him back a fraction of his independence.

Chapter Thirteen

Where There Is Despair, Hope

February, 2006

CAT HATED Valentine's Day. He wasn't the sort of hearts-and-flowers person who wanted or needed a special occasion full of candy and cupids, and it had always seemed pointless and commercialized. Maybe it was because he'd never had a boyfriend to share it with. Bryce didn't count; they'd been fooling around, but they weren't buying each other romantic trinkets or greeting cards. He knew plenty of guys who loved it, though, even if they sometimes liked to pretend otherwise. Zee, for example, had always gone overboard with every girlfriend.

Instead of home in bed with a sexy book, Cat was stuck at the cafe watching people order Valentine-themed coffees and desserts. It was crowded, so Mom needed both him and LR. She was busy at the register, decked out in pink and red. LR didn't enjoy the holiday any more than Cat did, but she had much more skill at looking happy while cashing out customers. Cat, tired and achier than usual, was grateful he was only responsible for picking up after the patrons.

It was snowing lightly, but the atmosphere inside was warm and cheerful, the post-work bustle building up. Cat heard the tinkle of the bell over the door and looked up in time to catch David's eye. The dimpled smile appeared, and David waved.

Mom stepped out from the back and saw David. She looked at Cat and shook her head, but she smiled. "Go on," she said. "We'll manage for a bit while you take a break." She called for LR and switched her out with one of the other employees so LR could take over Cat's duties.

Cat raised his eyebrows at her. This was the start of their busy time, and she was letting him go? She gestured to David then turned her back, returning to the kitchen. Cat motioned to David that he would be a minute. He put away the supplies he'd been using, washed his hands, and came out to the front of the store. By then, David had already ordered his coffee to go and had it in hand.

"I was in town buying Valentines," David said by way of explanation.

Cat tilted his head in question. David hadn't mentioned being in a relationship, but they hadn't seen each other in a while. A knot of disappointment formed in Cat's stomach even though he knew technically David was off-limits.

"For my family," David clarified. "My nieces and nephew—my sister's and my brother's kids. They're little, and we try to make it special for them. Here." He pulled out his wallet and opened it to the pictures then handed it to Cat.

There were several photos of three adorable children, a pair of brown-haired little girls and a blond boy. Cat flipped through, smiling. He handed the wallet back to David, who shoved it back in his pocket.

"Want to take a walk?" he asked.

Cat nodded, and David waited by the door for him to grab his jacket. They strolled down the main street, and Cat watched the people passing by. Even though it was cold, he and David didn't rush, taking their time to window-shop. They stopped outside a piercing place, and David laughed at the display in the window. It was a whole line of jewelry in the shape of pot leaves surrounded by Valentine decorations.

"Nothing says 'I love you' like some good, old-fashioned weed," David joked.

While they browsed the display, Cat absently reached up to press his fingers to the hole in his left ear.

"You have a piercing?" David asked. When Cat nodded, he said, "I've never seen you wear anything in it."

Cat had made sure the hole didn't close, but he hadn't worn an earring in months. He had been contemplating whether he should leave it alone, since he'd promised never to wear one again. Before he could think of a way to answer David, he felt the soft press of a finger and thumb against his earlobe. He raised his eyes to meet David's and nearly gasped at the sensation of drowning in their blue depths. David smiled, and Cat tried to remember how to move.

"You would look hot with an earring, especially with that new haircut," David said. His cheeks darkened. "I mean, I uh—sorry—I shouldn't have—"

His flustered stuttering brought Cat to his senses, and he reached up to touch David's hand, still lingering on his ear. He finally coaxed his mouth to recall the motion required for smiling, and David's breathy laugh revealed his relief.

"How did you manage to get one done, anyway?" David sighed at his mistake when Cat opened his mouth to offer a prayer in reply. "Never mind. I'm guessing that wasn't one of your better choices."

Cat scowled. Trying to convey his irritation, he flicked one of David's ears; he had both pierced. Cat suspected it had been far less risky for him—David's hemophilia was moderate rather than severe, so as long as he'd taken precautions, he probably hadn't had nearly the trouble Cat had with his own. Instead of glaring back at him, David only grinned.

"Yeah, yeah. Spare me the lecture. Since you already have the hole, I'm going to buy you a new earring," he said.

Cat pulled away, shaking his head. He didn't know what he and David were to each other, especially after the way David had touched him and complimented him, and he wasn't sure what a gift like that meant. Grasping David's arm, he tried to show him by tugging him away from the shop.

David wasn't having any of it. "I want to," he said. "Friends can buy each other Valentines, right? Let me do this for you."

Friends. That was all they were and all they ever would be. Cat swallowed heavily and nodded, coaxing his expression into something he hoped looked happy.

David pointed to the pot-leaf earring. "One of those?"

Cat covered his mouth and snickered behind his hand. He nodded again, and they entered the store. The man behind the counter was the same one who had done Cat's piercing in the first place, and he remembered him.

"I wondered if I'd see you again," he said cheerfully. "It's not every day I see such a beautiful ginger boy. Getting a new one today?"

Cat blushed and shook his head, looking to David. The artist grinned, making his thick mustache quiver. For a moment, the familiar impending panic crept up Cat's spine, but he remembered the beads in his pocket. He slid his hand in and touched them, soothing against his fingers. His breathing slowed and he relaxed.

In the meantime, David peered into the glass case and pointed to the specific earrings he liked. "Those," he said. "Can we see them?"

"Sure thing." The artist pulled them out and set them on the top of the case. He tilted his chin at David, but he addressed Cat. "Boyfriend?"

The word pulled on Cat's stomach in the same fluttering, tickling way David's laugh did. They weren't boyfriends, and Cat wasn't supposed to be thinking about that anyway. He shook his head, and the artist looked disappointed.

David set the earrings back down. "These are wonderful. Handmade?"

It was the artist's turn to look bashful. "Made them myself."

"We'll take them," David said.

"You sure he's not your boyfriend?"

Cat ducked his head, and the man laughed, a rich, booming sound. He wrapped the earrings in paper and set them in a little white box. David paid, and they paused beside the shop's door. David withdrew the box from the bag. He pulled out one of the earrings, closed the box, and put it back in the bag. Gently, he tugged on Cat's earlobe until he could slide the earring into place. The scent of his soap wafted to Cat's nostrils, and he inhaled, closing his eyes.

All too soon, David stepped back to admire the earring. He grinned. "It suits you," he said.

Cat smiled faintly, wishing David would move closer again. Instead, David pulled the box back out and removed the second earring. He took out one of his own and replaced it with the pot leaf, placing his on the opposite side of Cat's.

"We match," he remarked.

The wave of happiness washing over Cat was so intense it made him dizzy. It took almost a full minute for him to realize he wasn't lightheaded from happiness—he was starting to feel sick. It was too hot in the store, and he still had his jacket on. He looked around for a place to sit, but there weren't any chairs. In frustration, he gave a tiny grunt.

As soon as the sound escaped, David's demeanor changed to

concerned. "What's wrong?"

Cat didn't feel good enough by then to recite a full prayer. His throat burned as though it had been scraped raw. He managed a weak few words of the Hail Mary before leaning heavily against David.

"Okay, babe. I've got you."

David wrapped an arm around Cat's waist and helped him move to the wall, where Cat slid down to the floor. David put a hand on Cat's forehead and checked his pulse with the other.

"Your heart's a little fast, and you feel warm. Are you getting sick again?" David's brow creased. Cat nodded; the motion made his head hurt. "You're so pale." David looked back at the shop's owner. "Can he have some water?"

The owner disappeared in back and returned with a bottle of water, which he opened and handed to David.

After shedding his coat and sipping the water, Cat began to regain strength. Gradually, his head cleared. He put his hand out and pressed his fingers over David's heart, the only way he knew to thank him. How David had worked out so quickly what was wrong was a mystery; even Cat's parents weren't so aware. Curiosity must have shown on his face because David chuckled.

"I'm a nurse, and I've dealt with this my whole life, too."

Cat wasn't clear-headed enough to puzzle through what David meant. It sounded strange to him, knowing his constant health crises weren't solely related to hemophilia, but he couldn't piece together why. He rubbed his temples in a futile effort to bring his mind back to order.

While Cat wrestled with his muddled thoughts, David reached up and rubbed the back of Cat's neck gently. The result of the touch was a shiver that traveled from the top of Cat's head down to his belly. It had nothing to do with his oncoming fever. He sucked in his breath. It had been an eternity since he'd felt anything remotely like that kind of excitement, and he tensed, willing it to pass.

David dropped his hand. "Let's go," he said. "I'll walk you back to the cafe and tell your mom what happened. I can drive you home then, if you want."

He stood and offered Cat a hand, which he accepted. Cat stayed still for a moment to see if the dizziness had indeed passed. Relieved he was steady, he put a hand on David's arm to reassure him before putting his jacket back on. Nodding, David stepped outside, and Cat followed. David looped his arm around Cat's waist, and Cat accepted the support. The throbbing in his head and sandpaper behind his eyes temporarily dampened the intensity of his feelings for David and provided a welcome barrier.

It took over a week before Cat's fever broke and he began to recover from his cold. He was still sniffling, but at least the body aches were gone. Even a minor illness was a big deal now, and Mom had hovered—or made the others hover—the entire time in case he needed medical attention. Their constant presence made it harder to hide the intermittent dreams, enhanced by his elevated temperature. Each time he woke from a nightmare, he heard footfalls outside his door, someone making sure he was all right.

In the first few days, the pain was almost unbearable. Besides leaving him weak and exhausted, illness caused his residual pain to spike and lowered his tolerance for it. Every morning, he eyed the bottle of pills still sitting on his dresser. His refusal to take them after That Night and his recovery from the first surgeries had been as much an assertion of himself as his vows. Now, lying in bed with fire under his skin and aches in his joints, it was tempting to revisit taking something stronger than over-the-counter meds. He wouldn't, though. How—and even whether—he addressed his pain was at least one thing still under his power.

Instead, Cat made it through his lengthy sickness with plain Tylenol and the steady stream of texts from David, checking in on him and entertaining him with stories about work. He was on day shifts, so Cat lounged on the couch watching random daytime television and waiting for David to finish so they could message freely. Until being forced to stay home and do nothing, Cat hadn't given much thought to how dull his life had become. Even if he'd wanted to text something other than smileys and frowns, he had little to say about anything at all. He was sure David didn't care much about reality home improvement shows or reruns of old legal dramas.

At last, one morning he woke feeling significantly better. The dreams had been less intense than usual, and Cat was fairly well-rested. He remembered David wanted to meet up after work, and they had made plans to spend time together in the cafe if Cat was feeling up to it. In his excitement, Cat sat up a bit too fast, causing spots in his line of vision. He stayed still for a minute or two until it passed, frowning. Ever since That Night, a lot of his ongoing health problems had been worse, but that one was the most annoying. He wasn't used to doing things at a snail's pace.

After texting David a smiley and receiving a return message about what time David would arrive, Cat tossed back the blankets and stood. Having put away all his usual sleep attire, he'd resorted to sleeping naked or in his underwear most nights. He stood in front of his dresser, and the familiar longing to choose something stylish to wear under his clothes washed over him. He tried to force past it, reminding himself that David wouldn't see it anyway, but he couldn't resist. The urge was too strong; he knew what he wanted, and it wasn't any of the pairs of boring briefs neatly folded in his drawer.

Taking a deep breath, he drew himself up and walked to the closet with his head held high. All his lace and satin, of both the masculine and feminine varieties, rested peacefully in a clearly marked bin on the floor. He knelt down and drew it out, his hands shaking. No one would know. They would only ever see the outside, the jeans hiding the evidence. It wasn't really cheating if he was the only one who knew.

He didn't even need to search. The pair he wanted—deep blue with lace sides and a little bow in front—was right on top. He stood up, the panties in hand, and slid his used pair off. He'd barely gotten the blue ones on when there was a knock and his door opened. Cat yelped and put his hands in front of his crotch.

LR's eyes widened. "Oh, god! I'm sorry. I was just coming in to see if you were feeling better today. I thought you'd be dressed." Her brow furrowed. "Kitty-Cat? You okay?"

Her use of his pet name alerted him to her worry. He loved when she called him that, but he knew she was scared now, and it was because of something he'd done or was doing. He bit his lip and waited for her to say something.

"It's all right." She crossed the room and put her hand on his arm. "I'm here. God, you're shaking all over. You're not having a relapse, are you?"

He shook his head and held out his hands. She was right; he was trembling violently. In an instant, he realized his mistake. LR had seen his underwear, and she knew what he was doing. Her arms went around him, and she pulled him close.

"Sh," she murmured. "It's okay. I'm glad you're trying to be you again."

That was the wrong thing to say. Anger surged through him,

and he shoved her violently. He was always himself. Couldn't she see that? LR caught her balance and stood staring at him, her lips parted and her breathing ragged. When she could speak, her words sliced him open.

"We've tried, Cat. For months, we've all tried. I don't know how to get through to you. I'm only one person, and I can't do it anymore. Please, stop shutting us—me—out."

She turned around and walked out, closing the door behind her. Cat sagged back against his dresser and looked down at himself. He couldn't wear the underwear. Angrily, he yanked them off and threw them aside then pulled a bland pair of gray boxer briefs out of his drawer. He didn't need stupid lace and bows to be himself. He could be whomever he wanted no matter how he dressed. With a strangled sob, he threw on a ratty black shirt with a faded band logo and a pair of baggy jeans. Not even the thought of seeing David was enough to bring him out of the deep sadness descending on him.

Before he left his room, he put the lid back on the bin and shoved it into his closet. After delivering a kick to the bin that was more painful than satisfying, he walked out the door, leaving the blue panties tangled in the corner.

Chapter Fourteen

Where There Is Darkness, Light

March, 2006

Cat had begged off work early, since it was the middle of the week and there was nothing much happening at the cafe. He'd showed David's number to Mom, which she'd put in her own phone, as a way of letting her know who he would be with. His mother had given him one of her knowing looks, and he'd had to work hard not to roll his eyes at her. If he'd done so, she would have found a way to make things difficult for him. Cat loved his mother, and he was proud of the way she'd come so far since her days of fussing over him for every little mishap as though waiting for him to become dust. Unfortunately, she'd replaced that with something he thought was supposed to resemble tough love with regard to taking care of himself on his own. They were at a stand-off, and it was always touchy whether she would let him out without a lecture.

Since he'd come through his cold all right, she'd agreed on the condition he was "careful." Cat no longer had any certainty about what that meant; it could have been a reference to anything. He suspected her secret fear was that David would suggest something inappropriate and Cat would wind up nearly dead outside another gay bar. As it was parallel to one of his own fears, Cat saw no reason not to agree to her terms.

David came in at four, and LR was on the register. Her eyes lit up when she saw him, and Cat had to hold back storming over to the counter and shoving her. He wasn't impressed with the way she was flirting with him while she took his order. How dare she! Cat wasn't sure of David's age, but he had to be old enough that seventeen-year-old LR was far too young for him. Yet there she was, acting like she was plenty grown up to score a date with an adult man—one she knew perfectly well was there to see Cat, not her.

She didn't miss Cat's reaction. When she looked over to him, he narrowed his eyes at her, and she looked from Cat to David and back. Winking, she mouthed at Cat, *He's cute*, and Cat's annoyance with her dissipated as he caught on to her intentions. He knew he'd gone red, and he hoped David hadn't seen the exchange. From David's amused expression, Cat suspected he had, but he didn't say a word.

As the afternoon wound down, they walked through the town, deciding on a place to eat. David kept up a steady stream of chatter about work, his family, and the sorts of books he liked. Cat was glad he didn't have to explain anything of his own. He wasn't sure what David would make of his collection of cheap romance novels, especially since most of them weren't remotely gay. Half of them— kinky pirates and clinical descriptions aside—didn't even have any decent sex in them, so he couldn't excuse it by saying he read them for the penises.

There was a shop on the corner of Main Street and Arbor, the type with entries on two sides and sales racks that could be pushed outside when the weather was nice. A pair of older women called to David, and all four of them stepped inside the shop to get out of the wind. The women swept David away and began chatting with him, and Cat, not sure what else to do, looked through the clearance racks.

There wasn't much in there to interest him, but two things caught his eye. First, he saw a yellow bikini with hot pink polka dots. He mused that it would look terrible on him because of the color, but he liked the style. Next, he saw a skirt. It wasn't just any skirt, either. It was short, probably wouldn't even reach Cat's knees. The bright green material was stretchy, and Cat saw that the top of it would cling and mold to the shape of his body. The bottom flared with large pleats which would billow out if a person were to spin around in it. The whole thing was cute and sexy and flirty, exactly the sort of skirt Cat might have worn before That Night.

He fingered the fabric, his heart racing. There was no need for him to buy a new skirt, but everything in him longed for it. It would look perfect with a tank top, and he even had a pair of shoes that matched the color. He sighed softly, missing his old life.

A slight movement at his elbow alerted him to David's presence, and he whirled around, eyes wide and lips parted. He backed away from David, opening and closing his mouth.

"Sorry about making you wait. Do you like that one?" David asked. His voice was calm and quiet.

Cat shook his head vigorously and crossed his arms over his chest, gripping his upper arms. David had only ever seen him in his jeans and t-shirts; he had no idea what Cat's previous clothes had been like.

"It's okay," David assured him. "It would look nice on you."

Shaking his head again and hating how David read him so easily, Cat stepped back, away from the rack. He glanced at the skirt out of the corner of his eye. No, he told himself firmly. Not only did he not want it, he didn't want David to offer to buy him anything else or to know he'd once worn those kinds of clothes. He wasn't interested in gifts from someone who wasn't even a boyfriend, and certainly not because that person felt sorry for him. Cat took one last look at David, turned around, and fled up the street, heading back to the cafe.

If Cat's mother was surprised to see him, she didn't show it. She looked him over and drew him into a hug then sat him down at a corner table. The post-work crowd hadn't arrived yet. There were only three customers, and they all seemed too wrapped up in their own affairs to bother with Cat or his mother.

In an uncharacteristic gesture, she ran her fingers through his hair, sweeping his bangs from his forehead. "I wish you could tell me what's wrong."

Cat leaned his elbows on the table and leaned forward in misery. To soothe himself, he muttered, "My God, I offer you my prayers, works, joys, and sufferings of this day."

His mother sighed. "Oh, honey. I wish you would talk to me. Where's David?"

He closed his eyes and recited the prayer again, finishing it this time while rocking slightly in his seat.

"Damn it," his mother whispered. "What did that evil person do to my baby?"

Surprised and hurt at her words, Cat opened his eyes and looked at his mother, really looked. Her eyes were red, and there was strain around them as she worked to keep from crying. Worry lines creased her face where none had been before. He realized then that she hadn't been talking about David when she'd said *evil person.* Cat wondered how often since That Night she'd stayed up, perhaps taking out her old rosary and reciting the same prayers he did, even though it had probably been more than twenty-five years since she'd last done so. Cat suspected she was his age when she stopped.

He reached out and put his hand on hers, hoping to reassure her he was still there, still hanging on, still managing. She turned her hand enough to squeeze his fingers before pulling away.

"I'm going back to work. I'll bring you some tea. Sugar, spice, no milk?"

Cat nodded, and she got up from the table. While he waited for her to return, the bell over the door tinkled. When Cat caught sight of David, he shrank back against the wall, embarrassed both for showing his interest in the skirt and for his behavior afterward.

LR stepped up to take his order. She chatted with David while he waited, and Cat scowled. He didn't want to see either of them, so he got up and ducked into the hallway with the bathrooms, slipping into the supply closet. He peeked out in time to see his mother come back from the kitchen with his tea. She stopped at the table and set it down, looking around. Her shoulders slumped, and she sighed. When she turned, she nearly collided with David.

"Excuse me," he said.

Cat's mother pursed her lips. For a moment, Cat thought she might tell David off for not watching where he was going—or maybe for not keeping track of Cat. She surprised Cat by taking an entirely different route. Judging by the way David's eyes widened as she spoke, she'd caught him off-guard too.

"He needs a friend right now, not whatever it is you think you're doing." She eyed him up and down.

"That is what I'm doing," David insisted. "Being a friend."

"Right. Don't think I'm clueless about things just because he won't—or can't—talk about them. I know you've been seeing a lot of each other, and I saw the earring."

David didn't deny buying it, though how she'd known Cat hadn't bought it for himself was anyone's guess. "I'm not—" he tried, but she cut him off.

She leaned forward, and Cat barely heard what she said next. "He won't tell us who did this to him. It was bad. You weren't with him right after, but you are now, and you see what he's like.

Whatever happened, you need to tread very, very carefully here."

With that, she stepped around him and returned to the kitchen, but not without a meaningful glance at the bathroom hallway. David stood where he was for a moment, to-go cup in hand, tapping his fingers against the thick paper. Eventually, he turned around, and when he did, his eyes met Cat's. There was no way for Cat to pretend he hadn't noticed David, so he stepped all the way out from the hallway.

David tilted his head as an invitation and sat down in the same corner where Cat had been before David came in. Cat accepted the invitation to sit, perched across from David with his back rigid. David blew on his drink; Cat stirred his until David glared at him and put a hand on his to get him to stop. Cat looked down and made a valiant effort to hide his smirk; his nonverbal skills had evidently rubbed off on David. The attempt at concealing his amusement was unsuccessful. David grinned before his expression turned serious again.

He didn't waste any time getting right to the point. "I know you can't—or don't want to—tell me what happened back there, but maybe I can guess," he said.

Cat held out his hands to David in a "go ahead" gesture. He picked up his spoon again, but David reached out and touched his wrist. With a roll of his eyes, Cat left it alone.

"Okay," David said. "First, um..." He pressed his lips together, and Cat almost smirked again. David was obviously trying to phrase it as a yes or no question to avoid Cat's verbal vomit. David continued, "Are you embarrassed?"

Cat sighed and shifted in his seat. It wasn't as though he had something to hide. Before That Night, his life had been an open book. He was fairly certain there wasn't anyone left in town who hadn't seen him wear a skirt at some point. Concordia was a welcoming place, aside from a few conservative people—some religious, some not—who made it their personal mission to redeem the town from unnamed ruination. The church where Cat grew up tried to stay out of the town's politics, but they weren't welcoming. One reason his Grandpa Rowland had stopped going was due to their failure to progress. Not until his own coming out did Cat learn about Grandpa's relationships before he met and fell in love with Grandma. Cat suspected David thought he was trying not to be—as Bryce put it—"too gay." Cat shook his head, shrugged, and nodded. Embarrassment was the wrong word for it, but maybe it would do.

"You're not sure?" David ran his fingers over Cat's wrist, sending a shiver down Cat's spine. "I don't mind, you know. You'd look pretty like that." Cat gasped, but David misinterpreted his reaction and smiled. "I think there's more to it. You'd look pretty, sure, but I like the wild look on you, too. The skirt reminded me of cotton candy, all fluffy sugar. You, though—I think you're more like bittersweet chocolate."

The moment broke as David's words hit Cat. He'd made a promise that he wouldn't go back to the way he'd been before. His thoughts turned to the neatly lined up boxes of clothes in his closet, including the colorful, patterned, and lacy underwear. Pretty. *You're very pretty.* Cat's whole body began to shake, and he wrapped his arms around himself to hold it together.

"Lord Jesus Christ, have mercy on me, a sinner," he said.

"Cat?"

"Lord Jesus Christ, have mercy on me, a sinner."

David slid out of his seat and moved around the table to sit by Cat.

"Lord Jesus Christ, have mercy on me, a sinner." The shaking increased, and Cat had to draw in several breaths before he could continue. "Lord Jesus Christ, have mercy on me, a sinner."

David went to slide his arm around Cat, but he changed his mind when Cat pulled away. Instead, David reached out and rested his hand on the back of Cat's neck, rubbing gently. "Sh, it's okay. You're okay," he said. "Breathe."

Cat shook his head, which was starting to hurt. "Lord Jesus Christ, have mercy on me, a sinner." His voice broke on the last word, and he squeezed his eyes shut.

Warm arms went around him, and he leaned into David, slumping against his side in relief. David wasn't going to ask him anything else. He was saying something, but the words registered only as nonsense; Cat couldn't process them properly. He wriggled his arm free and reached into his pocket, his fingers connecting with the beads. His breathing slowed, and he heard David counting and felt his warm breath against his ear.

Quieter this time, Cat mumbled, "Lord Jesus Christ, have mercy on me, a sinner." He opened his eyes.

A shadow fell across the table, and he looked up to see his mother, hands on her hips and a frown on her face. She wasn't looking at him, though. Her gaze was trained on David.

"I'm sorry," David said. "I don't know what happened." He

glanced down at Cat. "Does she know?" he asked. "About the clothes, I mean."

Cat nodded, and his mother sighed and slid into a chair across from them. "So that's what this is about."

"Yes. He was looking at clothes, and I saw him. That's why he took off. When I tried to talk to him about it...well, this." David gestured at Cat.

All Cat could do was look up into his eyes and say, "Lord Jesus Christ, have mercy on me, a sinner." It was the best he could manage in the moment.

"I did warn you," his mother said, but there was no heat or anger in her voice. "I'm going to assume he didn't tell you. Hell, he didn't technically even tell us, just showed us something he'd written, and he hasn't said a word since except for reciting prayers he learned as a child."

"Tell me what?" David asked. The arm around Cat's shoulders tightened.

Cat glared at his mother. She was speaking as though he wasn't sitting right there. Of course, she had no way of knowing David had been with him the first time he'd panicked.

She looked between them. "I don't feel like I should violate whatever trust he's given both you and me. Cat's very religious in a way his father, sister, and I are not. He takes things seriously. After what happened to him, he...changed." She stood up. "When he's ready, he'll show you. Until then, as I said before, tread carefully." She walked away, leaving the two of them alone.

David pulled away a little. "Is that true? This is sort of a religious thing?"

Cat repeated his earlier sequence of head shake, shrug, and nod.

"Oh," David replied, and for a moment, Cat thought he was disappointed. His next words surprised Cat. "I don't know if you'd want to...and you don't have to if it's too much...but..." He paused. "Do you want to come to church with me sometime?"

Cat backed up and gave David what he hoped was a *what the hell* look. He didn't think he would be welcome, and he wondered why David attended.

David dispelled his fears. "It's an affirming church," he said. "You know, where they don't make a big thing over sexuality and gender, and anyone can be a member. If it makes a difference, Pastor Maryann's partner is another woman."

The pastor? Cat's mouth fell open in surprise. For having lived in Concordia his whole life, he had no idea such a church existed. David didn't say anything else, and Cat hid behind his tea while he contemplated a response. At last he set his cup down and nodded.

"Great!" David said. "This Sunday? I'll pick you up at nine-thirty." He took out his wallet, rifled through it, and handed Cat a business card with the name and address of the church on it. It wasn't in Concordia after all but the next town over. "You can show this to your family if they ask where I'm taking you."

Cat nodded again and took the card. A flush of pleasure crept up his neck when he realized David had understood and provided a means for him to communicate. As he drained his cup, he thought, *I can do this. It's just one day.*

CHAPTER FIFTEEN

WHERE THERE IS SADNESS, JOY

CAT PULLED on a pair of tiger-striped briefs and stood in front of his closet, pushing hangers back and forth as he warred with himself over what to wear. He was absolutely not going to church in a dress, no matter how tempting the idea was. Most of his less feminine clothes weren't appropriate either, being too casual for the occasion. His hand paused on his formal black trousers, the ones he'd worn in high school when he performed on stage with the orchestra. He assumed they still fit, as he'd stopped growing taller by the time he was seventeen, though he worried he might be too thin now as a result of all his illnesses.

He removed them from the hanger and dragged them on—they were indeed slightly loose—then frowned into the closet as though blaming it for not coughing a shirt back out at him. He had even fewer options there, and neither his formal white Oxford nor the numerous t-shirts with rude graphics seemed right. At last he spotted a violet button-down and pulled it out. He put it on and tucked it in, leaving the top few buttons undone, then threw on a belt before sliding his rosary into the pocket. At the mirror over his dresser, he fluffed his bangs and peered at his reflection. With his heart thumping, he opened the jewelry case and withdrew a small onyx stud. His hands shook as he put it in.

For a long time he stood there looking at himself. He wasn't sure if he liked his appearance or not, but it would have to do. When he put the lid back on the jewelry box, his hand brushed against a bag he hadn't noticed. He opened it and reached inside. His fingers closed around a small, slim box, and he took it out. With a gasp, he dropped it back onto his dresser. LR must have put it there; it was the only explanation for why he had a brand-new lip gloss—the fancy kind bought from someone with a home-based makeup business.

Cat gripped the edge of his dresser and breathed slowly to quell the storm of anxiety and frustration. He raised his eyes to the mirror, staring at his pale, freckled face and imagining what his lips would look like painted with the new gloss. As temptation rose, he tried to ignore the little thrill running up his spine, but it was no use. He had to open the tube and see what LR had given him. Less than nine months before, he'd have been excited to try it out. What would it hurt to peek now? He wouldn't have to wear it, and even if he did, it wouldn't need to mean anything other than keeping his lips from getting chapped. He took the tube out of the box and opened it.

When he unscrewed the top, the fragrance of candied flowers wafted to his nostrils. He eyed the bit of gloss clinging to the applicator tip. It was sheer but not shimmering, more like scented Vaseline. He hesitated for only a second before sweeping the applicator over his lips, making them shine. The sweet scent blossomed, and he inhaled, smiling. As he did so, he caught his reflection again and his mouth dropped open. It had made a difference. The little bit of gloss, and the rush of joy it brought him, was enough to make him look better than he had in months. Cat grinned at his image in the mirror, but his smile faded and his cheeks turned pink when he realized what he'd almost done. He turned away to look for a box of tissues so he could wipe his mouth before going out in public.

He was just in time to come face to face with Mom, hovering in his doorway. "Where are you going?" she asked.

Lip gloss woes forgotten, Cat twisted around and picked up the little card from his dresser to hand to Mom.

"Ah," she said when she saw it. She crossed to the bed and sat down, patting the spot next to her.

Obediently, Cat joined her.

"You look nice," she remarked, a soft smile on her lips.

Cat nodded in acknowledgment.

Mom reached up and smoothed his bangs. "You haven't been to church in a while." She sighed. "Do you know why I stopped going?" When Cat shook his head, she continued. "It was after you were born and we found out you had hemophilia."

Puzzled, Cat nodded and motioned for her to continue.

"Right, well, back then, it was still a very scary time for parents to face that diagnosis in their children. No matter how much assurance the doctors gave that you would not get sick from the life-saving treatments, it was barely past the time when there was no question you would have. Everyone kept telling me 'God doesn't make mistakes' and 'God does everything for a reason.'" Mom's eyes glistened, and she cleared her throat. "I had a lot of trouble believing 'God' would create a child with the intent of making the child suffer."

Cat leaned his head on Mom's shoulder, wishing he could reassure her but knowing the truth in her words. He *had* suffered, in more ways than she probably realized. It occurred to him she'd meant to keep him from all the pain, inadvertently causing him more. He sighed deeply.

"I also knew how genetics worked. This was in no way God's doing—it was *my* messed up genes which made you so sick. I couldn't even blame it on your father or share the responsibility with him. I'd known it was a possibility, but I thought maybe I wouldn't be the one to pass it on." She put her arms around Cat. "I spent your childhood trying to make up for what I'd done, trying to keep you from the consequences of my choice to have biological children." She shifted, causing Cat to sit up, and took his face in her hands. "With all my hard work, I still couldn't protect you from what happened at someone else's hands."

Cat stared at her, wishing he had a way to ask her if she regretted having him, regretted his very existence.

The hurt must have shown because she said, "Oh, my baby. I don't even for one second wish I'd chosen not to have you. I only wish I'd made better decisions while you were growing up instead of letting fear rule me." She didn't remove her hands to brush away the tears which now rolled down her cheeks. "I hope you'll give me a chance to do things differently now."

Cat wrapped his arms around her and held on. No matter how much he wished she'd let go sooner, she wasn't to blame for something out of her control. Mom sat back after a minute.

"Are you going with David?" she asked as she dried her eyes.

He nodded, and she squeezed his hand.

"If this is what you need, go with my blessing." She gave his arm one last gentle pat and stood up. "I like him, you know."

Cat watched her turn around and walk out and then finished getting ready for David to pick him up. He didn't wipe his lips clean after all.

When Cat heard the doorbell, he dashed down the stairs, hoping to get there first. LR beat him to it, opening the door to greet David and giving Cat a sly smile before she slipped past him and back up the stairs. Cat was in too good a mood to be annoyed by her, though, so he didn't react as he grabbed his coat from the rack. While he pulled it on, he caught David eying him up and down. His expression went from surprised to amused, and Cat flushed under the scrutiny. He crossed his arms and looked away. David reached out and pried his arms apart until Cat dropped them to his sides. Cat met David's gaze and was rewarded with a smile which made him even warmer.

"You look really nice," David said, a slight catch in his voice.

Cat glanced down at himself and realized David had never seen him this way. He'd seen Cat in a hospital gown, a handful of naughty t-shirts, and his cafe uniform—khakis and a light reddish-brown polo—but never dressed up. Cat ducked his head, pleased at the compliment but a little embarrassed at being overdressed. David was more casual in a pair of dark jeans and a blue-and-white striped shirt with a collar.

"It's a bit of a drive," David said. "It's just outside Concordia, in the country. Hope that's okay."

They spent the drive play-fighting over the radio station; Cat's classical contemporary won out over David's seventies rock. David lowered the volume, and Cat listened while he chatted about his mom and two older siblings. Before Cat knew it, they'd arrived at the church.

David pulled into a driveway and followed several cars up a low hill and around the church. It was a modern structure, an unusually shaped building which could have been for any purpose at all. There was nothing about it which proclaimed "church": no stained glass windows or belfry or cross adorning the front or roof. It was one story, made of pale brick. There was a small gravel parking lot at the back, and David chose a spot off to the side under some trees.

As Cat reached for the door handle, David stopped him. "Wait. I think maybe I should tell you a few things. You're Catholic, right?" When Cat nodded, David continued. "Well, this probably won't be anything like what you've been to. We don't belong to any denomination, and people are from all kinds of traditions. A lot of us were rejected by other churches or even our families." He tilted his head. "I guess you kind of know the history of Concordia, right?"

Cat did. Concordia had once been much more conservative, but over time, as it gained popularity with tourists, many things had changed. A large number of the businesses had always been quietly queer-owned and operated, including one of the local wineries, and people grew tired of hiding. Though it never gained the status of other well-known gay tourist towns, Concordia had developed its own rainbow flair. The majority of residents and visitors welcomed the changes, but there was still a strong conservative streak among long-established families. There were residents who wanted to see the town return to an older time. Some simply left people alone, but others were more vocal about their disapproval. Bryce's family came to Cat's mind, but he quickly turned his attention back to David to suppress the sorrow those thoughts produced.

"This church opened its doors during a time when some people still thought the town was a battleground on which to fight their bigoted war. We needed a safe place where people felt God's love, and this was it. Pastor Maryann was one of the founders. We tried to keep something of all the practices people brought in with them, so it's a little...unusual." He smiled. "You'll see."

Cat tilted his head and studied David. He wondered what he was in for, but he nodded, and David returned it.

When they climbed out, Cat pulled his jacket around him. The early March wind sent a chill right through him, and he shivered. David put an arm around him, and Cat glanced at the people on their way in. Even though David had assured him the church was welcoming, Cat wasn't sure how comfortable he felt giving the appearance that they were there as more than friends. No one seemed to have noticed, so he leaned on David and let him lead the way to the door.

The inside was as unimpressive as the outside. It was an ordinary church, with long, cushioned pews and a lectern at the front, but other than that, it was different from Cat's former church. It took a moment for Cat to figure it out. There was a band set up on one side of the low stage, and there were other unfamiliar elements—a projector and screen, for one, and the formal furnishings were missing. Cat wondered if they even took Holy

Communion there. It was well-lit rather than being dim, and there were no candles. As he watched people filter in, he noticed everyone simply took seats. He couldn't decide if the lack of solemn ceremony bothered him or intrigued him.

David led him to a pew toward the front in the side section. He slid into the row and said, "I usually sit closer to the back, but I figured you'd want to see better. We're on the side so you don't feel like you have the whole church behind you, but we're down front so you can take everything in." His smile turned to a puzzled frown when Cat didn't move. "What is it?"

Still unsure of proper etiquette, Cat stood beside the chairs. He bit his lip then hastily crossed himself before slipping in beside David, who nodded. Once they were seated, Cat turned to watch the other attendees filtering in. After what David had said, he wasn't surprised to see so many different people represented. A family with three little girls sat across the aisle from them, and the tiniest one squirmed off the seat to stand facing Cat. She stared at him until he waved to her, after which she turned away to hide her chubby cheeks against her mama's knee. Cat put a hand over his mouth to stifle his giggle.

A moment later, the girl slid out of her pew and approached Cat. She put her little hand on his cheek and said, "Freckles." She touched her own face. "Like me." Before Cat could react, she scurried back to her seat, leaving him grinning. Her mother looked ready to scold, but when she looked at Cat, he gave her a thumbs-up and she smiled instead.

They had only been seated a few minutes when the musicians filed in and picked up their instruments. Cat watched, fascinated. They'd had an organ at his old church, and they'd sung traditional liturgy. He had no idea what to expect. A peek at the calendar that morning had confirmed it was the first Sunday of Lent. Did this church do anything special? Drums and guitars seemed too much for such a somber occasion.

The music began, even though there were still stragglers out in the hall. Over the tune, a woman at the microphone invited them to stand and sing along. Cat got to his feet, shooting David a wary look. David only looked over and grinned, making Cat shrink back. He prepared himself to be jolted out of his skin with a rock concert.

It never arrived. The band was playing a hymn—unexpectedly one Cat recognized, though not from his former church. It was strange hearing *Amazing Grace* played in a more contemporary way, but it wasn't at all the raucous noise Cat had expected. The words were printed on the screen up front, and Cat blinked in confusion for a moment. These were not the familiar stanzas. Around him, people's voices joined together to sing the new words.

Amazing grace, how sweet the sound
That saved a soul like me
I once was lost, but now I'm found
God's love has set me free

Cat glanced sideways at David, who murmured, "I'll explain after."

With a nod, Cat turned back to the front. He didn't sing, but he mouthed the words along with the others, thinking about them. Several of the verses ran the same way with altered text. David didn't look his way again, but Cat caught the faint smile on his lips. The song ended, and the band played a couple more Cat didn't recognize. He felt more than heard the vibrations of David's rich voice; he wasn't bad.

Once they sat down, David leaned over to Cat. He said, "There's a reason we don't sing those words here. We've taken out all the references to 'blind' or 'deaf' or 'lame' as evidence of sin, and we don't sing of ourselves as *wretches*. Too many of us have been told we're born utterly evil with nothing good inside us or who we are is too damaged to deserve love. None of that is true."

He took Cat's hand in his and squeezed, and the raw pain which passed across his face caused Cat to suck in his breath. He wondered what David had seen in his lifetime to make him once believe himself to be broken beyond repair. He'd never tried to find a way to ask David for his story. He reached out with his free hand and touched David's shoulder, offering the only reassurance he could.

The moment passed, and David's expression closed off. He let go of Cat's hand and faced forward again, leaving Cat to sit with what he'd said. It was how Cat had seen himself since That Night, his soul fractured by his mistakes. He looked down at his hands, flexing his fingers and fanning them out across his thighs. He allowed himself to feel every ache in his joints, every tug on his skin from his scars, every new way in which his body protested ordinary motion. They were his evidence that nothing would repair the packaging. But was he a wretch, in pieces at the very core of his being as well? David didn't seem to think any of them were, but he didn't know how much Cat's actions had played a part in That

Night; even Bryce was unaware of the full truth.

While Cat contemplated, he lost track of what was happening around him. David nudged him, and he returned his attention to the church service. There was nothing else about it which felt familiar. David explained a few things as they went, and Cat had a paper bulletin to follow as well. He tried to take it all in, but it was overwhelming. Everything was so different. It wasn't until Pastor Maryann stood up to deliver what Cat would have called a homily and David—and the bulletin—called a sermon that he found something he understood.

She read the morning's text, from Genesis 9—God's promise to Noah. Cat squirmed; he'd never liked the story much, even though as a child he'd heard it over and over, read from a book with cute animal pictures and smiling cartoon people. When Pastor Maryann raised her eyes to the congregation, the words she delivered were nothing like Cat had expected.

"I don't know about you, but the story of Noah and the ark always creates more questions than it answers for me. I don't mean the ones even our children should ask, about how an earth-wide flood is geologically possible or how Noah acquired polar bears, raccoons, and kangaroos. No, I mean questions like, 'Why would a loving, merciful God commit such an act of genocide?'"

That was the part which had always frightened Cat. He understood God's promise never to destroy people again, but it warred with his idea of who God was. He nodded, and David glanced at him but said nothing.

Pastor Maryann continued, "I don't think this is a story to be taken so literally. What if the lesson we need to learn is that there is nothing in us too big for God to take care of? The whole Bible is full of stories about grand-scale redemption. What if God can do that for each and every one of us? Your past is in the past—washed, renewed, and fresh. Like Noah's landscape, it's changed, but also like Noah's landscape, it isn't beyond repair. The old is dead and gone, but the new has come, like the hope we have in the death and resurrection of our Lord. This is a season of reflection, a time to acknowledge our need for redemption and restoration as we await Easter morning."

She had more to say, but Cat's mind was already whirring a mile a minute, thinking about what she'd said and how it related to what David had said. Could he put the past behind him, start fresh? He didn't know.

Pastor Maryann concluded her sermon, and a string quartet stepped up to the stage. Cat admired their instruments, different from his own—they were all electric, smaller and thinner than his own cello, capable of their sharp, clear sound only via amplifier. The musicians began to play. Cat knew this hymn too—he'd played it himself. He watched the cellist, his fingers involuntarily marking the patterns along with her, and he could almost feel the bite of the strings against the pads.

David nudged him. "You play?" he whispered.

Cat didn't respond for a moment, swallowing the lump in his throat at the memories invoked by the melody. He nodded, and out of the corner of his eye, he caught David's smile.

"Play for me sometime?"

Cat shrugged. He hadn't played a single note in more than six months, but both the hymn and David's request gave him such a rush of longing he couldn't help the image which formed in his mind. He pictured David sitting on his bed, eyes closed as he listened to Cat drawing the bow across the strings. Cat turned to David and touched his shoulder, nodding. Heat prickled his neck when David grinned.

The rest of the band returned to the stage, the lead singer inviting the congregation to stand and sing the same hymn. Cat focused on the words as voices raised around him.

Forbid it, Lord, that I should boast
save in the death of Christ, my God!
All the vain things that charm me most,
I sacrifice them through his blood.

Cat leaned on David, turning his face into David's shoulder and breathing slowly. Was that what he'd done? Become charmed by vain things? He'd only wanted to be like everyone else. Now he'd made his sacrifices, given up those "vain things" he'd chased after. Did it cover him for everything he'd done wrong That Night?

Were the whole realm of nature mine,
That were a present far too small;
Love so amazing, so divine,
Demands my soul, my life, my all.

His *all*. Everything—all the things he'd done up until that point and all of who he was. Cat frowned. Maybe this was his sign from God, coming to church with David. It was Lent, a time of reflection and self-sacrifice. He'd always given something up for Lent, like the time he'd sworn off romance novels. Even after he was no longer attending Mass, he'd kept doing it every year. Now he had nothing left to give up except himself, the person he once was. He'd tried to do that already, but it was an incomplete effort.

An idea occurred to him. Could he, like Pastor Maryann had said, be washed, renewed, and fresh? He didn't know for sure, but he hoped it was true. He wanted to put it all behind him. If Cat couldn't be who he wanted anymore, maybe he could become someone different, erase the memory of who he had been. David had called him *pretty but wild.* He couldn't be pretty anymore, but maybe he could be what David had suggested. He would reinvent himself, someone different and better and stronger than he had been. It would be as though That Night had never happened.

The song ended, and Cat sat up straight. David slid an arm around him and murmured in his ear, "Are you all right?"

Cat nodded and looked over at David. Determination rose in him. What had been done was done—he didn't need anyone or anything to try to fix what was broken and lost. *I am not a wretch,* he thought. He was going to prove to everyone he was all right. He didn't need his parents or Shannon the physical therapist or Dr. Saliers or even David to look after him; he would be fine without their help. All he needed was to prove it to them.

He nodded at David again, and David sat back, apparently satisfied. *I want to wash away the past and become something new. I want my life back.*

PART V

TRIAL

AUGUST, 2013

LEAVING DR. Elyse's office, an idea occurred to Cat. Before he could find Micah and talk to him, he needed some time to gather his thoughts. He hopped into his truck, but instead of going home, he headed for the cemetery.

It was overcast, but the air didn't have the heavy feel of impending rain. July heat had given way to the slightly cooler August temperatures. Cat left his truck and trudged up the hill, the breeze stirring his hair. He found David's stone easily, though he'd only been to visit it twice before—at the funeral and around a year later, when the grief was still fresh. He didn't believe there was any reason to go; it was only a marker. David wasn't even buried there. He'd been cremated, per his wishes and those of his family.

Cat sat down on the grass facing the stone. He had no idea what to say. He closed his eyes and pictured David's loose curls, his blue eyes, and his dimpled smile. It seemed silly now, coming to talk to a dead person in a place that didn't even house his body. Yet there he was, staring at the dates of his lover's life and thinking about the frailty of his own. Regardless of what he'd told Dr. Elyse, he was still wary about new beginnings.

The thought stirred anger in him, and he tore at the grass in frustration. It wasn't supposed to work this way. He'd been meant to die first—he'd always known it. He should have died multiple times over the years, including eight years before when he'd been beaten nearly to death outside that club. So much was wrong with him that on any given day, he couldn't be sure anymore which parts would work and which wouldn't. How could he ask anyone else to spend his life, or even his summer, with that hanging over them?

He'd loved David, but he'd held back a bit of himself. David had, too. What made him feel guilty now wasn't that he could so easily fall for someone else but how much he wanted to do it. He wanted to let go and not be scared that he would leave a lover behind the way David left him. The desire terrified him for how utterly selfish it seemed; he wasn't sure anymore if he knew what real love looked like.

He reached out and ran his fingers over the stone. "You knew, didn't you?" he asked. "You knew how much time we both had, and you took a chance anyway." Cat swallowed back a sob. "I always thought it would be me, but you knew it would be you. Is that why you took the risk?" He sighed. "I'm sorry I didn't keep my promise, but it's not one I should have made to you."

Dr. Elyse's words came back to him, about opening his heart and making commitments rather than vows. A tiny, nagging thought wouldn't let go of him: Micah wouldn't expect anywhere near what he expected of himself. He couldn't know that for sure, of course. Micah was complicated at best. Cat was strong enough to handle Micah's demons—he knew intimately how easily the fuse could be lit by the smallest reminder. He'd counted on it, in fact, when he tried to avoid the very different kind of fire ignited by proximity with a man. Something had gone wrong, though. He'd clearly missed some vital piece of information, and setting Micah up with a friend hadn't been the right thing at all, maybe not for any of them.

A new worry hit Cat. Maybe it was too late; he had fled, and unlike all their previous arguments, this one had a feel of permanence. He'd threatened it, after all. Now it was up to him to make a move and hope there was still time to salvage the scraps. Something brushed at the edges of his memory, another time when he'd sewn together pieces of himself both physically and emotionally. He still bore the scars, but over time he'd come to see their elegance, to love them even. Anything with Micah worth saving would be the same. Slowly, Cat rose to his feet, brushing off his pants and stretching a little to relieve the aches in his joints. He returned to his truck and drove home without ever turning on the radio.

Cat tried to force down something to eat, but he wasn't feeling his best. He was achy, and he was still raw from spending the past few days wrapped up in his own thoughts. He contemplated a swim; that might ease his sore muscles. Remembering he'd left his swimsuit in his truck, he reached for the door to go retrieve it. The minute he swung it open, his heart gave a lurch.

Micah stood on the porch, his hand raised to knock. Even through a haze of weariness and pain, Cat was struck with the desire to simply stand there looking at him. Micah resembled David to a degree, with his tan skin and dark, curly hair, but that was where the similarities ended. Micah had a couple of inches on David, and he was broader and more filled out than David had been. Micah's eyes were deep, rich brown instead of blue. Even his curls were different—short, tight ringlets, darker and coarser. Cat wanted to put his fingers in them and tug, feeling their texture.

They were different in personality, too. Where David had been calm and confident, Micah was full of hurt and fear, heavy emotions coloring all his words and deeds. He'd confessed to Cat some of the more painful parts of his past, but Cat was certain there was more to it than what he chose to reveal—possibly more than he was aware of himself. It was his unflinching honesty which drew Cat in and made him want to know more while also giving him a desire to soothe those wounds.

Cat stiffened his spine, not trusting himself to keep from simply launching at Micah and kissing him instead of initiating the much-needed conversation they ought to be having. "What are you doing here?" he finally asked, the words coming out harsher than he intended.

"Are you okay?" Micah reached out but withdrew his hand and dropped it to his side. "You don't look good."

"I'm actually not feeling great," Cat admitted. "But I'm okay."

"Can I come in? I have your shirt." Micah held out a sunset-orange piece of material which may or may not have been a t-shirt.

This was it—the moment they could begin really talking or the moment either of them could destroy it all. Wherever this was going to go, Cat held all the cards, and he faced the reality of the decision he'd made while talking to Dr. Elyse. Instead of answering Micah directly, he stepped to the side, motioning for him to enter. As he watched Micah making his way across the living room threshold to the couch, he prayed, moving his lips but making no sound.

Oh, holy Saint Jude, apostle and martyr, help me now in my urgent need…

Spring

Chapter Sixteen

After This Our Exile

April 2006

Cat kept his three vows for the duration of Lent. During that time, he and David saw each other on and off, including at another visit to David's church. He only went every other weekend due to his hospital schedule. In between, Cat began putting in more hours in the cafe. This time, he worked on a new project—updating the building. It had been a long time since he'd tinkered with repair work, and it was pleasurable taking apart some of the equipment and replacing damaged parts. He changed a number of small things, noting with pride and a small degree of amusement that Mom was impressed.

It wasn't his only project. He did some minor work around the house as well. It was satisfying to note his parents' combination of exasperation and appreciation whenever they came home to something new. Mom was annoyed the day he decided to replace all the light switches on the second floor, since it required turning off the power to that part of the house. She did not complain, however, when the clothes dryer conked out and Cat managed to fix it while she was at the cafe.

His twentieth birthday came and went at the end of March, a quiet and entirely uneventful day. It was strange, being a whole two decades old. He felt as though he'd aged much more in the previous year than in the nineteen before. His body certainly agreed when his joints groaned every morning. There wasn't even dinner with his family or David, since everyone—including Cat—was working. Cat hadn't been upset. He looked forward to seeing David at the first meeting in April of their hemophilia group. With less than two weeks until Easter, Cat had a lot of planning to do if he was going to be successful with his transformation.

To Cat's surprise and disappointment, David didn't show up for the meeting. It was the first time he'd missed one since Cat joined, and Cat was lost without David to translate his nonverbal communication to the group. Cat's shirt of the week—the phrase "I think he's gay" with an arrow pointing down—earned him a few snickers and approving nods from the others. After that, Cat spent the entire meeting avoiding all eye contact and playing with the cuff of his sock. Delia only addressed him once, just to ask if he had anything he wanted to add. The only positive thing that happened was when, on their way out, Delia finally noticed his shirt and tried to hide both a slight frown and an amused snort. Cat finally looked up at her, and when their eyes met, he was shocked to see both tenderness and respect in her gaze. He gave the first smile he'd ever offered her, and when she returned it, her posture relaxed.

At home, Cat lay in bed on top of the covers, still dressed. He'd been able to distract himself from the clothes sitting in storage and the old life they represented for months, but now his attention turned to them as he contemplated the countdown to Easter. He didn't want the softness and lace anymore, but he had nothing with which to replace those things. Wearing shirts like the one he had on made it easier to process his bouts of disempowered, genderless feelings, but it didn't help him with figuring out how else to reorganize his life. It also didn't help him with missing David.

An idea struck him, and he sat up. He grabbed his phone and turned it so the camera faced his chest. He couldn't take the picture in the mirror; all the words would be backwards. The only option was to try it until he had a clear enough shot. It took four attempts, but he got what he wanted. He texted the photo to David then lay back down with his phone on the pillow beside him.

He'd almost fallen asleep when he got a reply. Eagerly, he retrieved the message.

Nice shirt.

Cat sent him a grin.

Sorry I missed you tonight.
Sad face.
I wasn't at the meeting because I'm not feeling good.
Sad face.
There was a long pause, and then David sent, *It's complicated.*
Question mark.
I'm fine. Don't worry.
Cat felt bad. He hadn't thought about it much before, the ways in which David was dealing with some of the same things he did. Before he could think of an appropriate reply, David texted again.
If I'd gone, I was going to ask if you wanted to go somewhere with me for your birthday.
Cat sent a smiley. He waited a moment then sent a question mark.
Anywhere you like. There was a long pause before another text came through. *Maybe we can talk. Or I can talk. You can recite prayers if you want.*
Grin.
I already called in sick for tomorrow. I don't want to get you sick, and I'm on days for a while. How about Friday? That's my next day off, and I should be better.
Smile.
Good. We can text in between. Sweet dreams.
Cat sent a bedtime prayer and set his phone aside once David responded with a smiley of his own. He hadn't been able to ask the question weighing on his mind, and David hadn't volunteered an answer. What did David mean by "maybe we can talk"? Cat wondered if it was about deciding what they were to each other. He wasn't sure anymore; even though he'd made a commitment not to get involved with anyone, he hadn't been able to control his growing attachment to David. A painful idea struck Cat, and he sucked in his breath. David was a nurse. It was possible he saw himself as Cat's caregiver, someone who might even replace Cat's family. It was equally possible that's how Cat saw him, too—not as a lover but as someone to take care of him. Those thoughts made Cat uncomfortable, and he didn't know how to address them.
He turned over and settled down. All night, his internal confusion produced anxiety-driven dreams and restless sleep.

For the next few days, Cat kept his secret fears about David to himself. Instead, he threw himself into practicing his cello. He'd begun after the first time David brought him to church. He wanted to be good enough to fulfill David's request to play for him. It wasn't hard to pick up again, but after more than six months of not playing at all, he was no longer at the level of someone who had once won competitions.

He kept to his room with the door shut, but he knew everyone could hear. Each time, he avoided looking at any member of his family. He already knew what he would see in their expressions—pride in his skill and happiness that he was playing again. Before, he would have relished their pleasure at his accomplishments. Now it was only a painful reminder that none of them knew he wasn't going back. He learned quickly he could no longer spend hours fine-tuning his performance, and he no longer had the energy he would have required as a professional. The contrast between his father's approval and his own disappointment were too much to bear.

Even so, Cat couldn't deny it felt good to play. After seeing the electric cello at David's church, Cat decided he wanted one for himself. One afternoon, he and LR stopped by the music store, where Cat used his birthday money to purchase several new pieces of sheet music, a booklet of blank staves for composition, and some high-quality rosin. He paused by the instruments, admiring the cellos. There were acoustic ones in all sizes, as well as electric ones. Cat liked one that was translucent green.

As he reached for the tag to see how much, he stopped, his hand outstretched. In the middle of the row was an unusual cello. Smaller, lighter than an acoustic, it was similar to the electric ones—but not identical. It wasn't flat like the others. Cat lowered his hand and stepped closer.

The shop's owner came up beside him. "Beautiful, isn't it?"

Cat whirled around. He nodded, his ears heating up at having been caught off-guard.

"It's a hybrid. It can be played acoustically in smaller spaces, such as a chamber hall or a church. But it's also meant to be electrified when played in a larger venue." The man smiled. "My own creation. I wanted to combine the sounds of both, something new and unique."

Cat reached for the price tag. His face fell when he saw how much it was, and he shook his head. Maybe he could save for a while. With a sad smile and a shrug of his shoulders, Cat turned away.

"If you change your mind, I'll be up front," the owner said, retreating from the line of cellos.

As he walked away, LR returned with a few items of her own. "Find something you like?"

Cat shrugged again, but he glanced back at the cello. When he returned his attention to LR, she grinned.

"It's a nice one," she said. "Probably not great if you're going back to school, but it looks like it could be fun to play. Ready to go pay?"

Nodding, Cat followed LR to the register, more determined than ever to find a way to purchase the beautiful instrument.

The day David was coming to take him out, Cat stood in front of his closet, clothes strewn everywhere. He sighed. Nothing seemed right. As he peered into his closet, hoping for inspiration, there was a series of tiny, light raps on his door. Puzzled, Cat crossed the room and opened it. His jaw dropped when he saw David.

"Hey," David said. "Sorry I'm early. Your mom said I should come up."

Cat, still in his pajamas—fortunately, he'd put something on after showering—waved at the closet to indicate he was still trying to decide on his clothes. David stepped around him. He glanced down at the boxes on the floor then up at Cat, his eyebrows raised in question.

With a shake of his head, Cat bent down and opened the top box. He pulled out a lacy white skirt and a pink blouse and scowled at them. He held them out to show David, then crumpled the skirt and tossed it aside, holding onto the blouse. He waved at all the other boxes with his free hand.

"Oh," David said, obviously still confused. "You'd look cute in that."

Cat rolled his eyes, annoyed at David's lack of understanding and his own inability to communicate clearly without words. He didn't have any means of explaining his dysphoria, his sense of wrongness and discomfort, to David. He wasn't convinced David would have understood even if Cat had spoken aloud; Cat didn't have words to describe the way he'd been feeling lost in a sea of gender nothingness. He huffed noisily then yanked out one of his rude t-shirts. He held it up side-by-side with the pink blouse.

"You don't want to wear those clothes?"

Cat threw the pink blouse aside and shook his head. He looked at the t-shirt and shrugged. It wasn't the most appropriate attire for a day out celebrating his birthday.

David bent down and retrieved the skirt and blouse. He folded both and tucked them back in their bin. He held out his hand until Cat delivered the t-shirt into it, and then David hung it back in his closet. He stood there for a few minutes before reaching in and drawing out a jewel-green v-neck and a black hooded sweatshirt. He handed them to Cat.

"Got any pants that would go with this? I like the green on you." David's cheeks turned slightly pink.

Cat pulled out a pair of black skinny jeans and held them up.

"Yeah, those'll do."

Cat motioned for David to turn around so he could get dressed. David arched an eyebrow, but he complied. In a moment, Cat was fully dressed again. David tilted his head and tapped his lips; Cat saw the gears in his head turning. A moment later, David's eyes flicked to the jewelry box on Cat's dresser. He crossed the room to rifle through it. When he turned around, he had the pot leaf in hand, which he passed to Cat to put in. He studied Cat for a few minutes, walking around him.

"You look fine," he said. "But I have an idea. Those shirts you wear to group—I keep thinking Delia's going to have puppies every time she reads them."

Ducking his head, Cat laughed. David was right; Delia hated his shirts. Once, she'd told him he was disrupting the group. Three people had come up to him later and told him she could bite them and he should just go on dressing however he wanted.

Grinning, David continued. "I think maybe instead of that skirt and blouse, we could try something new. You might not talk, but you sure can express yourself. I'll bet we could find a way for you to be both pretty and wild."

Cat raised an eyebrow at him, swallowing back the lump David's use of *pretty* caused.

"Don't give me that look," David admonished him. "Just come with me."

Before they left his bedroom, Cat eyed himself in the mirror. He grinned at his reflection then turned around to follow David out of the room. Downstairs, they stepped into the kitchen. LR and Mom were at the table, reading, and Dad was at the sink, rinsing dishes. Cat cleared his throat, and they all looked up.

LR rose from the table and came to stand next to Cat. She rolled her eyes and flicked his earring. At the same time, Mom said,

"Really, Cat?" Dad said nothing, but his lips twitched. Cat suspected the whole family secretly enjoyed it but weren't willing to say so. Their supportive teasing warmed him all the way to his toes. He took it as a sign of their growing acceptance of now-Cat versus then-Cat. With a cheerful wave, Cat followed David out to his car. This time, he let David pick the radio station.

The drive was longer than Cat had been expecting, and he looked at the car's dashboard clock then pointedly at David, who only gave him a mysterious smile. Eventually, they pulled in at the outlet mall in Watkins Glen. Cat's palms were clammy, and he swallowed several times to calm his nerves. He had a feeling he knew exactly what David had in mind.

"Come, Holy Spirit, fill the hearts of your faithful," he murmured.

"Cat," David said.

"And kindle them in the fire of your love."

David sighed and got out of the car. He came around to the passenger side and yanked open the door. "Cat."

"Send forth your Spirit and they shall be created."

"Cat!" David yelled, almost in his ear.

Cat finally looked up, startled to see David's scrunched nose and furrowed brow two inches from his face. Before he could open his mouth to recite the next line, David put a hand over it and made a warning noise in the back of his throat.

"Enough. I promised I'd take you shopping, and I meant it. You're a grown-up, and you have the right to say no. But at least let me show you a few things before you decide you're done. Okay?" He held out his hand.

Reluctantly, Cat accepted it and let David help him out of the car. He kept his head down and stayed close to David's side the whole time. David only huffed and ruffled Cat's hair with affection. Cat relaxed enough for his stomach to calm down, but he still shivered when they reached the entrance. He let go of David and took a deep breath then nodded. They crossed the threshold into the first store.

Inside, cool air wafted over them. David led him down the main aisle, and they stopped to look at a rack with several t-shirts of the variety Cat preferred. He looked down at the one he had on, which featured a pun involving a nightstand. David gave him a little push, and Cat went past to a rack of black tank tops. There were a number there with unfamiliar band names, strange designs, and rude words. Cat thumbed through them, wondering which ones he should get. He barely noticed when David stepped away.

A few minutes later, just as Cat pulled three he liked, David was back. In his hand was a black leather skirt with pockets and a slight flare to the bottom. Cat sucked in his breath. He looked up at David and drew his lower lip between his teeth, debating. The skirt was gorgeous—something he never would have picked for himself because he'd never thought much beyond what LR chose for him. Her tastes didn't tend to run in leather or innuendo-laced slogans.

He put out his hand and hovered inches away from touching the skirt. It looked buttery soft, and he was sure it would fit him. Desire to feel the leather against his legs warred with his instinct to protect himself. He wrapped his arms around himself and stood in the middle of the store, rocking slightly while he tried to decide which side was allowed to win.

"You'll look beautiful," David whispered.

That broke the spell. Cat shot out his hand and snagged the skirt from David then beelined for the dressing rooms. He shut himself inside and yanked off his jeans and shirt. First he pulled the first of the tank tops over his head. Then, with shaking hands, he pulled up the skirt and reached around to zip the back. Just as he'd expected, the fit was marvelous. It hugged his ass and made him look a bit like he had hips. The inside of the leather felt good against his bare thighs, tighter at the top and with as much swish at the bottom as leather afforded. Cat ran his hands over the skirt and turned this way and that to see himself in the mirrors.

The knock on the fitting room door startled him. "Cat? Are you going to show me?"

Cat unlatched the door and peeked out, relieved to see David right there. He motioned for David to come inside and hurried to lock the door again. David's lips twitched, but he didn't say anything. Cat pressed against the mirror and hunched so David couldn't quite see.

"Honey, you have to move your hands. Come on. Let me see, please."

Slowly, Cat lowered his hands and straightened up. He kept his arms at his sides and his back straight as though he were having an inspection. David made a twirling motion with his finger. Heat rose in Cat's cheeks, but he obeyed. He heard David's sharp intake of breath and whirled around to find David wide-eyed, staring at his chest. Cat looked down. The tank top he'd tried on was an aggressive shade of raspberry with a glittery heart a shade darker encircling the phrase "queer as fuck." David grinned.

"Cute, but it doesn't go with the skirt. Here." He handed Cat a white sleeveless button-down.

Cat motioned for him to turn around even though he was only taking off his shirt and even though David had already seen his bare ass in the hospital. That had been entirely different circumstances. Now Cat was acutely aware of his road map of scars, the way his abdomen bulged a little on one side, the way his stomach was so concave his ribs looked like a xylophone. It was one thing for David-as-nurse to see him; it was something else for David-as-friend to look at his body.

His fingers trembled so much he almost couldn't fasten the buttons, but eventually he smoothed out the fabric, tucking the bottom in and adjusting it. He tapped David on the shoulder. When David spun to face him, his expression was no longer amused. Instead, his eyes raked over Cat, causing heat to radiate down from the top of Cat's head to his toes. A peek in the mirror confirmed Cat had gone as red as it was humanly possible to be. Still David's gaze devoured him.

"Holy shit. Yes, you look gorgeous," David said, finding his voice. "We'll get that outfit." He cleared his throat then laughed. "The other shirt too, if you like."

There was nothing that could have prepared Cat for the way he felt hearing those words. He came alive, launching himself at David and pulling him into a hug. David laughed again, his chest rumbling against Cat. Overcome with excitement and joy, Cat pulled back to look David in the eye. He wanted to find a way to thank him. When their eyes met, there was a long pause. Cat felt David's firm muscles tense under his fingers, sensed the faint tremor which matched his own. He closed the distance between them at the same moment David did. Their mouths met, and an electric thrill pulsed down Cat's spine. His eyes closed, and for a long time he said with his lips what he couldn't convey in words.

Before Cat could properly enjoy the first kiss he'd had in months, David gasped and pulled back. "We can't."

Hurt, Cat stepped away and folded in on himself. David still looked stunned, though he didn't quite seem angry. For a long time, neither of them said anything.

David cleared his throat. "I'm sorry."

Cat shook his head. David didn't like him that way; there was nothing to apologize for. Cat knew he'd crossed a line. He made to turn away so he could get dressed in his own clothes again. A warm hand landed on his shoulder, and he looked at David.

"Wait. I didn't do that right. You have no idea how much I wanted to kiss you," David said, almost too quietly for Cat to hear. "I just can't. Not before we talk about it, okay?" He put up his hand. "It's not because of you. Please...trust me?"

The way he asked, hopeful and nervous, puzzled Cat. If David wanted to kiss him, and he wanted to kiss David, what was the problem if it wasn't Cat himself? There was no other appropriate response but to nod, regardless of how little he understood.

"When we're done shopping, come have lunch at my apartment," David suggested. "There are some things I need to tell you, and..." He paused and sighed. "You might not like all of them, but we can't be together unless I'm honest with you."

Cat's only answer was to reach out and touch David's cheek. He hoped David understood it to mean *I'm listening.*

He did. "Good. Then how about you change, and we'll go pay for that skirt." He winked, his joyful enthusiasm back in full force.

David slipped out of the dressing room. Cat put his other clothes back on and carried the shirts and skirt to the register, where David was waiting. He drew out his own money, but David only smiled and put a hand over Cat's.

"I've got this, remember? And then we can go find a few other stores." He leaned in and whispered, "There's a place I want to take you to find something nice for under that skirt."

Blushing furiously, Cat could only nod.

CHAPTER SEVENTEEN

TURN YOUR EYES OF MERCY TOWARD US

CAT STOOD just inside the door of David's tiny apartment, waiting for an invitation to come farther in. David took his hand and tugged him into the kitchen then pulled out a chair. Cat plopped into it and looked up.

"So...lunch. You're vegan, right?"

Cat stuck out his tongue and shook his head.

David laughed. "Okay."

He pulled some things out of the fridge and set them on the table. Cat pushed the carton of milk away with a grimace.

"You don't drink milk?" David asked.

Putting a hand on his stomach, Cat doubled over.

"Oh. It makes you sick. But you said you're not vegan. I can work with that. How about an omelet with everything except cheese?" David pulled a pan out of a cupboard.

Cat nodded and settled in happily to watch David work. He set ingredients on the counter and began cutting things up. After a few minutes, Cat wondered if he was being rude and stood up. He put his fingers on David's wrist to get his attention. When David paused to look at him, Cat gestured to the knife and held up a tomato. With a shrug, David handed him another knife and went back to work.

He had something on his mind, Cat could tell. He hoped it was an explanation for why he'd gotten so upset in the dressing room. Cat still felt guilty for crossing the line, and he hoped David would forgive him. He wasn't sure how to communicate how sorry he was, other than what he'd already done.

David gathered the chopped vegetables into bowls and began cracking eggs. As soon as he had the food cooking, Cat sat back down at the table to wait. In a short time, their food was done, and David delivered two steaming plates. He set a pitcher of water and two glasses on the table, and Cat helped himself.

As they ate, David didn't look at Cat. In fact, he mostly pushed his food around on his plate, and his hands trembled. Cat waited; David would speak when he was ready. The quiet didn't bother him in the least. He was glad David wanted him there at all. Eventually, David set his fork down and sighed.

"You want to know why I acted like such a jerk."

Cat didn't know how to respond. If he agreed, then he would be saying David had been a jerk—which Cat definitely didn't believe he had. If he disagreed, he would never get a proper answer about what had upset David about the kiss. Cat reached out and put his hand on top of David's, hoping to get across that he was willing to listen.

That seemed to have done the trick. David said, "I did want to kiss you. I promise, it's not because I don't like you."

He stood up and began clearing the table, scraping his plate into the trash and stacking the dishes on the counter. He turned to face Cat, leaning on the sink and drumming his fingers against the edge of the counter.

"I like you very much," he said, his voice soft and warm. "I didn't think it would go anywhere. I mean, I was your nurse—and trust me, I wasn't thinking about you like that when I was. But then the group...and all the times we saw each other...and..." He closed his eyes, and he looked like it hurt to find the right words.

There was a long silence, and Cat hardly breathed while he waited for David to speak again. Eventually, David opened his eyes and drew up his shoulders. He gave a sharp nod as though he'd decided something.

"I do want you, but I can't start any relationships without complete honesty," he said. "And after I tell you, I won't blame you if it's too much."

Cat tilted his head. He supposed he knew what David was going to say before he said it. Cat had lived too long with his own multiple health issues not to be aware of how those living with hemophilia were affected in parallel with other communities. He waited for David to continue.

Instead of explaining, David surprised Cat with a question. "Did you ever wonder why you're the only person in our hemophilia group with the severe form? It's the most common type."

Cat shook his head. He knew exactly why. Almost everyone older than Cat had already died. His mother's fears for him weren't entirely unfounded. He'd grown up having frequent blood draws, probably more than his health warranted. Never having needed a full blood transfusion until That Night—thanks in part to his mother's hypervigilance when it came to his health—he'd sensed their relief when he temporarily switched to recombinant factor and the surge in tension when he became reactive to it.

David cleared his throat. "Right. Well, I'm almost six years older than you are, and in that short a time..." Another long pause. "When I was about three, I had surgery. It should have been a minor procedure, and it would be for any other kid. Even for me it wasn't complicated, since I didn't need maintenance factor. They took precautions, of course. Infusions before, blood on standby. No big deal, right? Until it was." He crossed his arms. "Maybe I'm lucky HIV is the only thing I got out of the deal—that time."

Cat nodded. He knew too many people who hadn't lived as long as David had, so he thought there was more to the story. He folded his hands on the table and kept his eyes trained on David.

A look of frustration crossed his face. "It's bad enough that I dealt with my mom whispering things to school staff and thinking every other check-up the doctor might tell her I was about to die. At one point, they were sure I *was* dying, and it's pretty damn miraculous I came through it. Sometimes, I think it would have been easier if I had died. That was hard but nowhere near as hard as growing up and realizing I'm *not* going to drop over next week." He didn't speak for a moment, gripping the counter behind him. "My mom was a single parent with three kids. She couldn't afford meds. So she enrolled me in clinical trials so I could get treatment."

He lowered his arms and sighed. "I was homeschooled for a long time while I was in treatment. I was too sick for school, but Mom didn't want me to fall behind. It wasn't a good time for us. It also wasn't the end of the multiple things I've dealt with over the years. Remember when I said I didn't feel good the other night? Well, that's from the meds. I also have hepatitis C, though it's in remission. I've lost track of how many different things I've been on for everything. They work—I won't deny that—but the side effects are terrible. They make complications of the hemophilia worse, even though my type isn't severe. So, more meds to counterbalance." He snorted. "The meds don't work on the worst side effect of all."

Cat held out his hands, urging David to continue. He leaned forward to listen.

"I want what everyone else does—love and family, someone to come home to at night. Finding those has been nearly impossible."

Cat understood that, at least. Bryce had been caring toward Cat when it came to his health, but because he wasn't ready to be out, they weren't able to have what Cat wanted. He rose from his chair and went to stand beside David. Hesitating for only a moment, he put his hand on David's trembling arm. David reached up with his other hand and pressed it against Cat's then shifted away with a sigh.

"Women, men, it doesn't matter. Almost no one I've gone out with has stuck around for a second date, let alone more. It's like a deal breaker, every damn time. I know there are people out there who are okay with it, but why should I have to start every date with an apology? The nicer ones feel sorry for me, as though it makes any difference if they can believe it's 'not my fault.'" He made air quotes. "The less nice ones shame me or ask me invasive questions or believe I'm lying about how I got it to earn more sympathy. They don't understand what it was like to grow up with family members who wouldn't so much as hug me and nightmares about the exact way I would die. Besides, the stigma's the same either way. No one really cares how the fuck I got it, only that they don't want me to pass it on—like I can't figure out how not to do that or that I care so little about others I might share on purpose. To so many people, I'm filthy."

Cat thought back to some of the first words David said to him, all those months ago in the hospital. He'd advised Cat not to let one night dictate the rest of his life. It made sense now. Like Cat, David knew how it was to feel like something slimy, worth only as much as someone else dictated. The vile words popped into Cat's head before he could stop them. *You're very pretty, and I like pretty men.* Cat shivered and touched the pocket where he kept his rosary, quieting the voice in his head. David didn't deserve to feel like that any more than Cat did. He stepped closer, intending to reach out, but David turned around and began running water while he fished out a dish pan. He kept his back to Cat, filling the pan with hot water and adding soap. He shut off the tap and then spun to face

Cat again.

"Do you know how much I hate it when guys say they're *clean?* I know what that means—they think people like me aren't. But I'm not dirty or tainted, Cat. I'm not!" His voice broke on the last word. "None of us are."

Cat couldn't have agreed more—and didn't particularly care how David got HIV anyway—but how could he convey that to David? He looked at the pan of water. Stepping around David, he scooped a handful of soap bubbles. He held them in his palm for a moment then blew on them, sending them flying onto David's cheek and neck. David's eyes widened and his mouth fell open. Cat just grinned and did it again.

Clean, he thought, praying David understood. *You are clean.*

By that time, David had recovered himself. He gave Cat a sly glance and reached into the sink, gathering his own soapy missile. Not bothering with a gentle puff of air, he resorted to smearing the whole thing on Cat's head. Cat retaliated by dunking his hands and rubbing them all over David's shirt.

For the next few minutes, they soaked each other, laughing and splashing and leaving almost nothing to wash the dishes. Cat wiped his wet hands on David's jeans, and David grabbed him around the waist, pressing his back against the sink. They both giggled, and then, their faces inches apart, Cat waited. His heart hammered, and he held his breath. Before he could make a move, David's mouth was on his, hot and fierce.

Cat wound his arms around David's neck, drawing him closer. They pressed together, kissing hungrily. When David shifted to skim his hand up Cat's side under his wet t-shirt, Cat didn't resist. He'd already broken his vow of simplicity; in the scheme of things, what difference did it make if he broke another one before his deadline? His breathing sped up and he gasped into David's mouth.

Encouraged, David rubbed his thumb over Cat's nipple. It caused a spike of pleasure to radiate outward, spreading up to heat his neck and down to settle in his belly. His whole body reacted in a way it hadn't since That Night. Spurred on by David's gentle touch, his dick took notice and swelled against his fly.

David didn't miss the response. He pressed forward with his hips, allowing Cat to feel that he was aroused too. Cat fumbled to tug David's shirt free from his jeans so he could make David feel as good as he did. David's hand wandered down to squeeze between Cat's legs, rubbing gently until Cat thought he might explode. He pushed against David's hand, and David walked his fingers up to the button on Cat's jeans. He popped it open and slid the zipper down.

Just as David's hand began to slide inside the gap, an icy panic descended on Cat the same way it always did when he tried to feel good this way. Memories of the bathroom and Bryce tumbled through his mind, mixing with the fear of what had happened afterward. His already rapid breathing turned to hyperventilating, and he grabbed David's wrist to get him to stop. At the same time, the only functional part of Cat's mind warned him not to push David away after he'd been so open. With one hand, Cat gripped David's wandering fingers. With the other, he reached up to pull him closer, clutching his shirt and burying his face in David's shoulder. He was a trembling mess, but he wouldn't hurt the one person who had been patient with him.

To Cat's relief, David understood. He moved his hand away from Cat's fly and wrapped it around his back. He pulled him in and held him, whispering, "Sh," into his hair.

Anger flared in Cat's chest. Less at David's protective touch and more at himself, at his own weakness. He was tired of being afraid and furious at his body for not cooperating the way he wanted it to. He growled in frustration and pushed at David, who backed up against the counter. Cat stood in front of him, hands balled into fists and face flaming. His eyes met David's, and Cat saw the hurt in his expression. Cat's rage dissipated into misery, and he sank to the floor. His back to the fridge, he bent his knees up and grasped his hair in his hands.

The warm press of a shoulder against his caused Cat to turn his head. Wordlessly, David put an arm around him. He kept it loose, comforting rather than protective. Slowly, Cat came back to himself. After several minutes, they separated, and Cat looked up at David. He touched his cheek then moved his hand to press his fingers over David's heart. Reassuring, he hoped. He needed time before he would be ready for more than soapy kisses in the kitchen.

"I didn't mean to push," David said. "It's okay if you're not ready. When you are, I want—" He swallowed. "I want to be with you, if you'll have me."

The last of Cat's anger faded, and he nodded. He wanted to make new memories with David to erase the shame of That Night, but he had to have time. David stood and helped Cat to his feet. He leaned in to give Cat a gentle kiss as Cat zipped his fly again. Relief at David's understanding made Cat a little giddy. As a promise, Cat reached down and patted the front of David's jeans. David laughed, startling him.

"Looks like you're telling him, 'good dog,'" he said.

Cat grinned and winked. The resulting laugh that welled out of David was worth it. He wrapped his arms around Cat and rocked, shaking them both with his mirth. When he calmed down, he placed kiss after kiss on Cat's temple, each one feeling like a return promise. Cat pulled away just far enough to look David in the eye before giving him one last, long embrace.

They drew apart, and David looked at the spilled water, the mostly empty dish pan, and the dirty pile on the counter. "Guess I'd better get back to work," he remarked.

Grabbing a towel from the oven door handle, Cat held it up in offer. Side by side, they cleaned up the mess they'd made.

Chapter Eighteen

Show Unto Us the Blessed Fruit

THE NEXT couple of days were relatively uneventful, but Cat couldn't get his afternoon with David out of his mind, especially kissing in his kitchen. He warred between wanting to do it again and thinking it might be fine to go back to strictly keeping the vows he'd made. The whole day after their shopping trip, he hadn't been able to wear any of his new clothes. He'd stuck carefully to a plain t-shirt—not even one with a slogan—and jeans with an ordinary pair of briefs underneath. He holed up in his room, grateful David was working and wouldn't ask to see Cat in anything they'd bought.

The third night, he dreamed. At first, it was a terrifying press of darkness, and he fought against it until he felt a hand gripping his and the black faded around him to reveal David. Everything became heat and light, burning like the sun only in a way that made him desperately want more of it. The sensations rose and fell, and he chased them, seeking whatever would make the sun explode. He finally found David again, and they pressed together. It all blurred into a fiery ball of need and desire, consuming Cat from the inside out.

He woke suddenly, gasping, overheated and sweaty and spent. He flung back the covers, away from the splatters on his belly and chest. Gulping air, he tried to catch his breath. At last his heart rate slowed and he relaxed back into the pillows. For several minutes, he let the sticky mess cool on his skin, grateful he'd gone back to sleeping naked. When his head had cleared, he reached for the tissues on his nightstand. After cleaning up and tossing them into the trash, he relaxed again, enjoying the buzz in his veins.

It had been a long time since he'd come in his sleep. His mind went to the dream. It hadn't been especially sensual, just filled with random images. Yet the pleasure of it had been intense. David had been there, he remembered. The thought made his face hot, especially as he recalled the way David had held him in real life, had kissed him with such devotion, had rubbed him over the top of his jeans.

Both memories—dream-David and real-David—blended together, and the heat in Cat's face descended to his stomach and below. He'd come less than fifteen minutes prior, but he was already growing aroused again. He decided to take advantage of it and see if he could coax life into his dick on his own without panicking this time. He toyed with his foreskin, sliding it back and forth and running his thumb underneath it. His skin tingled with anticipation, and a pleasant ache developed in his balls. He let his penis rest against his palm, watching it swell when he rubbed it with the pads of his fingers.

Slow, he reminded himself. He had to take things easy, let it all happen naturally. He relaxed, closing his eyes and moving his hand at an unhurried pace. With the fingers of his other hand, he traced around each of his nipples. He'd always loved the feeling—the way his skin was so receptive to every touch. His nerves flared to life, and with them, the familiar body aches. He gritted his teeth, torn between pain and pleasure. His heart thumped as anxiety coiled in his gut, bound up with the pain where his thigh and hip met. He opened his eyes and twisted around to reach for his rosary on the night stand. The cool feel of the beads in his palm relaxed him, and his eyes fluttered shut again. He pictured David as he fingered both the beads and his cock, breathing steadily and counting in his head.

After a while, both the soreness and his panic receded, fading into the background as intense need built. A few drops of precome oozed out, and he smeared them with his index finger. He longed to grip himself and stroke hard and fast until he came, but he kept at the gentle teasing. It wouldn't do him any good to suffer another injury. Besides, this way, he could relearn how to bring himself off differently, keeping as still as possible. If he was going to allow David to touch him, he needed to know how to guide him.

He gasped at the sensory memory of David's skin on his...David's sensual mouth...the way they had both been so aroused. Cat panted, more liquid pooling at the tip of his penis. At the same time, he continued to touch his rosary, praying for peace and relief. He was so close, just a little more. His balls cramped and he let go of the beads to scrabble at the bed, trying to clutch the fitted sheet. He lifted his ass just as orgasm washed over him, hot come pulsing out to cover his hand and belly. With a forceful grunt, he released the tension and dropped back onto the bed.

He'd done it—masturbated to orgasm for the first time in months, and it hadn't hurt him. He ran his clean hand through his sweaty hair and let out a quavering laugh. Another box to check, a way he'd proved he wasn't utterly broken after all. Reaching over, he grabbed a wad of tissues and cleaned up so he could put something on, just in case LR decided to pay him an early morning visit. He grinned. If she weren't his sister, it might almost be worth the look on her face. He wondered if she'd heard him at all and if she would do what she used to before That Night. Whenever she claimed she could hear him jerking off, she would throw something at the wall between their rooms.

As he was getting up to find a pair of clean underwear, he heard the heavy thunk of a book. In response, Cat picked up his copy of the gay pirate book and threw it back, reveling in the faint laughter on the other side of the wall.

Easter weekend arrived, and Cat's nervous energy played havoc on his body. First he would attend church with David, and then his parents had invited David to dinner afterward. Cat had already made his decision about ending his Lent fast, but as the time drew nearer to showing everyone, he considered changing his mind. Consequently, he second-guessed himself on everything while getting ready for church, and the resulting tension made him feel ill.

He didn't usually bother trying to hide any of his symptoms; it was a hopeless cause anyway, with three people who knew him nearly as well as he knew himself. Easter morning, though, he made the effort to cover for how long he ended up in the bathroom. In the shower, he had to sit until the pain in his abdomen was manageable enough to stand. He wasn't sick, only nervous, and he didn't want anyone fussing or suggesting he shouldn't go to church. Despite being tense and sore, he privately enjoyed LR's irritated shriek when he emerged and implied he was taking so long because he was masturbating.

Back in his room, he toweled off and pulled his list from the wall. For a long time, he reread his vows, knowing what he was about to do. He couldn't bring himself to cross them all off, but he had a plan. He closed his eyes and inhaled deeply, steadying himself. After a few minutes, he was ready to choose his clothes. He stepped over to his closet and pushed the hangers around until he found what he wanted—the skirt he'd lovingly removed from its box the night before so he could press out the wrinkles. He touched the fabric, rubbing the lace between the pads of his finger and thumb and brushing against the maroon cotton before taking the skirt off the hanger.

He slipped it on then added a white button-down blouse. He crossed to his dresser and pulled a pearl teardrop earring out of his jewelry box. Satisfied, he peered at himself in the mirror, considering what to do with his face. As he opened up the case where he kept his lip gloss, there was a series of tiny, light raps on his door. Puzzled, Cat crossed the room and opened it to find LR.

When she saw what he was wearing, her eyes lit up. "Wait here," she commanded him then disappeared from the room.

A few minutes later, she was back, no longer in her bathrobe but wearing her matching skirt and a similar white blouse. Her hair was still wrapped in a towel. Cat couldn't help the grin stretching across his face.

"You look good," she said. Her smile faltered. "I don't want to say the wrong thing again, but can I tell you something?"

Cat tilted his head, curious about what she had on her mind. He nodded once, and she relaxed.

"I've missed this," she told him as she reached out to hold his hands. "I've always loved that I had a big brother and a big sister all rolled into one." She paused, biting her lip. "I love you, you know. Maybe one day, I'll have the courage to just be me the way you do." She sniffled.

Cat reached out and folded her into his arms. For a long time, they stood in the middle of his bedroom, holding each other tight. He tried to pour out on her all the feelings he couldn't put into words—his love for her, his gratitude, a lifetime of being first and best friends. A new feeling bloomed in his chest, a realization that this was one thing Landon hadn't been able to rip from him. No one could take away the years of friendship he had with LR. Peace spread through him from head to toe, the sacred healing of their bond.

Gentle throat-clearing alerted them to someone else's presence, and they let go. Cat and LR turned to the doorway, where Mom and Dad stood, both with soft smiles. LR pulled the towel from her head and shook her hair. She looked at Cat again.

"Are you going to church?" When he nodded, she said, "Um...can I come too?"

Surprised and pleased, Cat nodded. Mom suggested, "Why don't we all go? Do you think David would be all right with that?"

Cat nodded again, and the others all made to leave the room. He put up a hand to stop them then picked up his list from the dresser along with a black marker. He held both up, watching as three sets of eyebrows rose. With deliberate strokes, Cat carefully crossed off 2. *Vow of Simplicity. No clothes or jewelry other than jeans and t-shirts. Limit of one pair of ordinary sneakers. Absolutely no makeup of any kind.*

LR grinned. "Does that mean you'll let me do your makeup today?"

Cat crossed his arms and shook his head, eliciting light laughter from the others. LR exaggerated a pout, but then she shrugged and stepped around their parents. Mom and Dad retreated as well, leaving Cat to apply his lip gloss in peace.

He was putting on the final touches when he heard the doorbell. He capped the gloss and hurried down the stairs to answer it. When he opened the door and saw David, his jaw dropped. David was dressed in a light gray suit with an Easter egg blue shirt and a tie with stripes to match. Cat was nearly faint with longing at how handsome he looked. A delighted smile spread across David's face at almost the same moment, making Cat flush.

"Oh, wow," David said. "You look...amazing." He leaned in and kissed Cat's cheek.

Behind Cat, LR squeaked happily. "You two are so cute!"

Cat was tempted to aim a kick at her, but David chuckled. "Thanks, I think."

Mom and Dad reappeared, and Dad shook David's hand. "You must be David. I'm Gil."

Mom said, "Cat thought you wouldn't mind a little more company at the church service this morning."

"Sure. Is everyone ready?" David asked.

Cat nodded, and they all stepped out into the cool, sunny Easter morning.

After church, lunch was a quiet but happy celebration. Cat listened while his family peppered David with questions, periodically squeezing David's fingers under the table. Once they'd eaten and cleaned up, Cat had more to show them. He knew it would lead to expectations on their part, but he was determined to do it anyway. It made him jumpy. As soon as the last dish was in the dishwasher, he made to go upstairs, but LR stopped him.

"Wait here," she said. "We have something for you." She disappeared into the office. A moment later, she was back with an impressively large wrapped package.

Cat's eyebrows shot up, wondering what his family could possibly have gotten for him. They didn't generally do gifts at Easter, and it was long past his birthday. Besides, they'd all gotten him something already. He eyed LR suspiciously, but she only grinned. Everyone settled down in the living room, and all eyes were on Cat.

He ran his hand over the object, trying to guess what was inside. When he finally tore off the paper, he didn't bother hiding his delighted gasp. It was a cello case, smaller and lighter than the one up in his room. With shaking fingers, Cat unlatched the case and stared in at the gorgeous cello he'd seen in the shop. He ran his hands over the smooth surface, plucked the strings to hear their deep sound. There was a new bow, too, one of the fiberglass ones which had become more popular.

Cat leapt up from the table and grabbed first LR and then his parents, holding on to each of them in turn. He might not have wanted to make music his life's work anymore, but now he had a reason to begin playing again in earnest. For the first time in what felt like an eternity, Cat experienced a rush of joy so immense he couldn't contain his delighted laughter. When he caught sight of his parents and sister watching him, their faces alight with pleasure as well, it was almost too much. He turned to David, and to his surprise, he saw the same happiness in his eyes. Cat raised his eyebrows.

"Yes, I knew," David said. "It was your sister's idea, and she asked me to help."

Cat crossed the room and tugged on David's hand until he stood then wrapped him in a hug so enthusiastic it nearly knocked David back over. They let go, and Cat returned his attention to the cello, allowing the reality that it was his to sink in.

"Play for us," Dad suggested. There was a touch of longing and sadness in his voice, but he smiled.

Nodding, Cat sat down. He tuned the instrument then sat for

a moment, considering. Then he began to play. He started with the hymns from the church service, full of the solemn glory of the Easter celebration. When he finished, he paused to choose his next piece. He drew on his memory, recalling one of his favorite concerti, something he'd loved so much he could still play it without sheet music. The strains of Bach filled the house, and he closed his eyes as he immersed himself in the music.

When he finished, there was silence. He opened his eyes in the stillness to find everyone's emotions displayed plainly. David was the only one not brushing away tears, perhaps because he didn't have a lifetime of hearing Cat play.

"Beautiful," David murmured.

"Oh, Cat," LR whispered.

Cat set the cello back in its case. He motioned for everyone to wait. He ascended the stairs to his room, where he picked up the list and the marker he'd left on his dresser. It was now or never.

He returned to the living room and held the paper up. With the same care he'd used that morning, he drew a line through, *3. Vow of Chastity. No dates. No boyfriends. No sex. No jerking off.* Then he set the items on his chair and crossed the room to David. In one smooth movement, he sat down on David's lap and kissed him soundly on the lips, ignoring the light laughter around him.

Dad stood and picked up the paper. "You only have one left."

Cat nodded. His father hadn't asked the question Cat had anticipated—whether or not it meant Cat would cross it off too. He couldn't answer that yet, but having left behind the other vows, it was a matter of time. One day, he would need to break his silence, but he wasn't ready.

"So it's official?" LR asked, breaking the tension. "You and David."

Relaxing, Cat grinned and gave her a thumbs up. He turned to David and bit his lip, realizing he hadn't asked David's opinion on the matter. David only laughed and wrapped his arms around Cat.

"I think that's safe to say," he agreed, squeezing gently.

"Now we've established it, how about dessert?" Mom asked. "I think your father made the world's most perfect chocolate cake, and I want a piece."

Cat stood up and held out his hand to David. They hung back, and as soon as the others disappeared into the kitchen, David kissed Cat again. "Come over this week?" he asked. "I have Friday off." He blushed and added, "We don't have to do anything. Just dinner and a movie."

With a nod, Cat pressed David's hand in his own. David smiled, and they headed for the kitchen to join the others. Cat's cheeks heated as he thought, *But what if I want to do something?*

CHAPTER NINETEEN

OUR LIFE, OUR SWEETNESS, AND OUR HOPE

CAT LAY various items into a duffel bag, carefully choosing and making sure to pack extra things in case he wasn't in the mood to wear a particular outfit. David had done a lot to help him find his happy place, somewhere between jeans paired with rude shirts and flouncy skirts. He liked best the way he looked when he had a bit of both. The buttery leather skirt was his favorite, though he didn't take it with him this time. That was more for a night out, he thought. An image of David peeling it off him sprang to mind, and he flushed. Maybe another night.

While he was folding a shirt, LR knocked on his partially open door. He looked up as she pushed it open and grinned at her. She'd been the one who first supported him about being with David, and he thought she'd be happy that he was taking the next step. The smile faded when he saw her expression, and he frowned.

LR stalked to his bed and sat down, crossing her leg and wiggling her foot. She bit her lip. "Cat, are you sure you want to do this?"

He rolled his eyes, hoping to convey "I'm capable of making my own decisions." Huffing at her, he went back to folding.

"Are you looking to David to fix something?" Before he could answer, she continued, "I don't want to see anyone get hurt."

Shaking his head, Cat ignored her and went to his dresser to pack other things he needed. He and David had two whole days together, and Cat had promised to take weekend shifts at the cafe in order to make up for skipping out in the middle of the week. If she'd thought spending the time with David was a bad idea, she wouldn't have agreed.

LR sighed and said, "I know what you did before. You think none of us had a clue about you and Bryce? If you're using David, he's the one who will end up crushed. Even I can see he loves you in a way Bryce never did."

Cat glared at her and zipped his bag. He set it by the door and turned to face her, arms crossed over his chest. She had no business poking into his life that way. He barely restrained himself from giving her a rude gesture. How could she have known anything about the relationship he'd had with Bryce?

"I know I was excited for you about going out with him, but that was before you decided to go spend the night with him. You're a lot younger than he is. What he wants and what you want—two different things. He thinks he can save you."

With a sneer, Cat shared his opinion with her by giving her the finger.

LR gave an irritated growl and stood up. "Damn it, are you even listening to me?" She threw up her hands. "Of course you're not. You never do. I'm just your stupid kid sister, right? I'm young, not ignorant," she continued. "Sometimes, I get so sick of your shit. You have a real knack for making me feel like I'm the older one and I have to watch out for everything you do. I've had your back, but the whole last eight months sucked for me, too."

He wanted to respond. He wanted to tell her that if she thought it was so hard, for her, she should try living in his body for just one day. As if in agreement, his shoulder twinged. He shook it off and turned his icy glare on her, warning her to back the hell off.

"Oh, so that's how it is," she said. Her eyes were dark and sad rather than angry. "I know that look—the one that says you think everything is so tough for you, but the rest of us live in a magical, sunshiny fairy land. You have no idea." She stepped closer until she was right in front of him; he shrank back. "I only want to make sure this isn't going to end up actually killing you this time."

So that was it. She wasn't worried about where his relationship with David was going. She was terrified he might end up where he had with Bryce. Cat's anger dissipated. If he could have, he'd have told her it was all right. What he had with David wasn't built on the shaky foundation his relationship with Bryce had been. Besides, he had David's assurance they could wait until Cat was ready for more than dinner and a movie. LR didn't have all the details.

The only thing he could do was make it clear he was going, regardless of her opinion. He turned back to the bag on his bed, put the last few items in, and zipped it shut. He slung it over his shoulder and stood facing her. It wasn't LR's decision.

Her shoulders sagged. "If you're sure," she said.

He brushed her fingers with his and nodded before stepping around her and out of his room.

Cat thundered down the stairs to wait for David. His parents were sitting in the living room, and there was no doubt they were waiting for him, though they were trying to appear casual. He made a point of showing them his overnight bag, daring them to question his decision the way LR had. His mother's mouth was tense, but she kept quiet. His father tipped his chin down in acknowledgment. No one said a word.

He turned around and headed for the door, but before he reached it, LR called out from the stairs, "Wait!"

Pausing with his hand on the knob, Cat turned to look at her. She held up a finger to signal him to stay put, and then she raced back up the steps. A moment later, she was back, a small pouch in her hand. She pressed it into his palm and leaned in as if to kiss him on the cheek. Her face was hidden from their parents' view when she put her lips up to Cat's ear.

"Be safe, okay?" she whispered.

He reached up and grazed her cheek with his fingers, and she smiled. They'd made their peace from the argument in Cat's room, and her unconditional support meant more to him than he could express. With a squeeze of his hand, she let go and joined their parents in the living room. As Cat opened the door, he heard her suggest they put on a movie. He stepped out into the warm summer night and pulled the door shut softly behind him.

David was just pulling into the driveway. Cat tried to look casual as he approached, but judging by David's expression, he hadn't been entirely successful. He climbed in and settled his bag at his feet.

"What's in there?" David asked, pointing at the pouch.

Cat had almost forgotten it. He loosened the drawstring and pulled out the contents: two condoms and his rosary, which he'd forgotten in his hurry. David laughed so hard the car swerved.

"What the hell?" he said, still chuckling. "That's...different."

Cat pinched his arm. Despite the fact that he didn't know if they would use the condoms–that night or any other–Cat was touched by LR's thoughtfulness. He slid the beads of his rosary through his fingers and smiled.

"Do you use that?" David asked, his tone changing from amusement to curiosity.

Nodding, Cat slid the rosary back into the pouch.

David reached over and twined his fingers with Cat's. "Show me sometime?"

Cat tilted his head. David sounded sincere and a little shy. Again, Cat nodded. It was private, but he thought he could share it with David.

They arrived at David's apartment. It was still early, and they'd planned to make a night of it. David hadn't pressured Cat so far, and there was no reason to think they would do anything unless Cat was a fully willing participant. His nerves zinged, both from the anticipation and the anxiety that they might try more than kissing and loose fumbling. The doctor had left Cat with the impression it could go either way whether or not everything worked the way he wanted it to, but after his own experiments, he at least knew he *could*.

David had prepared a simple dinner which he'd left baking while he picked Cat up. Now he pulled it out of the oven, and Cat inhaled the scent of the vegetables and spices. It was some kind of casserole, and it smelled heavenly. He might have to ask David for the recipe and try it out on his family.

While David set food and drinks on the table, Cat browsed his selection of movies. He wasn't sure what to watch. They'd never talked about their tastes–not even in a one-sided way. He was surprised to find a wide range of interesting films, from artsy independent dramas to superheroes to romantic comedies, of both the gay and straight varieties. There were even a handful of what didn't quite look like porn but made Cat's eyebrows shoot up. He snickered, wondering what David would make of the books hidden under his mattress. He pulled out three films he'd never seen and set them on the coffee table for later.

A moment later, David entered the living room with their dinner. He set the plates on the coffee table and returned to the kitchen for their glasses. Once his hands were empty, he stepped over to Cat and touched his shoulder. Cat smiled up at him, and David rewarded him with a soft kiss.

"What did you pick?" he asked, holding out his hand for the movie.

Cat grinned and handed him one of the not-quite-porn films. David's eyes grew big, and his mouth dropped open. He closed it and then opened it again, rendered speechless. Cat laughed.

David recovered himself. "You know this one's not gay, right?" He cleared his throat, and a light blush tinted his cheeks.

Cat shrugged and took the movie back then handed David the stack he'd actually chosen. David rolled his eyes, but he smiled as he took the pile.

"How about this one?" He held up one of the romantic comedies—gay version.

They put in the movie and settled down to eat. Afterward, David stretched out on the couch with Cat nestled against his chest. Feeling content and relaxed, Cat drifted into a light doze with David's arms around him protectively, his fingers tracing patterns on Cat's hands.

He woke with a start when the movie ended and silence descended on the apartment. It was almost dark outside, the sky a deep, smoky blue. Cool breeze filtered in the open window, bringing the scent of an evening rain shower. Cat shivered, but not from cold. Tilting his head up to look at David, he reached to trace his finger along David's jaw in apology for falling asleep. David caught his hand and kissed it.

"It's all right. I'm glad you feel safe here," David murmured.

He bent his head forward enough to brush his lips against Cat's forehead then trail them down his cheek to reach his lips. The delicate kiss sent sparks up and down Cat's spine. He pulled himself up farther so they could kiss more deeply. David opened his mouth, and Cat licked into it. He tasted the spice from their meal, but instead of finding it unpleasant, he relished it. David moved his hand to Cat's thigh, and Cat wound an arm up and around the back of David's neck.

They stayed just like that, nearly still except for Cat's fingers on David's skin and David's hand rubbing gently up and down Cat's thigh. Cat's position was just right that he felt it as David grew aroused from the contact. The sensation gave Cat a rush, and he gasped. David slid his hand from Cat's thigh up his side and under his shirt to the soft skin of his belly. Cat, always so sensitive, giggled at the tickling, but David ignored him and continued his path until he found Cat's nipple. Laughter faded into a groan and then another gasp when Cat realized what was happening.

He was *hard.* Not just a bit, like he'd been in the kitchen the first time or the dozens of times they'd kissed since. No, this was an honest-to-goodness nearly full erection, like the ones he'd finally achieved alone. His pants were uncomfortably tight, and he had an intense desire to grab David's hand and move it lower. If David kept kissing him and touching him, he might even be able to come. Doing so alone was one thing, but achieving orgasm with someone else was entirely different. Cat discovered how much he'd missed being in contact with another person. The thought sent a ripple through him that had him arching his back slightly.

Panting, David withdrew his mouth. "Do you want to go in the bedroom?" he asked.

At Cat's vigorous nod, David shifted and Cat had to move to avoid being dumped on his ass. They stood up, and David took his hand. Cat paused in the hallway long enough to pick up his bag before being tugged into the bedroom.

David's room wasn't as tidy as Cat's. The bed was unmade, and there was a pile of clothes in the corner. The thought of stripping David down and adding to the pile had him almost too excited to notice that he was the one being undressed. David dragged on the hem of Cat's shirt, working it up over his chest until Cat raised his arms for David to pull it off. David fumbled with the fly of Cat's jeans, finally unzipping them and shoving them down.

If he was surprised at Cat's lacy red thong, he didn't say a word. His chest rose and fell as he stared, and Cat almost thought he might start drooling. He laughed softly and put a finger under David's chin, breaking the spell. David didn't even wait for Cat to help; he simply stripped down to his underwear—a classy pair of green and blue striped bikinis which Cat thought were both stylish and sexy. He wondered if it was a bad thing that he wanted to feel the soft material almost as much as he wanted to reach inside them and touch David's cock.

He decided it didn't matter and he could do both. David drew him in for another kiss, and Cat slipped his hand down between them. He rubbed David through the fabric of his underwear, groaning at the feel of David's rigid dick through the soft cotton. His mouth watered at the idea of kissing David over the top of the cloth. He was distracted, however, by the hand now massaging him through the lace at his crotch.

"Want you," David murmured into his shoulder. "Want to

make you feel so good." He stifled a whine against Cat's neck. "Want you to make me feel good. Is this okay?"

Cat nodded. David let go, and they lay down on the bed, still in their underwear. Cat was grateful. He wasn't ready to take his off yet. David backed off, hovering over Cat and looking down at him. He reached out with one finger, tracing the scars lining Cat's thighs and abdomen. They were still fresh enough they stood out against his pale skin, cutting a path through his freckles. Slowly, David peeled down Cat's thong, exposing his flesh.

"Shit," he said. "God, your dick is beautiful."

The heat his words created burned a fiery trail from the top of Cat's head straight down to his groin. He put a hand to himself, not out of shame but out of a need to relieve some of the pressure building inside. It surprised Cat to see David's hand shaking as he ran his first two fingers through the sparse red-gold hair between Cat's legs.

"I want to put my mouth on you," David said, barely controlling his voice. "But not yet. Right now, I just want to touch you."

He stripped off his underwear, and Cat's eyes widened in appreciation for his thick erection. Cat, too, pulled his thong the rest of the way off, tossing it onto the floor. David lay down next to him and rolled them both onto their sides so Cat's back was to his front. David's hard length brushed against the back of Cat's thigh.

David's breath tickled Cat's ear. "You'll have to help me. I'm going to touch you, but you can move my hand to wherever it feels good for you. If you need to stop for any reason—anything at all— squeeze my fingers, and I will stop without question. All right?"

Cat nodded and reached back to touch David's hair. He was ready to have David's hands on him, to feel pleasure together. Unsure how else to communicate his desire, he whispered, "Glory be to the Father..."

David chuckled, and the vibrations made his body move against Cat in a way which turned his prayer into a deep moan. David kissed his neck, and in the motion of his lips, Cat felt the smile still lingering there. It disappeared after a few moments of softly mouthing beneath Cat's ear.

"I know we have to be careful," David said, withdrawing a little. "Hold as still as you can."

Cat wasn't sure if he could. He was both so turned on and so excited that he was able to get to this point that he wasn't sure how he could keep from moving. David supplied the answer. He wrapped an arm underneath Cat, around his waist to hold him steady. With the fingers of that hand, he caressed Cat's nipple, rolling it and squeezing gently. He used his free hand to encircle Cat's erection, beginning with a slow, sensual pace.

As arousal built, it began to ache a bit, and not in a sexual way. The muscles deep in Cat's abdomen protested, and he was glad he had David to hold him so he wouldn't give in and thrust wildly as urgency grew simultaneously with pain. He closed his eyes, shifting his attention from the soreness to the glorious sensation of having someone touch his cock again. Pleasure rose, and he wanted to cry out, to yell David's name. Behind him, David's hips moved, hardly more than Cat's did but enough that Cat felt the hot, hard slide against his skin. Cat's hand, still gripping David's hair, tightened.

The deep muscle twinges mingled with intensifying need until Cat could hardly distinguish them. He was unsure whether he wanted it to go on forever or reach its peak. The realization caused a tremor and a fleeting moment of fear; he hadn't come with someone else since That Night with Bryce. He wanted to now, wanted David to be the first person he shared this with. Shutting out the prayers which tried to tumble from his mouth, he placed his hand on top of David's, closing his fingers to get David to grip him more firmly. Cat breathed with his mouth open, each inhalation a sharp gasp. He couldn't take much more.

David panted into his ear. "Oh, my god," he groaned. "Fuck...I'm sorry...I'm going to—I can't—"

Cat wished he could tell him it was all right. He let go of David's hand to reach back and touch his hip just before David made a strangled cry and wet heat erupted against Cat's thigh. The slippery feeling sent a ripple through Cat from the knowledge he'd been responsible. He groaned and pressed his eyes shut as he flew over the edge of his orgasm and splattered across the sheets, trembling at the burning ache that resulted.

They didn't move at all for a moment, just breathing and trying to get their bearings. Cat was still in a mild amount of pain, but he'd proved to himself that his body wasn't completely broken. The thought brought to mind how long it had been since being touched didn't hurt. It took Cat back to the previous summer, all those afternoons spent rolling around in Bryce's bed. Bryce had never left Cat with a sense of peace or contentment; sex for them had been about something different. It had been about the need both of them had to feel in control—Cat's desire to be *normal* and Bryce's rage against his parents' bigotry. Regret and anger filled him, and he buried his face in the pillow. By the time he felt David's arms around him, it was too late to stop the flood. He sobbed at the combination of relief and sorrow at how good and how right being with David felt compared with what he'd had before.

"Hey," David whispered. "It's okay. I've got you."

The gut-wrenching sobs subsided, replaced by panic and an overwhelming nausea at what he'd done. He and Bryce had used each other over and over all summer. David's gentle touch and loving acceptance was so far removed from Cat's previous experience he didn't know where to go with it. He gagged. Pulling out of David's arms, he moved as fast as he could, barely making it to the bathroom sink before throwing up everything still left in his stomach. Panting, he leaned over the basin and waited for the sweating and heaving to stop.

"Cat?"

He turned his head and looked up. David was in the doorway, concern etched on his face. A fresh wave of nausea hit and Cat retched again.

"Did—did my cooking make you sick?" David said. He stepped inside the bathroom and put a hand on Cat's back.

The shaking subsided, and Cat shook his head. He swallowed down the bile threatening to rise. He was sure this wasn't from the food and all from his reaction to what they'd done in the bedroom. He didn't want to hurt David by communicating that, though. He turned around, but his legs were too weak and he sank down to the floor in front of the sink. David crouched down in front of him.

"Do you need me to call someone?" David's voice was low and soothing. "Your therapist or your doctor?"

Cat shook his head again. He forced back the well of emotions threatening to break free again. David had worked out for himself what was wrong. Cat put his head in his hands. Once again, he bit back a prayer of apology for his crimes.

"I'm not angry," David said, firm and sure. "This is not your fault. If I hurt you, I'm so, so sorry. But you did nothing wrong. Understand?"

Cat slowly raised his head, letting his hands drop to his lap. His gaze met David's. There was no anger there, only concern. David moved to sit next to Cat, drawing him in and allowing Cat to rest his aching head on David's shoulder. They stayed that way, the cold from the tile floor seeping into the bare skin of their bottoms, until Cat finally raised his head again.

"Do you want to wash up before bed?" David asked. "We're both kind of a mess, and I should probably change the sheets at this point. You can shower if you want while I clean up in the room." He drew in his lower lip. "Do you still want to share my bed?"

At Cat's nod, David stood up and helped Cat to his feet. David showed Cat where everything was and left him in the bathroom. By the time Cat emerged from the shower, his bag was in the room and a soft towel sat folded on the toilet seat. Revived from feeling clean again, Cat smiled at David's thoughtfulness and reached for his toothbrush.

He returned to the bedroom, and David, still stark naked, eyed him up and down then laughed when he saw Cat's pajamas. It wasn't mocking, just full of delight, and Cat flushed all over. He loved the pajamas—they were new, bought for the occasion of his first overnight at a man's apartment. The boxers were black satin, covered with chili peppers. He'd bought a jewel-green tank top that exactly matched the green stems. One particularly large jalapeno was positioned directly over his penis.

"Hey, sexy," David said. He stepped over to Cat and ran his hands through the still-damp ginger strands of hair.

Cat leaned in to kiss David, wanting to reassure him he was okay, that he was fine with what they'd done. It might be a while before he was ready to try again, but this was enough for now. He knew he could, and that was all that mattered.

As Cat sat down on the bed, David said, "Do you need to infuse before you go to sleep?"

Knowing he'd taken the precaution of doing so ahead of time, Cat shook his head and pointed his thumb over his shoulder to indicate he'd done it at home. Understanding, David nodded. Cat swung his legs up onto the bed and sighed as the exposed parts of his skin touched the cool cotton of the fresh sheets. David drew the blanket up over him and pressed a kiss to his temple.

"I'll be in soon. I'm going to shower." He looked down at Cat and touched his cheek.

Cat stretched up his hand and pressed his fingers over David's heart. He relaxed back into the bed.

David retreated from the room. Cat remembered the little pouch with his rosary and considered rising to retrieve it, but he was too comfortable. He settled for closing his eyes and concentrating on the words of the Our Father. A deep sense of fulfillment washed over him, as though he'd been fed the bread of heaven itself, and his eyes flew open in surprise. His time with David had been the opposite of shameful—it had been blessed. Being held and touched had brought Cat something almost holy. Not because it was so good or so perfect but because it was another way he had reclaimed a piece of his soul.

He pulled the covers up under his chin, falling asleep to the sound of the shower.

CHAPTER TWENTY

TO THEE DO WE SEND UP OUR SIGHS

IN THE morning, Cat was stiff and sore, but not to the point he'd expected. It wasn't even as bad as after his first time with Bryce, when he'd broken several surface blood vessels. The aching didn't feel like much more than his usual. He stretched, his arm landing on a bump in the covers next to him, and he smiled.

David stirred and rolled over, his eyes opening slowly. He blinked and held still. Cat didn't care that neither of them had brushed their teeth yet. He leaned in and kissed David. Sliding down farther under the covers, Cat put his arm across David's waist.

"You're okay?" David murmured, looking Cat up and down.

Cat hummed. It was a different sound than he usually made, but he wanted David to understand again how good he'd made Cat feel the night before. There was still a long way to go, and Cat wasn't sure he wanted to do it again yet, but it had been an important step. The thought that it might not be their only time stirred Cat into the beginnings of arousal, but he hauled the idea back where it belonged, firmly under control.

Not before David noticed, though. "Did you want...?" David put a hand on Cat's hip, leaving it there with the question hanging.

Something woke in Cat. David was being gentle, but he was also the one in control. He was the one initiating, the one leading, even if he was waiting for Cat's response. Cat wondered for a moment if LR had been right that David wanted to save him. It resurrected Cat's need to prove himself. In one swift motion, he pushed David onto his back and straddled him, pinning him. Cat leaned down and took David's mouth with his own, hot and aggressive. David kissed back, groaning and writhing under Cat. It sent a thrill down Cat's spine, the heady rush of power. He ground against David, forgetting himself for a few minutes.

A sudden ache in his hip caused Cat to pull away with a sharp gasp. He grunted and put a hand at the juncture of his thigh, where it throbbed. He rolled off David and turned his back to him. A hundred things tumbled through his mind, and he curled in on himself. It was Bryce all over again, and LR's words to him blared like an alarm in his brain.

"Hey," David murmured.

Cat felt the bed shift, but David didn't touch him. Silently, not even uttering a prayer, Cat waited.

After a few minutes, David said, "It's okay, babe. We won't do anything until you're ready again."

I don't know if I'll ever be ready, Cat thought, but he nodded, keeping his back turned.

At last David touched his shoulder. "I'm not angry. You'll have to trust me when I say if you never want to have sex with me again, it's all right."

Cat rolled over to look at him. David was propped on one elbow, his other hand now resting on the bed between them. His expression was open and inviting. Cat sighed; he didn't know how to communicate his tangled emotional web. He reached out and touched David's cheek, drawing a smile.

"I thought maybe we could go somewhere today," David suggested, changing the subject. "We can spend the day out on the lake, and then we'll get dinner in the village. There's a great place we can eat. I've known the owner since I was little, even though I grew up in Painted Post. Her sister married my mom's brother."

Cat nodded. Whatever David had in mind was fine. All he wanted was to enjoy himself for the rest of their time together. Putting a hand on top of David's, he looked over at him and smiled.

They rose from the bed, and David pulled on a t-shirt. Otherwise, he had on nothing but his underwear. He kicked his clothes aside, and Cat rolled his eyes. If Cat needed a distraction later, he could always hang up David's shirts. Cat pulled on the sheet and bedspread, dragging them into place and smoothing them out. David, who had obviously expected Cat to be right behind him, turned around to see what the holdup was. He laughed as Cat patted down the last wrinkle.

Cat scrunched his nose at David, who laughed again and held out his hand. "Come on," he said. "Let's get cleaned up and get something to eat."

After a day spent picnicking by the lake and taking advantage of the pre-season tourist attractions, David took Cat out on the boardwalk. It was early evening, the sun low in the sky and the spring air turning chilly. Cat was glad he'd thought to bring a jacket with him.

David held his hand, and a few people smiled as they passed. This was the first time Cat had ever been so public about a relationship. On reflection, he would have loved to have been open with any of his past loves. His first crush had been on a trans boy, but Blaze only liked girls. His first real boyfriend had spent years coping with his own confusion about whether it was okay to like more than one gender—he'd gotten the impression from a lot of people the answer was "no," and Cat could only reassure him so much. Then there was Bryce, who was likely to stay in the closet until it killed him.

Cat thought back to the morning and his fears of doing to David what he'd done to Bryce. Or maybe what he and Bryce had done to each other. Cat wasn't clear on what their relationship had meant. He gave David's hand a squeeze, causing David to look over at him. His eyes were bright, and Cat loved the life and joy he saw reflected there. David was mellow, but he loved deeply and wanted the best for the people around him. Cat wasn't sure if what he felt was love, exactly, but when he was with David he was happy and content in a way he never had been before—certainly not in the previous eight months.

They approached the railing and stood looking out over the water. The breeze ruffled David's curls, and Cat longed to run his fingers through them. He'd always loved curly hair, and the thought of tangling his hands in David's sparked arousal. When David turned toward him, Cat seized the moment. He pulled out his phone and aimed it at David, startling him. Cat stuck out his tongue, and David laughed. Cat snapped another picture, and this time he grinned when he looked at it. David looked gorgeous, happy and free, his laughter evident even in the still photo.

"Let me see," David begged.

Cat sent it as a text. David pulled out his phone and looked, shaking his head at the picture. He stepped closer and bumped Cat gently with his shoulder. Cat stepped in front of him and slipped his arms around David's neck. He pulled him down the short distance to kiss him, threading his fingers in those luscious, long curls and tugging gently.

David groaned softly, and the vibrations traveled from where their lips connected all the way down Cat's spine. The pleasurable tingles made him tighten his ass muscles, and he wanted to press against David to increase the feeling. At the shift, David ended the kiss.

"Why don't we have dinner first," he suggested. "Then maybe we can take this back to my apartment."

He laughed at Cat's enthusiastic nod, and they moved away from the railing. With the sun setting over the water, they retraced their steps to David's car. Cat restrained his racing thoughts. He'd been eager but anxious the night before, and this morning he hadn't been in the right frame of mind. Whatever he and David decided to do—or not—after dinner was up to them. David's reassurance calmed him, and once again, he slid his hand into David's as they walked to the car.

David drove toward the south end of the village. They pulled into an alley which led to a small parking area. The place David had brought Cat for dinner was a small building right on the corner of the alley. Cat laughed when he saw the name—it was called The Neanderthal. David grabbed his hand and laughed along with him.

"I know—weird name. The owner, Gerri, used to tend the bar at a place over in Watkins Glen. She says she got the name from how a lot of women told her men act in typical bars. When she opened this one, the town had already gained a reputation for having a lot of gay-friendly businesses. She saw that a lot of women were going with their gay pals to clubs to avoid being hit on by assholes or because there was literally nowhere they could all go together and still be safe. The Neanderthal welcomes everyone, but jerks get thrown out on their butts at the first sign of trouble. It's a full restaurant until nine, and then it's strictly a bar with live music on the weekends."

Cat liked the sound of that. He'd enjoyed the place the guys took him, right up until things went wrong. Now he wasn't sure if he could be in a place like the club again, ever. He slid a hand into the pocket of his jeans, brushing his rosary beads with his fingers. It made him think of LR, who had remembered them even though he'd forgotten in the excitement over his days with David. Briefly, sadness flowed through him at how close she'd been to the truth even though he hadn't wanted to see it. He pushed the thought aside, wanting to enjoy his evening with David.

They stepped inside, and Cat was hit with the cool air and the sound of soft music and light chatter. The atmosphere was cozy, like an old-fashioned pub. Since it was a weeknight, there weren't many people inside. A group of friends sat in the booth at the back corner, laughing and talking. A young couple was enjoying their dinner, holding hands across the table. Her belly was round and full, and periodically she rested her hand on it, making small circles. The sweetness gave Cat a rush of joy. He realized he vaguely knew them; they lived a few houses down from his grandparents in the waterfront neighborhood.

A pair of men sat a few tables away from the young couple. They intrigued Cat, and he stood watching them while they waited for Gerri to appear. One of them was slim with mostly graying hair. He had a hoop in his nose and a tattoo peeking out from under the sleeve of his orange t-shirt. He was handsome in a mature, almost refined way, but there was a roughness about him too, as though he'd seen more than a man should in one lifetime. His companion was also good-looking. He was shorter and muscular, with smooth, dark skin. They leaned close over the table, looking at their bill. The gray-haired man gave the other one a light peck on the cheek and was rewarded with a hand ruffling his hair. He smiled and stood up. On their way past, they paused at the pregnant couple's table to chat.

Cat's attention was drawn from them by the appearance of a woman with curvy hips and curvier hair, swept up on top of her head with strands hanging down to frame her face. She spotted David and came right over, giving him a wide smile and a crushing hug.

"David! How are you?" she said. She turned her gaze to Cat and smiled, making her whole face light up. "And you are?"

Before Cat could open his mouth, David said, "Don't ask him that. He won't answer, unless he starts spouting Bible verses." Cat scowled at him, but David grinned. "This is Cat. Cat, Gerri."

Gerri looked him up and down. "He's adorable, David. So cute. Careful or I might snatch him up. You know how I feel about redheads." She winked, and a blush crept over Cat's face.

David swatted at her arm. "One, he's taken. Two, I think you're a bit more...woman than he prefers. Three, *you're* taken."

Her laugh was musical. "I figured. So he's your boyfriend?"

"Uh..." It was David's turn to blush. "We hadn't exactly defined it in words." When Cat delivered an elbow to his ribs, David amended his statement. "That is, yes. He is." He looked at Cat, his eyes sparkling with mirth, and Cat snorted.

"Sit wherever you like." Gerri gestured around. "It's obviously not busy tonight."

As they turned to find seats, the two men Cat had been watching approached. They greeted David, surprised and pleased to see him.

"This is my boyfriend, Cat," David said. He pointed to the gray-haired man. "Jones, and the other one's Alonzo."

Cat shook hands all around, but he felt far more shy among them than he had with Gerri. He smiled, but he pressed closer to David, his heart speeding up and his stomach tightening. In response, David draped an arm around Cat's shoulders, and Cat relaxed. David made small circles with his thumb on Cat's arm, but he remained tense in the presence of the strange men. It was one thing watching them from afar; it was another thing to have them close up, talking to him.

David exchanged a few more words with Jones and Alonzo then said goodnight to them. Cat tuned everything out until David led him to a table and sat him down. Cat's breathing was shallow by that time, and he was losing awareness of his surroundings. David touched his face, and slowly Cat came back to himself. He shook his head and looked up at David.

"It's okay," David said. "You're safe. Do you want to leave?"

Grateful that David spotted what was wrong, Cat shook his head again. He needed a few minutes, maybe some water, but he could manage. At that moment, Gerri stopped by their table with two glasses of water and two menus.

"Your server will be right out, fellas." She glanced at Cat. "Is he okay?"

"Yeah," David told her. "He's like me. I think he's just feeling a little weak. Who's our server?"

Gerri frowned. "Derek. Why?"

David stood up and pulled on Gerri's elbow. Cat couldn't hear what they were saying, but the loss of David's presence made him nervous. David had covered for him with Gerri, but now they were having a private conversation. He was relieved when Gerri ducked back behind the bar and David sat down again. David picked up a menu.

"Mm, almost everything here is good, and they're great about making stuff as you need it. Just show me what you want, and I'll order it the way you like."

Frowning, Cat tilted his chin in the direction Gerri had gone.

David lowered his menu. "I wanted Gerri's input on making tonight more relaxing for both of us." He put a hand on top of Cat's.

Cat smiled and settled in his seat, the fear from earlier melting away at David's thoughtfulness. He scanned his options. Eventually, he pointed to the catch of the day and a bowl of chicken and rice soup David said was the best anywhere in the village. A server arrived at their table, someone Cat guessed was probably not Derek, judging by her long, blond hair and full breasts, not to mention the name tag which read, "Samantha." She was cheerful and pleasant as she took their orders and disappeared in back.

While they waited, David talked. He never mentioned Cat's anxious reaction to Alonzo and Jones, but he put Cat's mind at ease about his friends. "So, no one actually knows Jones' first name. Or at least, he's never told any of us. He's former military–Vietnam. Not sure exactly how long he and Alonzo have been together. They considered getting married on vacation in Niagara Falls last year, but it wouldn't have been valid on the U.S. side. Guess the plan is to wait until it's legal here." David snorted. "It'll be a while."

As he talked, Cat relaxed. David trusted them, and there was no reason for Cat not to do so as well. It hit him then that he'd now made it through sex, a day at the lake, and meeting strange men in a social setting, all without the sense of dread which had plagued him for so many months. A grin spread across his face.

David stopped mid-sentence, obviously realizing Cat wasn't listening anymore. "What?"

Cat shook his head, grinning. "We give You thanks for all Your benefits, O Almighty God."

For a moment, David's eyes opened wide, and he stared at Cat. Then he laughed, full of a warmth and joy which caused Cat to feel as though his heart might burst. He reached across the table and held David's hand exactly as he'd seen Alonzo and Jones do. One more victory in Cat's column.

PART VI

Redemption

August, 2013

IT WAS Micah's last night in Concordia, and they were in his house. Cat had expected to feel something, sadness or longing or regret, maybe. He wasn't numb, but he wasn't experiencing any of those other things either. Instead, he felt whole and at peace. They'd managed a summer romance after all, even if it had only been a few weeks, and he'd given Micah a fairytale ending to his battle with the dragon in the form of Micah's spiteful brother. As much as Cat would miss waking up curled around another person, it felt more like a beginning than an ending.

Micah set the table while Cat prepared dinner. He shredded greens into bowls—mercifully, Micah would eat raw vegetables even if he gagged over the frozen ones—and tried to convince himself to be unhappy. Long-distance relationships didn't always work, and even though Micah was less than half a day's drive away, it wasn't a commute they could make all the time. Phone calls, emails, texts...they could do all those, but Cat wasn't sure they would.

And yet, the pain never arrived, not the way he thought it should have. The hole David had left was smaller, more manageable. Micah wasn't leaving him empty and broken; he was passing on more than he probably realized. He'd proved to Cat that his body, for all its scars, wasn't untouchable. Like Pandora's box, Cat had opened all Micah's wounds and let them out, but Micah had delivered hope before it, too, could float away. Cat snorted softly at his own sentimental thoughts.

A low chuckle behind him brought him into the moment, and

Micah's arms slid around his waist. "What's up?" Micah asked.

"Nothing," Cat said. "Thinking about you and what I want to do with your amazing mouth later."

"Mm. I'm not gonna be able to make it through dinner if you talk like that."

"Good thing it doesn't need to keep warm, then." Cat winked, and Micah's laughter rippled through both of them.

"I'm hungry, though. God, you make even vegan shit taste good."

"Thanks, I think," Cat replied. "And I keep telling you, I'm not vegan. You've seen me eat meat." He smacked Micah's hand with the salad tongs when he laughed. "You have such a filthy mind."

"Good point. Why are we discussing it when we could be eating this food—and then possibly each other?"

Cat snickered. "Almost ready. Here, put these on the table."

As they sat down at the table, Micah said softly, "Thank you."

"It was pretty easy to make," Cat replied, even though he knew Micah wasn't talking about the food.

"No." Micah fiddled with his fork but didn't pick it up. "For everything this summer. I don't think I'd have survived it without you and your friends."

Cat reached across the table and put his hand on Micah's. "You're welcome."

And that was all they said about the weeks they'd spent together fixing Micah's house and unraveling the damage to his soul. Nothing about taking on Micah's volatile older brother and his involvement in anti-gay spiritual violence. No words spilled over the boxes containing Micah's family secrets. No mentions of the delicate balance of their relationship or their shy firsts as they explored each other, mind and body.

Instead, Micah talked about his new novel, a buddy road trip to find a long-lost love. Cat detailed his work for a man who hovered the entire time he replaced a ceiling fan and how Cat suspected it was mostly an excuse to look at his ass while he worked. They speculated on a store in town which was being remodeled and wondered what sort of business would open up in it.

Despite what Micah had said, they lingered over dinner. They held hands on top of the table, and Micah slid his fingers up Cat's arm to trace the freckles there. Cat had no idea why Micah was so fascinated by them; maybe someday, Micah would explain. It should have made Cat feel strange, like an exotic pet, to have so much attention called to them, but it didn't. He'd hated them as a child—the mark of "mischief" in a redhead. When he was older, he thought they made him look like a kid. No one had specifically thought they were beautiful until Micah.

When they were through eating, they quietly cleaned the dishes, Micah leaning in to steal a kiss every so often. When the last of the plates were in the dishwasher and the water was swishing away, Micah leaned up against Cat, pressing him gently into the counter. This, Cat would miss—the way Micah panted for him and touched him greedily but with care and reserve so Cat wouldn't be injured. Micah had learned fast what would almost instantly set Cat's blood pounding yet be restrained enough to bring them both pleasure without pain.

Cat had a surprise for him, though, so he pushed against Micah's chest until he backed off, his head tilted in question. "Wait," Cat told him.

"Okay," Micah's eyebrows rose. "Everything all right? Are you feeling good enough for this? We don't have to—"

Cat cut him off with a kiss. "Sh. Yes, I feel fine, and yes, I want to make love with you *so much*. I've been half-hard all night. But you need to let me do a few things first." He stepped around Micah and twitched his ass, looking back and winking.

Micah laughed. "When you put it that way, what's another few minutes until I can have you in my arms?"

Without another glance, Cat picked up his backpack and dashed up to Micah's room. Micah had tidied up, which made Cat smile before he remembered why. Ordinarily, Micah was sloppy, but the lack of mess wasn't because of having company; it was because he would be heading home in the morning. Still, it made Cat's arrangements easier with clean surfaces to work on.

He opened his bag and began setting votive candles on the dresser, lining them up. In front of them, he set a round incense burner with a cone of his favorite honeysuckle in the bowl. He lit first the candles then the incense, blowing gently on the cone until the smoke drifted up to the ceiling. Once it was going, he opened the window a crack so they wouldn't be overwhelmed, and then he returned to his bag. He withdrew the leather pouch with his rosary and took it out, fingering the beads before laying it in front of the incense.

Cat pulled his phone out of his pocket and set it on the dresser by the incense burner. He removed a bright red-orange lacy negligee and a matching pair of panties from his bag. His heart sped up; he'd been feminine with Micah before—the leather skirt, his lip gloss and nail polish, the bathing suit which Micah drooled over—but he'd never shown him anything like this. He'd bought it that afternoon, wanting to reveal every part of himself. Micah had touched his external scars, but Cat had never explained what made it so meaningful that Micah had once called him *pretty*.

From the depths of his bag, Cat retrieved a number of toys, the ones they'd discovered they liked best together. He laid them out on the table beside the luxurious new king-size bed their friend Jones had picked out. Neither Cat nor Micah was particularly big, and the sheer size of it amused Cat. They hardly needed so much space, but it had been fun finding out what they could do with it. Cat set the bottle of lube next to everything else and returned to the dresser with the candles.

He slid his short denim cutoffs down and then his underwear before pulling his sleeveless t-shirt off. For a moment, he stood naked in front of the incense and candles, the same way he had when he'd prayed over Micah the last time they'd fought and almost lost each other. Slowly, he pulled on the panties then slipped the negligee over his head. It had thin straps and a fitted top, the rest flowing down over his belly and stopping at his hips so a bit of the underpants peeked out underneath. The material, though lacy, was soft against his skin, and Cat sighed with pleasure at the sensation.

With a last glance in the mirror, he fluffed his bangs and picked up his phone to text Micah that he was ready. In no time, the bedroom door opened, and Micah peered in. Cat watched him as he took it all in, the candles and the incense and the rosary.

"Are we pray—" Micah's words cut off when he turned to look at Cat, replaced by a sharp intake of breath. "Oh. Oh, my god. You're beautiful," he choked. "So damn gorgeous."

His eyes filled with tears, and Cat was reminded of why Micah was so willing to take care with him. No one had cared for Micah either, and now here Cat stood, baring all of himself in a display of wanton trust. Cat crossed the room and wrapped his arms around Micah.

"Sh, honey," he said. "I'm here. I'm not going anywhere."

Micah trembled in his arms, but in a moment, he was under control again. Not in a forced way but in a manner which told Cat he was truly all right. Cat stepped back and took Micah's hands in his.

"I want to make love all night," he said softly. "I want you touch me the way this—" he let go of Micah to gesture at his lacy ensemble "—makes me look." He gazed up into Micah's eyes, silently pleading for Micah to comprehend how much he'd revealed of himself by what he wore. Micah still saw him as a man, and Cat needed to communicate the truth to him in a way he hadn't been able to before without knowing Micah so intimately. "Make me feel pretty," he whispered.

"Oh, yes." Micah put his fingers under Cat's chin and tilted his face to kiss him. When he withdrew to look at Cat, there was no question he'd understood; it was reflected in his eyes. "Oh, god, yes."

When Micah kissed him again, they lost and then found themselves in each other, and for a little while, Cat could forget it was their last night together.

Summer

Chapter Twenty-One

Hail Mary, Full of Grace

July, 2006

Summer had always been Cat's favorite season. The pace was unhurried, but the town was alive with tourists. The lake front's outdoor diners were busy, and every shop had a steady stream of customers. Down at the beach, there were children all over, and every so often there was an extra-loud shout from the playground in the corner park. Every year, the two-week summer festival brought people to the water for music, food, and traveling vendors.

Cat bought a new bathing suit for the occasion, a version of the hot pink one he'd seen at the end of winter. This one was dark blue with white stripes. He liked it so much he bought it in solid sea green as well, but David said he preferred the blue and white. Cat matched it with a pair of white swim trunks, and when he stood in front of the mirror in David's bathroom to apply his lip gloss, David came up behind him and kissed his shoulder.

"Hot," David murmured, trailing a finger down Cat's back.

Smiling, Cat leaned into his touch for a moment before stepping away. David had promised him a day out, and Cat didn't want to get caught up in each other and miss all the fun. If it didn't go well, it could put a damper on their afternoon. The frustration of still feeling so at odds with his body rendered their lovemaking difficult even on good days. There was no such thing between them as a quickie; everything required careful planning and communication. They'd been taking things slowly since April, trying to figure out what Cat was comfortable with. True to his word, David never pressed, and Cat was always free to stop anything he wasn't enjoying. The trouble was, even he didn't always know what he wanted or needed.

Cat caught David's gaze in the mirror as he exited the bathroom. Nothing in his expression indicated he was disappointed, and Cat relaxed. He reached into his bag, and his fingers brushed his MedicAlert tag. He'd always kept it somewhere on himself, whether in a pocket or his backpack, but he'd never worn it. He considered it briefly, but in the end, he left it at the bottom of his bag, under his towel. It was a step he wasn't ready for, even though he'd taken several others in recent weeks.

Dr. Stern had cleared him with a new treatment plan now that he could take the recombinant factor. He still had to use a higher dose, but one of the benefits was less chance of a spontaneous bleed. Cat considered it worth everything they'd done so far. In fact, Cat had felt good enough in a number of ways that he'd made his own changes. He wasn't seeing Shannon anymore, for one thing. She hadn't said he could stop, but Cat didn't see the point. His parents hadn't been happy, but they hadn't questioned him.

They weren't aware he'd also stopped seeing Dr. Saliers. He simply hadn't made another appointment. At least, he assumed they didn't know. They hadn't seen her for a while either, to his knowledge. He'd also stopped attending the group with David. It felt weird to go together now they were intimate, even if he was fairly sure there was at least one other couple among the members. It didn't matter; Cat didn't see a need for either of those things anymore. He hadn't had a panic attack in weeks, and Dr. Saliers had provided him with what he needed to cope with the manageable amount of anxiety he had left. He didn't see where she fit in anymore.

He did feel mildly guilty for not telling David he'd stopped. Obviously David knew about the group meetings and understood, but he didn't know Cat wasn't seeing his therapist. David would have urged him to continue, but he'd have been wasting his time.

Cat zipped his bag and shouldered it then turned to face David. With a grin, David held out his hand and led Cat out of the apartment. He toted a few things they needed for an afternoon at the summer festival which he threw into the trunk along with Cat's bag. They drove into town and parked at the far end of the boardwalk. Once they had their bags, they walked hand in hand toward the beach.

It was overwhelming at first, being out among so many people. Cat tried not to come across to David as clingy, but he stuck close as they made their way through the festival tents and stands. David held onto his hand, and Cat began to relax. They spent the day doing the sorts of touristy things Cat liked but hadn't done in years. Living on the lake, boat rides and the boardwalk and sandcastles were almost background noise. With David, though, they were new again. Outside of the summer festival, Cat's friends never bothered much with the sorts of things the summer renters and visitors did. David was different; he didn't seem to mind helping Cat make up for lost time.

As the afternoon wound down, they stopped at the grand stand to listen to the music. It was a group Cat had never heard before, and he was mesmerized by their sound. They were an Irish electric strings band—three fiddles and a cello, all with unusual instruments, plus someone on drums and a quartet of singers. Cat was absorbed in the music for some time.

When the song ended, Cat glanced at David out of the corner of his eye. To his surprise, David was watching him, seeming transfixed by Cat's delight in the music. He leaned in, pausing to wait for Cat's nod before kissing him. A wave of excitement and desire shot through Cat, and he flushed all over. Tucking those feelings away and hoping to resurrect them later, Cat turned back to the music.

The band started another song, and David wrapped his arms around Cat from behind. He put his mouth close to Cat's ear. "They're good, aren't they?"

Cat nodded, and he stayed in David's embrace until the end of the set. It was a good thing they were going home soon because Cat wanted to take advantage of a rare time he didn't have to coax his body to be in harmony with his mental and emotional arousal. He closed his eyes and concentrated on the sensations—David's warmth through his t-shirt against Cat's back; the scent of food cooking and sunscreen and lake water; the way the voices and instruments wove in and out of each other in perfect harmony. Cat was *alive* and *well* in a way he hadn't been for months.

The song ended, and Cat opened his eyes. He turned in

David's arms to look up at him. David's eyes were dark and full of promise, setting Cat's nerves tingling. Cat pressed his fingertips over David's heart, and David put his hand on top of Cat's. He leaned close.

"Want to get out of here?"

Oh, yes. Cat did. He nodded, drawing a grin from David.

A different band began setting up on the stage, so they wandered away. They threaded their fingers together as they meandered among the vendors back toward the car. The walk cooled them both down. Far from being awkward, the silence between them was comfortable. It was good, having a boyfriend with whom he could be open, one who didn't make demands on how he should live. While lost in thought, Cat had stopped paying attention to where they were going. Consequently, he nearly ran into someone. He pulled up short when he heard voices.

"Hey! Watch it," someone said.

"Sorry about that," David replied. He took hold of Cat's elbow. "Come on."

Cat looked up, and his mouth dropped open when he saw who it was. Even if he'd chosen to speak, he wouldn't have been able to just then. It was Bryce, flanked by Zee and Ezra. Cat stepped back, half hiding himself behind David. Sensing the shift, David turned slightly to him with a puzzled frown. As Cat took in the three of them, his gaze dropped and his blood ran cold. Bryce had his hand linked with Ezra's in the same way Cat was joined to David. He raised his eyes to meet Bryce's, and he registered the flicker of guilt across Bryce's face just before his expression turned to stone.

"Are you okay?" David whispered when Cat shivered and pressed closer.

Unable to move in any other way, Cat shook his head, and David furrowed his brow. He looked from Cat to the others.

"Cat," Zee said. "How are you?" His words were careful, but his voice trembled.

The urge to recite prayers at Zee rose, but Cat forced it down. He didn't dare respond. When had whatever it was between Bryce and Ezra started, and why hadn't any of them said a word to him? The only three people who had any idea what happened That Night had remained as silent to Cat as he was to the world. Hurt and confusion made his stomach twist, followed by guilt for not finding a way to contact them, either.

A gentle press of fingers against his palm brought Cat back to life. David was there, grounding him. Grief and shame gave way to anger over the way people he'd called friends had behaved in the past year. Cat stepped around David and faced them, standing with his back as straight as he could comfortably make it. He looked them in the eye one by one. Zee seemed resigned; Ezra appeared embarrassed and uncomfortable. It was Bryce's look that hurt most of all; his face was still a mask, but his eyes were sad.

"It's been a while, man," Ezra said, breaking the awkward silence.

Long enough they hadn't recognized him right away. Long enough Ezra had somehow convinced Bryce it was all right to hold hands in public. Cat snorted as he waved between them.

Bryce let go of Ezra's hand. "You're still not talking?"

Cat shrugged.

With a sigh, Bryce looked away. When he returned his gaze to Cat, all traces of regret were gone. "Yes. We're seeing each other." He sneered at David. "It's not like you haven't moved on too."

"Wait, what?" Ezra turned to Bryce. "Were you two a thing?"

Bryce lifted one shoulder. "I guess you could call it that, yeah. Didn't work out."

No one seemed to know what to say after that. Ezra still appeared confused, looking from Cat to Bryce and back again. Cat's mind flashed back to the previous summer when it had been Bryce at his side instead of David. Back then, Bryce had hidden everything and had wanted Cat to do the same. Surely now Bryce's parents knew about Ezra, since the town was small enough that even with all the tourists someone was sure to notice them. Ezra, who was so many things Cat was not. All the weeks of arguing came flooding back to Cat—about the way he dressed or walked or acted. How many of Bryce's excuses had been reasons to break things off with Cat and lay the blame on someone else's shoulders?

Zee broke the tension. "We're heading for the stage. Maybe we'll see you around."

He clapped Ezra on the shoulder, and the two of them stepped around David. Bryce didn't move. When the others had gone a few paces, they turned around and looked back. Bryce eyed Cat up and down, his gaze lingering on Cat's bikini top before rising to meet Cat's. He opened and closed his mouth a few times before he finally spoke.

"I, um...I've missed you. We all have."

Not enough to do anything about it. Cat huffed, but his

annoyance turned to sorrow. He'd missed them as well, but it was long past when they could pick up where they'd left off.

Bryce frowned. "Ezra and me...it's complicated," he said. "We had to do something, you know? Had to move forward. Maybe it's time you grew up too. Stop trying so hard to prove who you are."

He turned around and jogged to catch up with Zee and Ezra. His words burned holes in Cat so all he could do was stand there, watching. Bryce had been referring to the way Cat was dressed, but what he'd said dug deep, unearthing everything Cat had carefully closed away. In a few sentences, he'd pulled back the curtain to reveal a lifetime of concealed pain. Bryce was wrong; Cat hadn't been trying to prove who he was. He'd been trying to prove all the things he wasn't—all the labels everyone else had tried to pin on him. Cat didn't realize he was shaking until David touched his arm and he recoiled at the contact.

"Shit," David said. "What an asswipe. Come on, let's get you home."

It didn't matter that David was probably right. Bryce had been one of his best friends for years before That Night. Not only had David insulted him, he'd treated Cat passively, as though he couldn't decide for himself what he required. He'd been too protective, babying—assuming he had to take Cat home like a child in need of a nap. Unleashing his fury at the way everything felt suddenly upside down, Cat hauled back his fist and punched David in the arm as hard as he could. Admittedly, it wasn't all that hard, but it was still satisfying. He stormed off, not caring whether David followed him.

David called his name, but Cat ignored him. He darted among the other people. Later, he would text David and ask his forgiveness, but for now he needed to get away. It was a bit of a walk to the center of town, but once he made it back to the cafe, he could stay there until he found a ride home. He reached the sidewalk where the shops began and headed toward the cafe.

There were fewer people out on the street than on the beach, but it was still busy. Cat ducked under an awning to catch his breath and cool down in the shade. As a group of people walked past a store on the other side of the road, the door opened and a man stepped out. When the man emerged from the shadow of the building, Cat's world collapsed.

For as long as Cat lived, that face would haunt him, deeply embedded in every brain cell. With a sharp gasp, Cat backed up and hunched against the storefront. He lost track of everything except the galloping of his heart and the pounding in his ears. He gulped air. Sinking down, he bent his knees to his chest and gripped his head.

A voice beside him said, "Are you all right? Can I help?"

The sun was behind the person, leaving their face shrouded in shadow. Cat pressed harder against the wall. Whoever it was had crouched down beside him. Cat couldn't look. What if it was *him?*

"Here, let me help you."

The words echoed around Cat, and he recoiled. Everything in him screamed, *No!* He froze for a moment before he mumbled, "Lord Jesus Christ, have mercy on me, a sinner."

"Are you sick? Is there someone I can call?"

A hand rested on Cat's elbow. He yelped and yanked his arm away. "Lord Jesus Christ, have mercy on me, a sinner." His breath came in ragged gasps.

There were more voices around him, but it was an incomprehensible buzz. Shadows fell across the place where Cat was tucked into the corner. He continued to mumble his prayer, his heart thundering. There was something he was supposed to do when this happened, but he couldn't remember what it was. His thoughts slid against each other, disjointed. If David were there, he would know what to do. The idea took root. If only he could remember where David was or how to find him.

"Cat!" A shout rose above the other sounds in the street, breaking into Cat's confusion.

Cat had to reach out to David, bring him closer. He drew in air and hollered, "Lord Jesus Christ, have mercy on me, a sinner!"

"Cat!"

Again, louder this time. "Lord Jesus Christ, have mercy on me, a sinner!"

Before David reached him, the stranger had his hand back on Cat. The person called over their shoulder. Cat flinched and folded in on himself, the prayer he'd been reciting still turning in his head. He opened his mouth to continue. The whole time, the stranger kept talking, but the words no longer made sense. He didn't hear David anymore either. The tension coiled in his muscles until Cat hurt all over. Someone was screaming; Cat wondered if it was him.

"I'm here." David sounded out of breath. The screaming stopped, and David said, "You need to step away. He's having a panic attack."

One more time, Cat opened his mouth, saying the only thing that came to mind. "David!"

And then the whole world was dark.

CHAPTER TWENTY-TWO

BLESSED ARE YOU AMONG WOMEN

WHEN CAT woke, he heard the steady beeping of a hospital monitor. The sound was familiar enough to be comforting, despite the unease of knowing where he was. He'd been out with David and had panicked to the point he'd blacked out.

His head hurt. He reached up and discovered one side had a thick bandage. Somehow, he'd hit his head. That wasn't good news. His brain seemed to be working, though, and the pain he'd been in before was otherwise better. He assumed they'd given him a lot of different things, and he wouldn't have long before they made him sick. He lay still in hopes of putting that part off, closing his eyes again.

Hearing a sniffle at his elbow, Cat dared crack one eye open to peek over. David was hunched beside him, hands folded and head down. Was he crying? Cat had never seen him so distraught before. What had him so upset?

"I'm so sorry," he said. "Please, love. Just...talk to me. Please."

Cat licked his lips. He touched David's shoulder, and David looked up. His face was wet. He grasped Cat's hand and stroked it with his thumb.

"I'm okay," Cat whispered. The dryness in his throat made him cough, and he groaned quietly.

"You—you spoke," David said with an awed hush.

"Yeah."

David shook his head. "No, I mean back in town. You said my name."

Cat adjusted his position, and David helped him sit up. He didn't know where to start. "I needed you."

"Can you tell me what happened?" David leaned in, brushing Cat's hair with his free hand.

The question was too big to answer in a sentence or two. After almost a year, Cat had broken the first vow he'd made after That Night. *What happened* was more than running away from David and being caught unaware by the sight of Landon on Main Street. How could he sum up everything going on inside his head, and did he even want to? He'd convinced himself he was *better*, that the past was over and he could live with his new reality. A single moment shattered the illusion, and he didn't know what to do with it.

Except...he did know. He had to find a way to name what had happened to him and face it. When Bryce admonished him to stop proving himself, he'd hit on more than he'd intended. Even if Cat didn't owe David the truth, he owed it to himself. Cat sighed and looked away from David, afraid to meet his gaze and be tempted to tell him everything before he was ready. He shook his head.

David's shoulders slumped. "You ran off after we saw your friends."

Friends. Cat scoffed. Former friends was more like it. None of them had been capable of dealing with the aftermath of That Night. Once again, Bryce's words banged around in his head, colliding with the memory of Landon's face across the street. A nauseating mixture of shame and anxiety pooled in Cat's belly. His palms became clammy, and he gasped.

"Breathe," David said. He kept his hand linked to Cat's. "You're safe."

In his head, Cat counted to ten, and the tension ebbed. "I saw *him*." Cat squeezed his eyes shut.

"Who?" David frowned.

"L—the man who—" Cat choked on the words.

"Oh, love." The grip on his hand tightened. "Hey." David put his other hand on Cat's cheek. "Look at me." When Cat turned toward him, David said, "This is not your fault. The scum who hurt you did all of this."

Before Cat could respond, the curtain around his bed slid aside, and the rest of his family came in. LR bent down and kissed his cheek.

"Hey, Kitty-Cat. I brought you this." She tucked a small bear under his chin, and he looked up to offer her a small smile.

"Is he all right?" Dad asked David. "I'm glad you were nearby."

"I'm fine," Cat said. The three startled glances he received in reply amused him.

"Honey?" Mom stepped closer, and Cat patted the bed next to him. She sat down, careful of the IV tubing.

"I'm okay, Mom." It surprised him how much he liked the way the word *Mom* felt as it slid off his tongue. "For now," he added. He slumped back against the pillows. The twenty or so words he'd spoken since waking up had exhausted him.

Mom leaned in and kissed his forehead. "Take your time. The nurse said someone will be in to see you in a little while. Are you in pain?"

Determined not to hide the truth from her anymore, he nodded and touched his head. Mom stood and slipped around the curtain to the door. LR made herself comfortable on Cat's other side. She rolled her eyes at him, but she was smiling.

"You don't do anything halfway, do you? Ann Marie was down there shopping with her cousins and saw the whole thing."

Cat stuck his tongue out at her. He wasn't quite ready to say something snide back, so instead, he reached out and poked her in the ribs. She squealed, which earned her a huff from the nurse who walked in at that moment with a small cup in her hand.

"Here you go," the nurse said, handing Cat the pills and pouring him a cup of water.

Grateful, Cat accepted them. As he was handing the cup to Mom to set on the table, a doctor knocked and breezed in.

"How are you feeling?" she asked.

Cat shrugged. He'd been better, but he'd definitely been much worse.

"Doesn't look like a concussion, only a bit of a bump and some scrapes. We'll keep you for a little while longer, just to make sure, but I think we can take out the IV. It's a good thing your friend told us you have hemophilia, though—you might want to think about a medic alert tag." She made a few notes, patted him on the leg, and retreated from the room.

A short while later, the nurse was back to remove the IV. The others talked quietly, and Cat let the sounds carry him while the nurse worked. Just as he'd come up with a plan for how to restructure his life in the aftermath of That Night, he needed one now for how to move forward. One word at a time, he would find his voice again.

The nurse finished, and Cat hauled himself to sitting. He groaned, remembering exactly why he hated being on a drip. Four heads turned in his direction.

"I'm fine!" he assured them, then grunted. "I really, really need to pee." When all four of the others immediately stepped closer, he had to hold back a giggle. "Geez, you guys. Do you want to draw straws?"

The atmosphere lightened considerably, and laughter followed him as he let Mom help him up and into the bathroom.

One step at a time, Cat put the pieces back in order. It took a while, but he finally had his whole plan laid out. In the interim, he didn't see David. It wasn't that he didn't want to, but if he didn't take care of the rest first, he would fall back into relying on David to interpret his thoughts. He texted, using words, to ask for more time and to explain why.

It was strange, making his own appointments with Dr. Stern and with Shannon. The only call he didn't make was to Dr. Saliers. He asked Mom to do it. He suspected she'd long since figured out he hadn't been going—his mother wasn't clueless—but he needed to be honest and tell her directly. Another way to strengthen the fragile bond they'd had over the previous year.

At one time, Cat might have been surprised by her lack of anger or disappointment; not anymore. Without question, she did as he requested and scheduled his appointment for the same day as his trip to the doctor and physical therapist. In one bandage-ripping afternoon, he'd have it all taken care of. Afterward, he could fall apart with David if he needed to, collect his thoughts before laying it all bare before his family.

He selected his clothes with his usual care—the glittery, raspberry-colored "queer as fuck" t-shirt, his old favorite pair of denim capris, and his pot earring. After making his lips shine with the lip gloss LR had given him, he threw a change of clothes, his rosary, and a few other necessities in his duffel bag. As he did so, he came across his medic alert tag. With shaking fingers, he withdrew it and slipped it over his head, tucking it into his shirt. Satisfied, he descended the stairs and entered the kitchen, walking into a scene similar to the day David had taken him shopping.

"I have some appointments. Can I borrow the car?"

"Go ahead," Dad replied. "I can drop your mom off at the cafe." He glanced at LR. "Unless you need to go somewhere."

LR looked up from her book. "Nope. Ann Marie is picking me up later."

"I'll be back long enough to drop off the car. I'm spending the night at David's." Cat held his breath.

"No problem," Mom said, sliding the last plate into the dishwasher. "Did you two want to have dinner here first?"

Cat exhaled. "No, that's all right. I think we have plans."

And that was it, a lack of fanfare or worry or questions about every detail of his day. He shouldered his bag, accepted the keys from Dad, and left with a wave over his shoulder.

His first stop was Dr. Stern's office. One thing Cat had determined in the hospital was that he needed better pain management. It had been true since long before That Night, but afterward, he'd denied it or accepted pain as a consequence. He'd taken the heavy meds after his sessions with Shannon, but they left him with no choice but to sleep off the effects and hope he woke with less pain. Surely there had to be something in between.

Since he wasn't having a full exam, only a consultation, he remained dressed while he sat on the end of the exam table waiting. Dr. Stern entered. His eyebrows shot up when he saw Cat's shirt, but he composed himself and turned around to wash his hands.

"Hey, Dr. Stern."

The doctor glanced back over his shoulder. "Afternoon, Cat." He didn't remark on Cat's return to speech, but a hint of a smile touched the corners of his lips.

He dried his hands and began a cursory exam. "So, what brings you in?"

Cat swallowed his nerves. "I'm in a lot of pain."

Dr. Stern finished looking Cat over. "We can definitely do something about that. If you're willing, I have a number of options for you."

Half an hour later, Cat was armed with two new prescriptions and a date with another specialist to discuss the joint stripping Dr. Stern had mentioned previously. As Cat had suspected, it was more than a single incident which had caused some of his problems. There were long-term consequences of both his reactivity to the recombinant clotting factor and the damage done to his body That Night. Some of what Dr. Stern said left Cat disappointed, but he would deal with it later when he could talk to his parents about the decisions he'd made.

His next stop was to see Shannon. When she greeted him, he

gave her the finger for old times' sake. She only laughed and rolled her eyes. Once they were alone in the consultation room, Cat let her in on the secret.

"I'm here to talk about what comes next," he said.

Shannon jerked, so startled she dropped her pen. "You're talking!"

"I could go back to flipping you off," Cat offered, grinning.

"You're going to do that anyway." She picked her pen up from the floor and poised over her clipboard. "All right. Last time, I made a note that I thought you could probably maintain what we've done with the series of exercises I gave you. We can revisit in a few months to see how you're doing. Sound fair?"

"Definitely. I'm having surgery again, though, so I'll have to come in afterward for a while."

Shannon beamed. "I'll be here when you need me."

Loaded down with accessories to maintain his exercise regimen, Cat left Shannon and headed for his car. He took a few deep breaths to clear his mind before putting his things inside and climbing behind the wheel. One last stop, but it was the hardest. *I can do this. David is waiting for me. Just this and then I can go to him.* He started the car and pulled away from the physical therapy building.

Outside Dr. Saliers' office, he paused. Telling her he'd begun speaking again wouldn't be as casual as with Dr. Stern or as lighthearted as with Shannon. He'd made Mom promise not to tell her, to let Cat do it himself. Now that the moment had arrived, Cat's body was taut with anticipation. He reached into his pocket to feel his rosary, cool against his warm fingers. He closed his eyes, but no prayers came to mind. Bracing himself, he stepped inside.

When he was seated across the desk from Dr. Saliers, she pulled out her rosary and laid it in front of her. Cat took his out as well, but he held onto it. He drew in a deep breath, held it for a moment, then let it out slowly. Where to begin? He swallowed.

"You haven't been in for a while." Her voice held no judgment, only a reminder of where they stood. "Did you want to start with prayer?"

He shook his head.

"All right. You'll have to help me understand what you need. Is there something I can help you with today?"

Cat nodded then licked his lips. "I—" His hand tightened around his rosary as a flicker of realization passed over Dr. Saliers' face. Her eyes were on him. Waiting. "I started talking again."

As always, Dr. Saliers remained calm. "How has that felt?"

"Strange," Cat admitted. "Not bad. Not necessarily good, either." He paused, staring at his lap for a long time before looking back up. "Dr. Saliers?"

She smiled. Not a smirk with a note of triumph, but genuine pleasure at the sound of her name. "You can call me Elyse, Becket."

He sighed. "Then can you stop calling me Becket? I hate it. I go by Cat."

"Fair enough, Cat."

After another long silence, Cat said, "I had...a really bad panic attack." He looked up at her. "I can't keep doing this, holding it all in." He began to shake.

"It's all right. Take your time. We can say prayers, or I can help you breathe. Or both."

"Um...b-both."

Together, they brought Cat to a place where he was more calm and centered. Once he had relaxed, he rested his hands on top of the desk, still clutching his rosary. He looked at Dr. Elyse—he couldn't bring himself to think of her only by first name—and took one last deep breath before he began.

"I want to tell you what happened."

"You mean between your last visit and now? Or about what's going on today?"

"No." Cat was down to a whisper. "I want to tell you about the man who beat me until I almost died." His pulse bounded.

"You're always free to speak here. Nothing you say will leave this office."

Cat closed his eyes, allowing himself to reach into the memories of That Night. Scenes passed through his mind, out of order and disconnected. He tried to sort them into some kind of sequence. When he opened his eyes, he took a few slow breaths before he began.

"I don't remember everything, only that it started with my birthday and my friends taking me to this gay club..."

CHAPTER TWENTY-THREE

HOLY MARY, MOTHER OF GOD

CAT DROPPED his bag inside the entryway of David's apartment. He ached, both from the emotional upheaval of the day and because he allowed himself to really feel it this time. They'd picked up his meds from Linder's Drugs on the way to David's, and Cat reached in to pull out one of the bottles. Between meds to boost his clotting factor, for pain, for anxiety, and a renewal of his script for antibiotics, it looked like he'd brought half the pharmacy home with him. It was mildly discouraging. David led him to the couch, and Cat sank down onto it, rolling the pills in his hand.

"You want something to drink so you can take them?"

David's nervous energy bothered Cat. It was as though he didn't know how to bring up what had happened or all the ways it would change them. Cat nodded then remembered he was speaking now.

"Yes, thanks. Just water."

Cat leaned back against the couch cushions, listening to the clink of the ice and the sound of the tap. A moment later, David was at his elbow.

"Here."

Cat accepted the glass and swallowed the pills before he could change his mind. He set the glass on the coffee table and patted the cushion next to him. "Please sit." Once David had settled in, Cat didn't waste time. "I think we should probably talk about this." His mild anxiety bubbled over into a nervous chuckle. "Or I can talk, and you can gesticulate or whatever."

That dragged a smile out of David and eased the tension. "Okay," he said.

"I told my therapist everything—or as near to everything as I remember. I need to tell my family, too, but I want to practice on you first."

It had been one thing, telling Dr. Elyse. His parents—or rather, their insurance company—paid her to listen to him without judgment. His family needed to know, but they were too close, and they would all have something to say about it. Cat needed someone who was neither before he could take on the heavy task of exposing his flaws to his parents and then the police.

"I'm here," David said, his voice and his hand on Cat's reassuring. "I'm listening."

Cat took a deep breath and let it out slowly. "I went to a club. A guy we knew sneaked us in, and it wasn't the first time. We'd been doing it all summer. My friend Bryce—the one we saw at the festival—and I had an agreement, sort of. I don't know what we were. More than fuck buddies, less than boyfriends. He wasn't out, and we'd been arguing a lot." Cat swallowed. "He kept saying I was 'too gay,' meaning too girlie. I am who I am, and I told him to bite me. Two hours later, we were screwing in the club bathroom. It was kind of gross. I didn't care. I wanted to go hard and fast because we were agreed it was our last time. I got hurt."

David held Cat's hand the whole time as Cat poured out to him everything from That Night. He didn't soften anything, choosing instead to lay it all out in vivid detail. When he was through, he closed his eyes, took a cleansing breath, and said a quick prayer before looking at David again. Cat was surprised to find David's expression remained open and warm. There was no pity, but there was no judgment, either. He had the same relaxed, inviting posture he always did.

"You know none of this is your fault, right?"

"I don't know." Cat shifted away from David and lay back against the cushion. "I shouldn't have been with Bryce in the bathroom. I shouldn't have followed a virtual stranger. Maybe I should have said no to that club in the first place." He held up a hand when David opened his mouth to protest. "Don't," he said. "Let me finish. You need to know why I lost it at the festival and why I'm not sure where we go from here."

"All right." David's brow creased.

"He said—he told me I was pretty and he liked pretty men. I

know what that means because Bryce thought it too. He wanted me to play a part, to be a plaything for his fantasies. He kept saying it was my fault, that if I'd accepted his offer he wouldn't have to hurt me. I didn't understand it at the time because I was terrified, and then he knocked me out. If I'd been the kind of pretty boy he'd intended me to be, I never would have—" Cat stopped short, realizing what he'd said. He wasn't any man's toy and never had been. If he'd gone with Landon, he might not only have been beaten in a parking lot. Landon would never have accepted who he was, and Bryce never really had either. Cat sucked in his breath.

"What?" David asked, sounding worried.

"It wasn't my fault," Cat said. "Oh, God."

Cat collapsed against David's chest, strong arms reaching around to hold onto him. He didn't cry—not because he was out of tears but because he saw no need. Instead, he clung to David, shaking and repeating, "It wasn't my fault."

At last he sat up. David took his face in his hands. "No, love. It wasn't your fault at all. Not ever."

"I couldn't be what he wanted." Cat sighed. "I couldn't be what Bryce wanted, either. You asked me to help you understand what I need, but the truth is, I don't know. I never had the chance to figure it out."

"It's all right," David reassured him. "We can figure it out together."

Cat shook his head. "You don't understand. Bryce had expectations, and it's why he kept after me about being too feminine. He'd never cared so much until we were fucking. The first time, he let me top because he thought it might be easier with my hemophilia, and I didn't tell him the truth. Afterward, he got ideas about what it was supposed to be like, and so we tried it the other way around. I was so-so about it anyway, but...it was bad. Really bad. It hurt like hell because of my other problems, and I nearly—" Cat grimaced, searching for a polite way to explain before deciding David could handle it. "I almost shit all over him, and it triggered my irritable bowel. God, this is embarrassing. Anyway, I refused after that. So when I couldn't be who Bryce wanted, he was angry with me. Instead of trying to work it out, we were both too immature and took out our frustrations on each other."

After Landon beat him—Cat wouldn't even in his own head go back to denying reality—Cat had tried to suppress his beauty. In different ways, Landon and Bryce had both left him with the feeling he was *wrong* somehow. If he was pretty, the only men who wanted him would be ones who used his prettiness to validate their masculinity. Cat didn't know how to explain it to David.

He didn't need to. "You like to be in control," David said. "They saw you as passive."

Cat nodded. "That's part of it, yes." His ears heated. "Especially in bed."

"Ah," David replied, catching on. "I'm beginning to understand why you were so aggressive after our first time. You thought I'd see you that way too?"

"Yes." Cat chewed his lip. "You were always so protective. I assumed you wanted us to play those roles. I was angry with you at the festival because I thought you were treating me like some delicate flower. You'd almost done the same thing when we were in bed."

"Why didn't you—" David cut himself off.

"Tell you? I didn't know how. I'm not sure we should have been having sex before I could talk to you. I'm sorry."

"It's just as much on me as on you, maybe more. I made assumptions too." David sighed. "Maybe I did treat you like you needed my help."

They sat in silence for a long time. Cat stalled by sipping his water until the glass was empty, and then he set it back down. He put a hand on David's arm. "Why are you with me? Is it because you saw me as someone you could take care of? Or because you think you have to settle for someone like me?"

"Of course not!" David pulled away from Cat as though his touch burned. "What about you? I could ask the same thing."

"You don't think I've been questioning my motives? Wondering if I was depending on you too much?"

After a pause, David let out a low chuckle. "Listen to us. We've done what any couple does, and yet here we sit, examining it under a microscope. I'm with you because I like you. I enjoy spending time together. I..." He blew out a noisy breath. "I love you."

The words were almost visible in the air between them. In the span of four heart beats, images flashed through Cat's mind—Bryce, Landon, the club, months spent trying to keep his head above water. Overshadowing it all was David, gentle and patient. Cat reached out for David's hand.

"I love you too."

He'd said it, admitted it both to himself and to David for the first time. Instead of scrambling to take it back or cover for it or hide from it, he wanted to say those words over and over. The best he could do was lean in, wrap his arms around David, and kiss him.

Cat pulled back. "I love you."

David drew him close again, initiating the kiss this time. Joy radiated out from the center of Cat's chest, all the way to his fingers and toes. He sighed happily into their embrace. David ran his hand up to cradle the back of Cat's head. Their position was awkward, though, so Cat shifted.

"I love you," he mumbled against David's lips right before shoving David onto his back and pouncing like his name's sake to capture his mouth again.

David's laughter sent delicious ripples through Cat, making him lightheaded. They barely moved, both of them conscious of Cat's tolerance. Even so, the tiny motions of David's hips and the press of their bodies from chest to thigh caused desire to surge through Cat like an electric current. He tried to hold back, but now that he'd found his voice again, he couldn't keep silent.

"Oh...god...*David*," he breathed. "You feel *so good*."

The urgent groan wrenching itself from David only served to fuel Cat's need. As he dove back in for another kiss, David put a hand on his chest to stop him. Cat sat up and tilted his head in question.

Panting, David asked, "You want to take this into the bedroom?"

Cat braced himself with a hand on either side of David's head and gazed down at him. "On one condition."

"What's that?"

"It's my turn to lead. I want to explore every inch of you this time."

David answered with another groan and pushed lightly on Cat's chest. Cat almost flew off him, standing up and holding out a hand to help David up. A string of discarded garments and echoes of their laughter chased them down the hallway into David's room. They made it in record time, rushing to close the door and shed the rest of their clothes as soon as possible. Inside, David scooped Cat up in an almost ridiculous feat—they were nearly the same size—and carted him to the bed. Cat stretched out, unashamed now to display his naked form. A moment later, David joined him.

"I'm all yours," he said, right before Cat shut him up with a thousand kisses.

In the morning, Cat packed his bag to return home. He and David made love again in the shower, leaving Cat refreshed in every way. He clung to the feeling, hoping it would be enough to carry him through the conversation with his family.

David was working evenings for the coming weeks. When he dropped Cat off, he promised to return the next morning so he could be there when Cat called the police. Cat leaned in the driver's side window and kissed David. When he withdrew, David rubbed his forehead.

"You okay?" Cat asked.

"Yeah, just a headache." He smiled, but it was a little stiff. "Nothing..." He rubbed his eyes with his fingers and shook his head. "Sorry. Nothing a little sleep won't cure. We were pretty busy last night."

Cat grinned. "I didn't hear you complaining."

"No." David laughed, but it sounded strained. "I'll rest over at my mom's place before work, I promise."

"Good. I'll see you tomorrow," Cat said. "I love you."

David reached up and rested his palm against Cat's cheek. "I love you too."

Cat retreated to the porch to watch David drive away, tucking his concern in the back of his mind. He needed a clear head before talking to his family. He waited until the car was out of sight before entering the house. He had visions of everyone sitting around in the living room, waiting for his arrival. Instead, he was pleasantly surprised to find that only LR was there, curled up with a packet of SUNY Binghamton freshman orientation info. He swallowed heavily, thinking about how much had changed in a single year. One of his parents was cooking because the scent of bacon wafted from the kitchen, and there were the faint sounds of dishes clattering.

He plunked himself down next to LR, who eyed him sideways. He put out his hand to reach for hers, but he hesitated midway. She glanced down then set aside her papers and drew him against her. For a long time, he half-lay with his head on her shoulder and her hand carding through his hair. He closed his eyes, willing himself not to cry.

Eventually, LR sat him up and faced him. She took his cheeks in her hands. "I know I'm supposed to be the little sister," she said. "But I'm going to pretend for a sec that I'm not, okay?"

"Okay," Cat replied.

"This was not your fault. That is all." She kissed his forehead. "I love you, Kitty-Cat."

That was it; he was done for. He'd held it in, even with David, choosing to drown himself in a night of making love. Now, though, there was no holding back. He let go and sobbed—deep, painful bursts of sorrow and shame. LR wrapped her arms around him and rocked, her cheek pressed against his head. Her own hot tears wet his hair.

There was a clunk from the kitchen. In moments, a second set of arms joined LR's. Mom was behind him, draped over his back so she could reach both of them in her firm embrace. In the other room, there was a splash and a sizzle of something boiling over, but none of them moved. Cat heard the metal clink of a lid being removed and the sizzling ceased. The next thing he was aware of was Dad's head in his lap and his strong arms reaching around all of them.

When he'd run out of tears, Cat pushed a little with his back and his parents sat up. Mom rubbed his shoulder. LR grabbed a tissue and handed him the box, which he accepted gratefully. Once his face was mostly dry, he leaned against the couch and closed his eyes. Crying almost never made him feel better; it only left him achy and tired. It helped, though, to be able to release his hurt with his family.

"Honey?" his mother asked. "Are you—are you all right?"

"No," he said. "I don't think I ever will be."

He looked over at his mother. Her eyes were wet and red-rimmed, but they were full of understanding. His gaze drifted to LR, and she nodded. She set her hand on his arm.

Cat took a deep breath and looked at each of them in turn before beginning. "I have to tell you what really happened."

For the third time, he told the story. He didn't go into detail on some things, but he didn't spare them the truth about the nature of his relationship with Bryce and how he'd been in such a vulnerable position. It would come up again, and he didn't want them to hear it for the first time when he told the police. If they had doubts about his culpability, he needed to know. When he was through, he sat back, exhausted.

"I'm going to tell the police," he said. "But I need to know where all of you stand."

Mom frowned. "What?"

"Mom, I know what he means." She took a deep breath. "Can I?" she asked him.

"Yeah."

LR cleared her throat. "He thinks we might blame him, and I get why." She fiddled with the hem of her skirt. "I helped him get ready. Is it my fault too?"

"I see." Their mother pursed her lips. "This is not on either of you. I might not be thrilled Cat went to a bar or felt he needed to hide having sex by doing it in a bathroom. But he didn't deserve anything that happened, and no one else is to blame except the man who hurt him." She cupped his face in her hands. "Do you understand me? This is not your fault."

Cat asked, "Do you know why I did those things?"

"No," Mom replied. "Will you tell us?"

"Because all my life, I heard 'you can't do that.' You and Dad were full of that shit." He didn't apologize, even when his mother flinched. "The long, long list of things I wasn't allowed to do like other kids. It's why I let Zee drag me to that place to pierce my ear and why I started having sex with Bryce without telling anyone and why I went to a club I wasn't anywhere near old enough to go in. I wanted to do everything you said I couldn't do." He threw up his hands. "Remember when Dad used to try to get me to be 'all boy'? You were so pissed at him for letting me do stuff. Then when I told you I was gay and started dressing...differently, Dad let up on that. He'd been afraid I'd grow up to be scared of myself. Well, congratulations, I didn't. Instead, I got beaten up outside a club. I don't even know who I am anymore."

He put his hands to his head and ran them through his hair, out of words to express his frustration. In the spring, he'd been certain he could let it go, but all the big things he'd kept suppressed for months threatened to erupt. He had to tell them what else he'd decided, but he didn't know how. The silence was heavier than it had been when Cat was still refusing to speak. The only sounds were the quiet ticking of the clock and Cat's agitated breathing.

A soft throat-clearing broke the moment. Dad said, "I think maybe we have a lot to talk about, but we don't have to do it on empty stomachs. Why don't I finish cooking, and we can work through this together while we eat?" He stood up and retreated to the kitchen.

Mom rose as well. "I'll go help your father."

LR got to her feet and held out a hand to Cat. When he was

up, she leaned in. "I know I was part of the problem, but I'm on your side, Kitty. You have something in mind, don't you?" When he nodded, she squeezed his hand. "Please trust me to back you up."

"I do trust you," he said. "I promise."

They sat around the dining room table, and at first, the only conversation had to do with passing food around. Cat picked the vegetables out of his omelet and ate them first. He mostly shoved the food back and forth on his plate, taking small bites when his mother raised her eyebrow at him. Eventually, he set down his fork and looked around the table.

"I need to say this before I lose my nerve and go back to not speaking," he said, lowering his gaze to his plate.

"We're listening," Dad said.

Cat took a deep breath and blew it out slowly. "I'm tired of feeling useless."

"You're not useless, honey," Mom started, but he held up his hand.

"No, Mom. Dr. Stern said I need to be on disability because from here on out, how many days I can work is questionable. He also said it's not just because of the injuries. I don't want to do that yet. I will when I have to, but until then, I need to do something. Not working in the cafe because you feel obligated to have me there." He glared at Mom to prevent her from protesting. "I need something of my own."

"So, what is it you want to do?" his father asked.

"I'm not book-smart like LR, and I couldn't do all those classes anyway. I don't want to be a professional musician anymore, even though I could have before all this happened. I don't have the ability to sit and play for hours, and I certainly can't conduct." He cleared his throat. "I want to train as an electrician."

Three sets of eyes went wide, and a ripple of amusement ran through Cat that he'd managed to shock all of them at once. After a minute, understanding dawned all around.

Cat continued, "I've always been good with my hands. I like fixing stuff. Even without training, I updated the wiring in the cafe. With proper skills, I could do that for anyone who wanted me, and it means I can keep my own hours. For now, I still get to be on your health plan, so I don't have to worry that I'm not working enough to pay for my supplies and meds."

"If this is what you want, then we can make that happen," Dad said.

"It is." Cat paused. "'We' don't have to do anything. I already did it myself—I'm registered for classes for the fall semester."

"Then it's settled. I'll be glad to have you back with me on campus." Dad smiled. "I think, though, that we ought to talk about some of what you said earlier. None of us realized you were feeling that way. I can't speak for anyone else, but it's important to me to hear what you have to say."

Cat closed his eyes. He didn't have the words to explain how even though he loved David, he still worried he would end up more like his patient than his lover. David had more to offer than Cat could give in return. Cat also wasn't ready to tell them about his struggle to feel at home in his body. He could, however, tell them how he wanted them all to stop treating him like a fragile bird.

"The thing is," he began, "I'm not a delicate piece of glass, and I need all of you to stop acting like I am."

Chapter Twenty-Four

Pray for Us Sinners

In the morning, Cat was up early to shower and dress. The first thing he did once he returned to his room was pull out a pair of his favorite underwear, needing to feel the comfort of the satin against his skin. He sent David a quick text, and then he rifled through his closet, searching for a shirt. It went without saying that he needed to wear something conservative, no matter how uncomfortable it made him. He hated that he wouldn't be taken seriously otherwise, but if he was going to make a statement about Landon's attack, he didn't need to be dismissed based on his clothes.

He pulled out his white button-down shirt and black pants, his standard school concert uniform. He smiled as he recalled how pissed off his conductor was the first time he added a sequined teal bow tie—school color—in place of standard black. After laying the clothes carefully on the bed, he returned to his dresser and took out two more items—a pair of black socks and a camisole undershirt. He didn't have to tell anyone what was underneath his button-down, after all. He slipped on the undershirt and allowed himself a few minutes to enjoy the brush of the fabric.

He wriggled into the trousers and buttoned the shirt, tucking it in before adding a belt. From the recesses of his closet, he took out the one tie he owned. He hadn't worn it in years, and he didn't recall why he had it in the first place. Probably a gift from his Nana. At his dresser, he fumbled with it until he finally had the knot done properly. He paused with his hand on his jewelry box, but he didn't open the lid. No earring today, and no lip gloss either. He turned around to look at himself in the full-length mirror on the back of his door and gasped, tears springing to his eyes. He hated what he saw.

He looked like a man. An ordinary, professional man, someone who went to an office every day and put numbers in a computer. He didn't want to be the person in the mirror. He wished desperately that he could add a bit of makeup and paint his nails, anything to make him look less dull. With a heavy sigh he sat down on his bed to pull on his socks.

At the light rap on his door, he stood up to open it. LR stepped in. She smiled, but it appeared more pitying than pleased.

"You look...nice," she said.

"No, I don't." Cat returned to his dresser to fiddle with his hair, combing it into something equally boring as his attire.

"You do," LR insisted. "But you don't look like *you*."

Cat spun around to face her. "Bryce was right."

"Uh...okay. About what?" LR frowned.

"He always said I was girlie." Cat swallowed. "He was right, though, wasn't he? I am."

"Yes," LR agreed. "Very much. So what?"

"So—" Cat stopped in his tracks. *So nothing.* A smile crept across his face. "It's not a bad thing."

LR laughed. "Of course not!"

"I mean, it's true. I always wanted to be like you, in a way."

"Nah." LR shook her head. "I'm the only one who can pull off being me. You have to find who you are, Kitty-Cat."

He exhaled on a light laugh. "I'm not even sure. You know, I tried looking it up. There are all these words for who I might be— fairy, femme, gender-bender, gender fluid, genderqueer... genderfuck." He giggled.

LR put a hand to her mouth to hold back her own giggle. She lowered her fingers and said, "I like that last one. It suits you, for some reason."

"Maybe all those shirts I wear?" he suggested.

"Could be. I don't know, I think it's more about how you always like giving the finger to anyone who isn't okay with who you are." She laughed again. "I'm happy to call you a genderfuck, but you probably don't want to ask Mom and Dad to."

Cat waggled his eyebrows. "I don't know...I'd like to hear that come out of Mom's mouth. Would be hilarious. Not Dad, though."

He cringed. "Besides, he'd launch into some lesson on the German origins of the word 'fuck' or some such thing."

"Oh, god. Did he do that to you too the first time he heard you say it?"

"Yep."

When they had themselves under control again, LR asked, "When's David getting here?"

Cat shrugged. "He said nine when he dropped me off yesterday. I haven't talked to him since. I texted before I got dressed, but I haven't heard from him yet."

"Maybe he was already on his way. It's nearly nine now. Let's go wait downstairs."

Cat ate breakfast in silence while he waited. LR, seated to his right, had her orientation packet out again to memorize the campus map. The sheer ordinariness of it relaxed him enough to ask her about it.

"Oh," she said. "Well, I want to have everything planned out as much as I can in advance."

For the first time, Cat realized she was nervous about going away to school, even though it wasn't far. "You'll figure it out," he reassured her.

She smiled. "I know. It's just that I'm afraid I'm going to look like such a small-town little girl when I get there." She laughed. "That sounds silly, doesn't it?"

"No," he told her. "Not at all."

By the time they finished eating, David still hadn't shown up. He hadn't called or texted either. Cat sent another message, but his phone remained stubbornly silent. Cat wondered if this was how David had felt all those months when Cat wasn't talking. What could possibly have happened for him to forget he was supposed to be there?

LR commented, "I thought David would be here by now. Do you want me to call Mom or Dad?"

Cat shrugged. "Yeah, I guess so."

Mom had offered to stay home and let one of the other employees take care of things, but Cat had told her David would be there. He couldn't imagine why David hadn't at least called to say he'd be late or that he couldn't come.

LR called her, and she said she'd be home within the half hour. She urged Cat to call the police, since there would be a wait before someone showed up at the house. Drawing on every ounce of strength he had, he picked up his phone and hit the numbers.

When the dispatcher answered, he said in a shaking voice, "Yes, um, I'd like to report a violent crime."

The same officer came to the house who had been at the hospital when Cat woke up after Landon attacked him. There was a woman with him as well, and Cat was grateful. He wasn't sure he'd be able to get through it if he had to talk to the man alone, even with LR and Mom with him and even though Officer Kerwin was warm and kind. LR silently slipped him his rosary, which he kept in his hand the whole time. Afterward, he wasn't sure how he'd managed to get the entire story out, but he did.

Both officers assured him they would look into it, although neither sounded hopeful that much would come of it. They had the photos of Cat's injuries, and they would take statements from his friends, but proving a specific individual was responsible would be far more difficult without direct witnesses. He hadn't left any evidence behind.

Cat had known that going in, but he'd been determined to tell his story. He couldn't keep it inside forever; for him, it would mean he couldn't heal if he couldn't speak about it. That had been an epic failure. Now the hard work would begin, but maybe it wouldn't be so bad with David at his side.

Speaking of which, he had no idea where David was. Mom had shown up just before the police, and she and LR sat with him while he talked. After, Mom returned to the cafe, and LR stayed with him. He considered calling his therapist, but he already had an appointment scheduled in a few days. Despite his commitment to speaking out, he didn't need more talking at the moment. Going over what happened four times in three days had been plenty for the time being.

He left LR in the living room, watching a cheesy romantic comedy to distract herself from worrying about school. Her eyes were on him as he ascended the stairs, but she was wise enough not to ask him anything. Inside his room, Cat flopped onto his bed with his legs hanging over the side. He loosened his tie. As he lowered his hand to the bed, his fingers brushed against his pocket, reminding him his rosary was still in there. He pulled the beads out and held them up.

In all the time he'd been reciting prayers over the past eleven months, he had never concentrated on the words or what they meant. They were automatic responses or like repetitive motion, but they were largely meaningless in any personal sense. Cat sat up, dropping the rosary on the bed. He stood and walked to the mirror to stand in front of it.

He removed his tie, undoing the knot and sliding it out from his collar. He glanced back to the rosary on the bed then retreated to pick it up. He returned to the mirror and formed the sign of the cross, kissing the crucifix. He put the rosary back in his pants pocket with the crucifix hanging out. One by one, he slipped the buttons of his shirt through their holes, leaving it open to reveal the camisole underneath. As he did so, he said the Our Father. When he was through, he let the shirt fall from his shoulders onto the floor behind him.

Next, he unbuckled his belt. He touched the beads, one for each Hail Mary. He drew the belt through its loops and dropped it next to him. The whole time, he kept his eyes on his reflection, watching himself undress and his lips and tongue forming the prayers. He paused before continuing. This was not a day for a full rosary, and though it was out of order, he chose the Sorrowful Mysteries for his meditation. Likely Nana would have been horrified, but he reasoned she would have been horrified already by his life over the previous year.

He unbuttoned his pants and pulled down the zipper as he asked mercy for his sins. He took the rosary from his pocket and looped it over his arm so he could drop his pants. He recited the second Our Father and stepped out of them as he said, "deliver us from evil." He didn't close his eyes as he recited the Hail Marys, instead focusing on his image in the mirror and thinking about the ways in which he and Bryce had unintentionally wounded each other. Silently, he prayed peace on Bryce and Ezra, discovering it hurt less to imagine them together than to see Bryce slowly destroying himself alone.

Holding his rosary in one hand, he used the other to pull off his socks as he offered his body in self-sacrifice. He'd denied himself the pleasures he was sure had been responsible for both Bryce and Landon. Now, as he worked his way through the second decade on the chain, he wondered what *sacrifice* really meant. Perhaps he had yet to find out, but he knew it wasn't going to come from denying who he was.

His hands shook as he removed his camisole. Lips barely moving as he prayed, he tossed the undershirt aside and touched the pink scar on his side. It was lighter now, but the skin was still rough along its length. It would forever remind him of what had happened and what had become of him since. He hadn't been wrong—he wasn't made of glass. Yet he hadn't been right either, not exactly. There were no perfect categories of "normal" and "not normal." There was only acceptance—or not—of what *was*.

Finally, he stripped off his underwear. Naked before God and himself, he examined every flawed inch of his body. His tent, as the Apostle Paul called it. His dwelling place on Earth. Every scar, every bulge, every blotch and freckle. He hesitated then began to touch himself all over as he recited the Hail Marys again. His fingers found places which made him wince in pain or breathe in pleasure. It was his, for all the trials it had seen him through. Could he really learn to love it and call it home?

He knelt on the carpet, lowering his bottom so he sat on his folded legs. At last he bowed his head and let himself go. A deep sense of peace flowed through his veins, washing him in forgiveness—for himself, for Bryce, for his family. He finished the last decade, but he remained where he was, allowing the rage and shame and sorrow plaguing him to bleed out, replaced by love and comfort. He looked up and refused to flinch at his reflection. In all its joy and agony, the person in the mirror was him.

Cat whispered the prayer to St. Michael and crossed himself. He kissed the crucifix and rose to his feet. The calm he'd found while praying lingered as he gathered his discarded clothes and dropped them on the bed. He clung to the feeling in silent awe as he put his underwear and camisole back on. He hung his shirt and pants back in the closet and took out a fresh pair of pajama pants, black ones covered in pink flamingos.

He stopped in the bathroom to wash his face before heading back downstairs. Without a word, he joined LR on the couch to finish the movie. They'd both seen it before, so it was mindless fun, distracting enough to let Cat rest for a bit. He shifted so LR could lie against him, and he took a turn being the protective one. He wanted to transfer his sense of holy comfort to her somehow. The sounds of the film faded to the background as Cat silently spoke peace over his sister and stroked her hair.

When the movie was over, he still hadn't heard from David. Cat was somewhere between angry and worried sick. He called several more times and sent numerous texts, but there was still no response.

"LR?" Cat asked.

She looked up from a book she was reading. "Hmm?"

"I'm...I'm scared. I don't know where David is."

She frowned. "He should at least have called. Look, I don't know. Maybe this was too much for him. Give him some time, okay? It's been a rough few days. You went from sounding like a walking prayer book to full conversation. He doesn't know you the way we do, and maybe he's not sure how he feels." From the expression on her face, she didn't believe what she was saying any more than Cat did.

He shook his head. "That can't be it. As soon as Dad gets home from his class, I'm going to see if he'll let me take the car."

LR nodded. "I can help you make your case if you want."

"Thanks. I'd like that."

After that, he kept quiet and looked for ways to distract himself while he waited, though he couldn't help sneaking peaks at his phone every so often. Whatever was going on with David, Cat had to get to the bottom of it.

CHAPTER TWENTY-FIVE

NOW AND AT THE HOUR OF OUR DEATH

AS SOON as Dad arrived home, Cat pounced on him for the car keys. Dad handed them over on his way to his study, calling over his shoulder for Cat to drop LR at the cafe for work on his way. Cat threw on a pair of jeans and a plain pink t-shirt, and he and LR headed for town.

They didn't speak during the tense drive. LR kissed his cheek before she slid out of the passenger seat, giving him one last sympathetic nod. Once she was inside, Cat rushed to David's apartment. One of the other tenants held the door for him on her way out after he explained who he was there to see.

David wasn't home. Cat knocked for what seemed like ages, but no one answered. Then he remembered David was probably back at work, since it was so late in the afternoon. The plan had been for him to stay with Cat while the police were there and then head to work for the evening shift. Cat tried to recall which floor he worked on so he could call, but he didn't remember which medical unit he'd been admitted to when they met. Any time Cat had been there since, he'd stayed in hematology-oncology.

Considering all the options, Cat decided to simply drive there to find him. It would take less time to consult someone at the main desk than to call around hunting and be transferred multiple times. He parked in the ramp garage and entered through the main floor. He went to the information desk. The woman seated there looked up as he approached.

"Can I help you?"

"Yes. I'm looking for David Simms." Cat bounced as he waited, nervous energy surging through him.

The receptionist gave him a terse smile. "Is he a patient?" she prompted.

"Uh...no. He works here. I can't remember what unit." Cat took a pen from the cup on the desk and toyed with it.

The receptionist clacked on the keyboard, made a few clicks, and looked up. "He's on twenty-three hundred, but he's not in today." She clicked again.

"Crap," Cat muttered. The receptionist raised her eyebrows and he apologized. "I thought he was working."

He wandered away from the desk, heading in the general direction of the parking garage. His pocket vibrated, and he pulled out his phone. It was a text from an unfamiliar number. When he opened it, he frowned.

Is this Cat's phone?

Fear squeezed his chest. What if it was a message from Landon, now that Cat had gone to the police? Landon knew Ezra's cousin. He could easily find Cat's phone number. Cat had to breathe deeply and touch the rosary in his pocket before he deleted the text and slid his phone away. Almost as soon as it was back in his pocket, it vibrated again.

Is this Cat's phone?

He glared at the text. Whoever it was needed to stop. They already had his number, so responding wouldn't provide any new information. He sent back, *Who wants to know?*

This is David's mom.

Something didn't feel right. Cat's pulse quickened, and he had to sit down on the bench by the exit. His fingers trembled as he sent back, *I don't know where he is. Haven't seen him in a couple days.*

I know.

Cat frowned. This *definitely* wasn't right. *Okay?*

He's in the hospital.

Almost dropping his phone, Cat sucked air into his lungs. That explained a lot. *Which one?*

Regional. He's asking for you.

I'm here now, Cat messaged. *What floor?*

She gave him the information, and Cat crossed to the elevators. The whole ride, he shook. No wonder David hadn't come to stay with him when he called the police. It wasn't out of forgetfulness or avoiding Cat but because he was sick. Cat resisted the temptation to push the floor button again. By the time the elevator stopped, he was a wreck. He took off for the nurses' station, careening around the corner to get there faster even though he knew there wasn't much point.

When he reached the desk, he was out of breath. He gasped out, "David Simms."

"And you are?" the nurse asked.

"Oh, my god. I just want to see him. He's my—" Cat stopped. Would David get in trouble if he said it? He wasn't used to being open about a relationship.

A short, slender woman bearing a striking resemblance to David emerged from the room behind him. "That's his boyfriend. He's fine."

Thanking God that David's mother was of that stripe and not the one Bryce's family was, Cat followed her into the room. David lay in the bed, connected everywhere to various monitors. His left arm rested on the bed, and even from the doorway Cat saw his left eye was partially closed. It was strange, seeing someone from this side of hospital care. Cat looked to David's mother.

"I'm sorry, dear," she said. "This isn't how I'd have liked to tell you what was going on. I'm Marion, by the way." She extended a hand, which Cat accepted.

"I'm Cat." He bit his lip, embarrassed. "But you knew that."

"Cat," David said. The word slurred a little, and David's lips only moved on one side.

"Hey, baby." Cat stepped carefully around all the plugs. "What happened?"

"Stroke," David mumbled. "A-a small one."

Marion, who still stood at the foot of the bed, added, "It affected his left side. It's not as bad as they thought, and they're hopeful that physical therapy will help."

"Oh," was all Cat could say. He put his hand out but didn't touch David.

"'S okay," David said. "'S my good side."

Cat took his hand. "That's why you didn't come," he said.

"Yeah. S-sorry, sweetheart. Want...wanted to. Even after."

"You're hardly in shape to." Cat rubbed his thumb over David's hand and looked over to Marion.

She sighed. "I was out getting groceries before he came over. When I got home, he was already there, but I could tell something was wrong. I'd barely been there five minutes when he collapsed."

"Any idea what caused it?" Cat asked.

She looked down at David. "How much did you tell him?"

"Ever-everything," David replied.

Marion turned back to Cat. "It's the meds," she said. "This is one of the complications. He's at risk for bleeding, especially into his brain."

Cat nodded. He knew from what David had said before that it was risky, but he'd managed so far. Cat reached up and stroked his hand over David's curls. "I'm glad you're all right."

David wriggled, and it looked like he was trying to sit up. "Nuh!" he said.

Cat pushed him back down gently. "Be careful."

"'M fine!"

"Babe, if you were fine, you wouldn't be here. Let me help, okay?"

With a grunt, David batted Cat's hand away. He frowned at Cat with his unaffected eyebrow. "G'way."

Taken aback, Cat withdrew. "Whatever I did, I'm sorry."

David collapsed back against the pillows and stopped straining. Something beeped, and a nurse came in to look. He turned his head away from Cat, making it clear their conversation was over. Marion retreated from the bed and motioned for Cat to follow her.

Out in the hallway, they talked in whispers. Marion said, "I don't know what's wrong. He's been on and off like this since he woke up. I'm sure he's frustrated. It's not clear what the outcome is, and I think he's just not sure how to deal with it."

Cat nodded. "I can understand that."

"Maybe for now you should leave him. Let me talk to him, and you can come back tomorrow. He won't be sent home until they're sure the risk for another one has passed anyway."

"Okay."

Cat returned to the elevators and retraced his steps. David had asked to see him, but now he didn't want him there. Cat had no idea why. If David was worried that he'd failed in some way, Cat could reassure him he hadn't. Sure, he'd been upset at first, but knowing what happened made a difference. Somehow, he had to get through to David. They'd gotten this far; Cat wasn't letting go without a fight.

It took a week. Cat returned to the hospital the next day, but David wouldn't so much as look at him. While his instinct was to assume David had changed his mind about them, Cat knew without a doubt it wasn't about him. If it had been, David never would have treated him with such gentleness after Cat's trip to the emergency department during the summer festival. No, this was entirely about whatever was going on in David's head that he wouldn't—or couldn't—share. Cat knew something about silence and the many, many ways to break it.

Every day, his father dropped him off on his way to work. He stayed until the afternoon, when LR brought their mother's car to pick him up so he could spend a few hours working. His time at the hospital kept him busy enough that he didn't need to dwell on the police report or what might or might not come of it. Instead, he focused all his energy into sitting at David's bedside and doing what David had done for him—keeping up a one-sided conversation. The only difference was that David pretended not to listen.

By the third day, all the tubes and wires were gone, only reattached for meds and monitoring twice each shift. David was sitting up in bed, and he was able to feed himself. It was slow and one-handed, but he could do it mostly on his own. How much function returned to his left side remained to be seen after physical therapy. Marion kept Cat filled in on the details.

David wasn't entirely keeping quiet. He occasionally grumbled about various things. Cat wondered if he should take up knitting as another hobby. He was fairly handy and well-coordinated, and it amused him to imagine creating a scarf while he waited for David to make a move. Cat even had an old pink knit hat a friend had given him in middle school; he could find a pattern and make a similar cap for David. Then Cat remembered how much he hated that sort of thing and went back to devising a different plan.

On the fourth day, it struck him. When LR picked him up, he said, "Tell Mom I'll be there in half an hour. There's something I need to do first."

LR scrunched her nose at him. "What exactly do you want me to tell her?"

He shrugged. "Tell her the truth. I had to go buy something for David. Or make something up if you think it would be a better story."

She didn't question him further. Once she'd parked the car, he got out and took off down the street. He knew exactly where to go. He'd seen what he wanted there when they'd been displayed in the window a couple of months ago. The bell over the door tinkled as he entered the tattoo and piercing shop.

At the sound, the owner emerged from the back. "Well, hey!" he said. "How're you doing?"

Cat gave him a bright smile. "Doing fine."

The owner jumped. "You weren't so talkative last time I saw you."

"Things change. Listen, do you still have the hemp rosaries with the hand-painted beads?"

"Sure do." The owner motioned Cat over to the case. "What are you looking for?"

David wasn't Catholic, nor was he part of any other tradition which used prayer beads, but it hardly mattered. Cat scanned the various offerings then pointed to one at the end of the row.

"That one," he said.

The owner wrapped it up for Cat. "Interesting choice," he remarked.

"Oh, it's not for me. It's a gift." Cat smiled.

"Ah," the owner replied with a wink. "I see."

"But I'll also take...that one." He pointed to another one, quite different from the first. The one he picked for himself had rose-colored stones and a detailed pewter crucifix. "I need to replace my old one." He pulled it out of his pocket. "Can you put this medallion on it for me?"

"Sure can," the owner replied. He glanced at it and laughed. "Philomena?"

"Patron Saint of blood disorders," Cat said. "I have hemophilia." It might have been the first time Cat hadn't felt as though he should explain or excuse himself when he said it.

Once Cat was out of the store, he took the rosary he'd bought for David out of its paper to examine it more carefully. It was made of black hemp cord, and instead of beads, it was knotted. The cross was hand carved from soapstone, and there was an oval pendant of Agatha, Patron Saint of nurses. Cat ran his finger over it, imagining David's hands touching where his had. He slid the rosary back into its bag, pocketed it, and walked the short distance back to the cafe for his shift.

The next morning, he made sure to have his own new rosary securely in his pocket. He laid David's in a small box and wrapped it with silver paper before slipping it into his bag. After a quick shower, he chose his clothes carefully. For the previous few days, he'd played it safe, keeping to jeans and t-shirts. Admittedly, he'd gone a bit wild with the colors, and he'd successfully found nail polish to match every last one. Still, he hadn't wanted to attract any more attention than David might like.

That day, however, he chose differently. First, he picked out his underwear. Even though David was in a hospital bed and wasn't going to see it, he selected a fabulous pair of purple and black skull print low-rise briefs. Over that, he threw on a pair of cut-off denim shorts, cuffed at the bottom—just short enough to satisfy Cat's sense of self but just long enough the hospital staff wasn't likely to throw him out on his jeans-clad ass. He snorted to himself when he pulled out a shirt—black sleeveless, a little on the sheer side, and featuring a panda on the front. He fluffed his bangs, grinning at the purple streak LR had helped him put in the night before.

He put on his purple Converse, lacing them up before sitting back down on his bed to work on his nails, alternating purple, white, and black. He usually didn't care for black polish, as it was unpleasant both going on and coming off, but he considered David worth the effort. As a final touch, he broke into his supply of flavored lip glosses, choosing something called Candy Apple Kiss. It was tinted scarlet and tasted like a cinnamon red-hot. He stood in front of the mirror to admire the full effect.

When he stepped out of his room at last, he met LR in the hallway. She looked him up and down, her mouth open and her eyes popping. A slow grin spread across her face and she almost launched herself at Cat to wrap her arms around him.

"Watch the nails!" Cat warned.

"You look gorgeous!" she exclaimed, backing up to have a better look. She kept her hands on his shoulders. "Beautiful. There is no possible way David could resist you like that."

He huffed. "That is so not the point of what I'm wearing, you know."

"Maybe not, but he's going to love it. He's always been cool about how you look."

Cat shrugged. David had accepted him however he dressed and whatever way he chose to present. "I have to go. See you later," he said.

She leaned in and whispered, "I'm glad to have you back, Kitty-Cat. All of you." She kissed his cheek and slipped past him into her room.

The whole way to the hospital, Cat almost vibrated with excitement. Dad had to tell him three times to settle down, but it was impossible to keep still. At the entrance, he waved over his shoulder and almost ran inside.

He only received two sneering glances on his way up to David's floor. He also had one whistle—from a woman with a cleaning cart—and two high fives, one from a security guard and one from a patient waiting with transport services for the elevator Cat vacated. A male tech at the nurse's station gave Cat a once-over and grinned, and the nurse at the desk stared as he walked past to David's room. He rapped a cheerful beat on the door and went in without waiting for an answer.

If Marion was surprised by his outfit, she didn't show it. She greeted him with a simple, "Hello dear," and a kiss on the cheek. She mentioned something about going for coffee and ducked out.

When David looked up at Cat, his mouth dropped open. Cat sauntered up to the bed. "You like?" he asked, twirling around. He twitched his ass at David and silently cheered when it earned him a poorly covered chuckle.

Cat sat down next to David's bed. "I brought you something," he said. He set the wrapped box on top David's blanket-covered legs. "Open it, and I'll teach you how to use it."

David gave him a small frown, but then he huffed and opened the gift. When he withdrew the rosary, his lips parted in an O of surprise. He touched the knots and the cross, stopping at the pendant. He tilted his head as though waiting for Cat to say more.

"That's Agatha. She's the Patron Saint of nurses. And that," Cat pointed to the rosary, "is your first rosary. Handmade, of course. I seem to recall promising I'd show you how to use it. Give me a minute to get mine out, and I will. Just watch what I do first."

Cat reached into his pocket and withdrew his new beads. Taking them in hand, he kissed the cross. David didn't move. Cat realized David had never seen him use it—only heard the prayers, and some that weren't part of the rosary. His eyes never left Cat's fingers.

When he was through with a basic chaplet, Cat took David's hands in his. "Your turn," he said. "I'll help you."

Together, they made their way through the hemp knots, taking their time. At some point, Cat's gaze drifted to the door, and he spotted Marion. She neither entered nor left, and Cat returned his attention to David. When they were through, Cat touched David's hand and took the rosary from him, putting it away in its box.

When David turned to look at Cat, his eyes were red-rimmed.

"I'm sorry, baby," he said. "So sorry."

"For what?" Cat asked, genuinely perplexed. David had nothing to apologize for.

"For not being there when you needed me the day you called the police." His words still ran together a little, but they seemed to come more easily than they had been.

"Oh, honey, it's okay. I was fine."

David shook his head. "No! I was supposed to take care of you, and I couldn't." He was obviously working hard to control his spiraling emotions, and Cat reached out for him.

"That's not how it works," Cat said. "You did take care of me when I needed it. And then I was strong enough to do it on my own."

"It's not just that. The doctors say I'll be ready to go home in a day or two, but I don't know when I'll be able to work again, if ever. What happens when I can't even take care of myself anymore?" David said, his voice full of regret and anguish.

"Then *I* take care of *you*," Cat said. "We're both on borrowed time, and neither of us has a lot of tomorrows. So we do for each other, and that has to be good enough."

David clasped his hand and held it silently for a long moment. "It's good enough."

Leaning in, Cat kept his eyes locked on David's. "I wasn't there for you this time either, but I promise, never again. I should have listened to my gut when you said you had a headache. I'm not going to leave you to suffer alone like that."

"Me neither." David's good hand trembled as he lifted it to Cat's cheek. "I love you."

"I love you too."

Cat looked up to see Marion brushing at her eyes, and he smiled. David had given him the gift of himself; the least he could do was return the favor, whatever the future held for them. He'd meant what he said—he would stand by David as he recovered, whether he could work or not and whether he had another stroke or not. This wasn't the end of the road for them. It was only the beginning.

Epilogue

Father, Son, and Holy Ghost

October, 2013

CAT OPENED one eye, squinting at the light filtering through the small gap in his curtains. He inhaled long and slow, breathing in the warm scent of Micah's skin, then cuddled closer and closed his eyes again. So warm. So sleepy. So glad to finally have his man back with him for good, especially after everything it took to get there together. Micah had showed up on his doorstep three weeks earlier, full of promises and possibilities, after over a month apart. It only took one night together for Cat to know he never wanted to be without Micah again.

Fragments of the dream he'd been having floated back. Something about David, but nothing which felt painful or sad. Whatever it had been, Cat was left only with pleasant memories and the comforting reality of the man beside him.

Micah stirred. "No work today?" he mumbled.

"Mm-mm." Cat yawned. "Told Mom I was taking the day off."

"Why?" Micah shifted, and Cat felt him come fully awake. "Are you okay?"

"Yes, of course."

Cat thought it might be better proof if he showed Micah. He ran his fingers through Micah's dark, curly chest hair and pressed his mouth to one of his nipples. Micah wasn't nearly as sensitive as Cat, but Cat loved the feel of the tiny nub on his lips. He put out his tongue and flicked, making Micah laugh.

"So then why aren't you working at the cafe?" Micah asked. God, he was persistent.

Cat rolled onto his back. "Because it's not often we get to enjoy staying in bed for the morning. Can we get back to snuggling now?"

"Sure." Micah grinned and gently adjusted them both until he was spooning Cat.

He kissed Cat's shoulder then traced a design with his index finger. Cat hummed, enjoying the soft touch. Micah licked the same place and sighed, the sound so utterly content Cat couldn't help giggling.

"What are you doing?"

Micah nibbled Cat's shoulder with his lips. "I love this spot," he said. "You have a pattern of freckles, just here." He kissed it again. "I want to give it a name."

Cat laughed harder. "What?"

"Like...like a constellation." Micah sounded shy.

"Oh, yeah? What does it look like?" Cat's interest was piqued. Micah was more than a little obsessed with his freckles, but this was a new revelation about his relationship with them.

"It looks like..." There was a pause. "A cat." Micah chuckled. "I'll name it Whiskers, the Great Kitten."

Cat rolled over and shoved Micah playfully. "You are so fricking weird."

"You love my weird." Micah fell silent and still, and for a moment Cat was worried he'd upset him.

"Honey? You okay?"

"Yeah." Micah closed his eyes, and after a moment, his breathing evened out. "I'm good." He looked at Cat again and ran a hand through Cat's hair. "A little embarrassed."

"No shame," Cat reminded him.

"No shame," Micah agreed.

Cat kissed him softly, cupping Micah's jaw and enjoying the feel of his scruff. Cat had almost no body hair; he didn't even need to shave his face more than every few days at most. Micah wasn't really hairy, but he had enough it was a turn-on. Cat's hand wandered down, brushing against the fuzz on Micah's chest and tracing the bit below his navel as it disappeared into his boxers. When he slid his hand inside to tease the coarse pubic hair, Micah rewarded him with a quiet groan.

Keeping his hand still, Cat murmured, "Would you like it if I touched you?"

"Yeah."

Cat moved his hand farther inside Micah's underwear, pleased that Micah was already stiffening. "Can I blow you?" Cat asked. He wondered how Micah was feeling that morning; sometimes, even when he was hard, the answer was no, and they lay together talking instead.

"Yes..." Hesitant, unsure. Then more firmly, "Yes."

Cat reached around him to pull open the drawer and extract a condom. They were still using them, even after several weeks, because Cat was adjusting to being in constant contact with another person. Once he checked in with his doctor, he thought they could probably go without. For the moment, this was fine. Cat set it on the bed and tugged on Micah's boxers until they cleared his hips. He drew them down and tossed them off the bed then used his palms and fingers to slowly work Micah into a full erection.

"Did you buy new ones?" Micah asked then made a breathy, sexy noise as Cat rolled on the condom.

"Yeah." Cat moved so he hovered an inch from Micah's dick. His mouth watered a little. "Chocolate, but there are other flavors in the drawer."

"Oh, my god."

Cat wasn't sure whether Micah was responding to the flavored condoms or to the fact that Cat had just lowered his mouth to suck on the tip of his penis. It didn't matter. Cat took his time, a luxury they hadn't had in the morning since Micah moved back from Rochester. They were both still a little slow and sleepy, which Cat thought made for some of the best sex. It meant he didn't have to feel awkward or frustrated about asking to take things easy.

As usual, Cat knew Micah struggled to stay in the moment. Every inhalation shook with his warring needs for control and release. Cat ran his hands along Micah's thighs, closing his eyes and silently praying peace over him while he sucked. Even if Micah couldn't see or feel it, Cat had a deep sense of God's presence when they made love, as though the Holy Ghost herself was on them. He shivered, overwhelmed by the powerful sense of worshiping with their whole bodies.

Micah was close, if Cat judged by the tiny sounds he made and the slight motions of his hips as he tried to keep still both for his own sake and for Cat's. When Cat cupped his balls, rolling them a little, Micah choked on a cry and dug his heels into the mattress as he came. He let out his breath and relaxed onto the bed.

Cat pulled away and sat back, watching to see how Micah was. Sometimes he was all right, but most of the time he cried afterward. He said once he'd always hidden it until he met Cat, who made it safe for him to expel the years of shame. Cat could never understand that; didn't Micah's previous lovers know those feelings were as sacred as sex itself? He crawled up to curl his body against Micah's, resting his head on Micah's chest and listening to his heart.

In a few minutes, a lazy smile spread across Micah's face. "I'm...okay today. That felt really good." The flush on his cheeks darkened, and Cat touched one, understanding how much it took for Micah to admit to enjoying himself.

Once Micah had cleaned up, he lay facing Cat. He slid his hand between Cat's legs, rubbing him over the top of his pajamas, and Cat hummed happily. He had no problem making sure Micah knew exactly how much he liked what he was experiencing, and he hoped his open display of his desire might encourage Micah. He shoved his pajamas and lacy blue underpants down to mid-thigh, urging Micah to continue touching him.

"Yeah," he said. "Keep going."

Micah did, for another minute or two, but then he stopped. "Can—can I try something?"

Cat raised an eyebrow at him. "Sure, but I was really liking that."

With a huffy laugh, Micah said, "I want to rim you, but I wasn't sure if it was all right."

"Oh!" Cat nodded. He loved how Micah was becoming more comfortable talking about what they were doing. They couldn't have managed any other way, but the need to communicate clearly was an immense help to Micah in his own healing process. "It should be fine. My stomach's been okay for a while." It was his turn to feel slight embarrassment, and he was grateful he didn't need to clarify.

"Do I, um, need a dam?" Less comfortable to talk about, but still a good sign Micah could say it. Cat's heart swelled with pride in him.

"No, I don't think so," Cat said. "I would if I were doing you, but you should be good. You can if you like, though. They're in the drawer." He grinned. "Vanilla mint."

Micah laughed. "Could be worse, but I'll skip it. Turn over?"

Cat stripped off his clothes and snagged the towel Micah had used. He spread it underneath himself then rolled onto his stomach and adjusted into a position which wasn't too hard on his body but would be good for both of them. He closed his eyes and leaned on his crossed arms, relaxing when he felt Micah's warm hands on his back. For several minutes, that's all they did, the soft touch soothing in all the places Cat often ached. He sighed and stretched a little into it. Behind him, Micah made a sound somewhere between a cough and a laugh. Cat peered over his shoulder at Micah's amused smile.

"You look like a real cat when you do that." Another low chuckle.

Growling, Cat faced down again. Micah was not going to distract him.

Tender kisses landed all over his shoulders and down his back, following the path of Micah's hands. Humor left behind, Cat immersed himself in the moment, delighting in the way Micah made his body sing like his cello. He groaned when Micah's fingers spread him open and hissed at the first touch of Micah's tongue to his hole. Every nerve was alight, his already sensitive skin prickling with fire. Love and lust, bound together, fueled the burn.

Cat kept his hands on the bed, wanting to feel only the wet heat of Micah's mouth and nothing else. He could easily come this way and had before, though not with Micah. As always, he used his voice more than his body to keep himself from needing to move. He whispered encouragements and moaned his pleasure and shouted his impending climax, hurtling over the edge when Micah's tongue slid down to probe firmly behind his balls. Hot come sprayed onto the towel beneath him, and Cat lost all sense of his surroundings for a moment. He spasmed then collapsed, flushed and panting.

Micah lay back down on his side of the bed and pulled Cat close, reaching for the towel to fold it and clean Cat while he descended back to awareness. Cat's eyes closed partway, and he hovered in the space between orgasm and sleep, the room drifting in and out of focus. Micah drew the comforter back up over them, wrapping them once again in warmth.

They stayed in bed for a long time, dozing followed by light conversation about nothing in particular. Eventually, they got up and made their way to the kitchen. Micah cooked breakfast, which amused Cat even though it also pleased and surprised him.

While they ate, Cat said, "I'd like you to come somewhere with me today."

"Oh?"

"I don't know how you'll feel about it, but I think...I need this." Cat reached over and took Micah's hand. "For both of us."

They finished breakfast then showered—separately—and dressed. When they were ready, they headed out in Cat's silver truck. He pulled onto a tree-lined access road, following it until the cemetery came into view. Risking a glance, he saw Micah's puzzled expression, but he didn't explain. He parked on the side of the road and climbed out, waiting for Micah to do the same.

They held hands as Cat led Micah up the small rise to David's stone. Beneath their feet, leaves crunched, and a slight breeze ruffled their hair. Though it was late October, the air was pleasant and sunlight filtered through the trees, warming them. Cat stopped beside David's grave site and brushed a few stray leaves from the stone. He wanted to lay it all out for Micah, give him the story start to finish about what really happened the night he was beaten and how he'd recovered. He wanted to explain about Dr. Elyse and David and everything that had given him back his faith. It was too soon, though. Micah needed time to heal first, and they needed time together to build on the sacred and fragile trust they'd won with each other. Instead, Cat would give Micah a seed, a tiny bit of reassurance that he was ready to let go of the past.

"There's something I wanted to tell you," Cat said.

"Okay." Micah squeezed his hand. "Anything."

"LR said she told you how David died, more or less, but it's not the whole story. We should have been together, and I've always felt guilty for letting him die alone." Cat put up a hand to stop Micah from interrupting. "It's not like we had a big fight or anything. He had some work party to go to, and I'd agreed to be his date. Only I wasn't feeling great and begged off. He hadn't been feeling well either, but he went anyway. I could have too, but I chose not to. If I'd gone, I'd have been in the car with him."

Understanding crossed Micah's face. "And you'd have died too."

"Probably. It's hard to say—he died from a head injury and a stroke, but it wasn't clear which happened first. The passenger side was a wreck from smashing into the guard rail. I'm not sure I'd have survived it."

"Do you—do you ever wish—" Micah's Adam's apple bobbed.

"No," Cat said, keeping his voice gentle. "I wish I'd been with him, but I do not wish I'd died." He touched Micah's cheek, seeing with fresh perspective what was in Micah's heart. Micah had confessed how many times he'd tried to end his life, and Cat wanted to make sure he knew Cat wasn't ashamed of him even if he'd never felt the same way.

"Good." Micah turned his face to kiss Cat's palm. He closed his eyes, and his breath was warm on Cat's skin. "It's a shitty place to be, wanting to die."

"I know, honey. And I know how hard you've worked to stay alive too." Withdrawing his hand, Cat said, "When we were first together, he had a stroke, and I wasn't with him. I made this ridiculous promise I wouldn't let that happen again. He recovered well enough, and we were together for a couple more years, but his health wasn't good. After he died, I felt for a long time like I'd abandoned him when he needed me. If I'd been with him, maybe I'd have been the one driving. Maybe I could have saved him. And then I was angry because he'd left me. If he'd stayed home with me, he might have been able to get help. When I met you, I still felt at fault, and then I felt awful for being glad I was alive to have a chance with you. I couldn't let go because I know my expiration date is probably a lot sooner than yours, and I didn't want to make any more empty promises." He looked down at the stone. "Part of me is always going to love and miss David, but it doesn't change how much I love you." Cat drew in a deep breath, held it for a few seconds, and let it out. "I'm ready to stop feeling guilty for what I did and didn't do in the past or what I might or might not do in the future."

Micah reached for him, drawing him in and holding him, stroking his hair. When they released each other, there were no tears, no hot shame boiling in Cat's belly, no sense of having done the wrong thing. There was only a deep feeling of peace. He looked up at Micah and smiled.

"One more thing to do today," he said.

"Oh?" Micah's eyebrows shot up.

"It's time for you to meet my parents," he said. "For real, I mean. You've sort of met Mom in the cafe, but I never introduced you."

"Wow," Micah said, his voice soft. "I don't think I've ever met a lover's parents before, aside from Zayne's. And she hardly counts—'lover' is a bit of a stretch."

It was Cat's turn to look askance at Micah. "Oh, really? Thought you two had a thing."

Micah laughed. "Not quite. We used to make out sometimes, and we got off together once, fully clothed, back in high school.

Freaked us both the hell out, for different reasons. It should not surprise you that I puked after."

Cat clapped a hand over his mouth to stifle his laughter. When he'd recovered, he said, "Yeah, definitely not shocked. Anyway, you'll like my parents."

"Do I get to ask them embarrassing questions like why they named you Becket?"

"Oh, dear God. You could have asked *me*, you know. I'll tell you."

"You will?"

Cat rolled his eyes. "Sure. Already told you, I'm named for the Archbishop of Canterbury. He was a dissident who fought the establishment to keep Henry the Second from having power over the church. He's sometimes seen as a symbol of religious freedom, though that's a bit debatable given the Church's history. My middle name—Justice—should be self-explanatory."

"I never knew that was your middle name. How about your sister?"

"Ah, yeah. Well, she's not named for President Reagan any more than I'm named for Samuel Beckett. It's my grandmother's maiden name, so they used that spelling, but most people say it wrong—it's pronounced *Ree*-gan, like the character in *King Lear*. Her first name, though, was chosen for the same reason as my middle name. Do not ask me why they spelled Libertee funny because that I don't know."

"Seriously?" Micah asked. At Cat's nod, he said, "Who'd have thought?"

They'd begun walking away from David's stone, still holding hands. Micah swung their arms between them a little, making Cat feel like a kid again but in a good way. They were quiet for a few minutes, the only sound coming from the shuffle of leaves under their feet.

"There's one more thing," Cat said.

"All right," Micah replied.

"I sort of...didn't tell my parents...that you're ten years older than I am."

Micah laughed, a deep, rich sound rising from his chest. He stopped walking, grabbed Cat and pulled him close, rocking him a little. "Oh, my love. Well, I suppose they're about to find out. Will it matter to them?"

Cat drew back enough to beam up at him. "No," he said. "Not

even a bit. As long as I'm happy, that's all they want for me these days." He pressed in close again and rested his cheek against Micah's chest. "And I am, honey. I'm happier than I have been in years."

"Me too," Micah murmured into Cat's hair.

They let go again, ready to make their way to the truck and back into the world. Whatever else came their way, they had each other for now, and that was all that mattered.

ABOUT THE AUTHOR
A.M. Leibowitz is a queer spouse, parent, feminist, and book-lover falling somewhere on the Geek-Nerd Spectrum. They keep warm through the long, cold western New York winters by writing about life, relationships, hope, and happy-for-now endings. In between noveling and editing, they blog coffee-fueled, quirky commentary on faith, culture, writing, books, and their family.

Check out *Passing on Faith* by A. M. Leibowitz

Following his father's death, Micah Forbes believes he can finally put the family who rejected him and their religious bigotry behind him. In a cruel twist, his older brother calls to tell him he's inherited their father's abandoned vacation home.

Micah discovers the house comes complete with a long list of repairs, boxes full of family secrets, and a handful of quirky neighbors. Despite not wanting to get in too deep, he can't help the spark of interest stirred when the sexy redhead next door offers his help. Everything about the enigmatic Cat Rowland throws Micah off-balance, from his gender-bending sense of fashion to his handy repair skills to his deep spirituality. Before long, Micah is swept up by Cat and his friends, but Cat himself keeps his heart carefully protected.

When Micah's past and his present collide in a painful way, his self-destructive coping habits threaten to overwhelm him. To save himself, he needs to open his soul and let someone in. Cat has the key to unlock him, if he can let down his guard and trust his faith enough to catch Micah as he falls.

Read more from A. M. Leibowitz

Phin Patterson is an educational consultant dissatisfied with his job and his life. On a mission to complete one last assignment before escaping his unfulfilling career and figure out what he wants, he accepts a commission from Donald Murdock at the New York State Education Department. Suddenly, he finds himself on his way to evaluate a tiny school in New York's Southern Tier, not far from the town where he grew up. Now his only goal is to get in, do his job, and get out before anyone from his past remembers him.

That turns out to be easier said than done. Dani Sloane, the sharp-witted administrative assistant to the principal, learns the truth about why Phin is really there. With the help of her friends, she sets out to unmask him and force the local board of education to stop the plans that could ruin their school. Discovering that her sometime-lover is an old business associate of Phin's only complicates both the situation and their relationship.

Meanwhile, Phin, who has committed himself to keeping his emotional distance, can't resist the charm of the town and its residents—especially the school psychologist, who turns out to be an old friend he hasn't seen in over twenty years. While Dani works to take him down and save her school, Phin wrestles with learning how to do the right thing, including telling the truth to the man with whom he's already falling in love.

www.ingramcontent.com/pod-product-compliance
Lightning Source LLC
Chambersburg PA
CBHW070921190726
48292CB00004B/1049